Wicked Trials

Petal
& THORN

Petal and Thorn Books is an imprint of Thorn House Publishing Inc

Copyright © 2021 Elena Lawson
ISBN-13: 978-1-989723-17-3

This is a work of fiction. Characters, incidents and dialogs are products of the author's imagination and are not to be construed as real. Any resemblance to actual events is strictly coincidental.

Cover design & formatting: Pretty In Ink Creations

Edited by: Jennifer Jones @ Bookends Editing

Rook

ONE

Ava Jade stood there, a phantom in my room, dressed in light. Her lithe silhouette watched expectantly from the foot of my bed.

What was she doing in here? Grey had been changing the lock on the spare room door when I made my way past to my own bed.

She was asleep inside, face down on the pillow.

Out cold.

They were locking her in.

I didn't doubt she'd have no trouble getting free, but I didn't expect retribution so soon. No light leaked through the edges of my blackout curtains, which meant it'd barely been an hour or two since she passed out.

"Ava Jade?"

My voice sounded hollow. Dull, as though spoken through cloth.

Her lips tipped into a sharp, one-sided grin as she lifted a blade, the glint of the steel spearing into my eyes as it caught the light from the hallway behind her. She twirled it in her fingers.

My cock hardened.

"Come to exact your revenge?" I asked, slowly kicking off the thick blanket covering my naked body. I tucked my hands behind my head on the pillow to prop myself up. Getting a better view of her.

"Go ahead, Ghost," I baited her, adjusting my hips on the mattress to afford her an unobstructed view of my cock.

Her haughty gaze lowered, taking it in. Taking me in as though she were consuming every inch.

She threw the blade.

I closed my eyes.

It *thunked* into the wood of my headboard, and the sting of air on a fresh cut brought me roaring back to life. I lifted two fingers to my cheek, and they came away wet.

I groaned, biting my lip ring, the movement making the sting deepen.

"Come on then," I goaded her, happy to take the punishment for my brothers' actions if *she* was to be my executioner. "I'm ready."

Her eyes sparked as she vaulted over the footboard and was atop me in an instant, a new blade at my throat. I shivered, tipping my head back to afford her a better angle.

She leaned in, her warm breath brushing beneath my ear. "If I wanted to kill you, you'd already be dead."

"Then what do you want?"

Her fist closed around my cock, and I stiffened, my body reacting to her touch in a way it'd *never* reacted before.

My nerve endings blazed.

Hot.

So *fucking* hot. *Burning.*

But I'd burn to ash for her. She only had to light the match.

Ava Jade ran the blade at my throat down to my collarbone, skimming it over my chest and down my stomach, toward my rock-solid cock still clutched in her fist.

Her fingers, tight around my girth, slipped a little and the tiny amount of friction made me groan, my hips aching to thrust into her palm as the sharp edge of the blade skated around the base of my manhood.

Fucking hell.

"Tell me what *you* want…" she coaxed, her tone a wicked combination of desire and hatred.

My lips parted on a breathy sigh.

"Cut me. Burn me. Bleed me. I'm yours."

She shifted her weight, and I bucked as her mouth closed over the head of my cock, warm and wet and…

"Rook!"

Corvus' voice echoed down the hall, and I clenched my teeth, inhaling sharply as Ava Jade curled her tongue around the tip.

Not now, Corvus.

"Rook, get up."

I moved, plunging my hands into her hair to hold her there, my fingers twisting into the silky locks as my hips thrusted upward, fucking her mouth as she held her blade to my femoral artery, pressing firm enough to let me know who was really in charge here.

Something knocked into my chest, and I woke with a curse on my lips, scrambling to sit up, my head spinning, still drunk on the feel of her.

"The fuck, Corv?"

"Get out of bed," he ordered, ornery as ever with a

sour sneer on his lips. Fuck, just because *he* couldn't sleep didn't mean he had to ruin it for the rest of us. I happened to have been having the best fucking dream I'd had in years.

The *only* dream I'd had in years. So rare and so real I thought…

"You have a test in Sociology today," Corv grumbled, tugging my bedroom door shut behind him as he left.

"We're leaving in ten," he called from outside.

I fell back onto my pillow, letting my hand fall to my sweat slicked chest.

I didn't dream.

Hadn't since I was a kid.

When sleep claimed me, it was a dark thing. A numb thing.

And when I woke, it was as though no time at all passed between night and morning. The only evidence it had was the light of the new day, my sore muscles, and morning wood.

I lifted the blanket to glare down at the swollen head of my cock, aching for a release. The visual of Ava Jade in my head, so crisp only a few seconds ago, was already beginning to fade. I clutched at it, willing it to stay with eyes squeezed tightly shut.

But it was fleeting, vanishing before I could trap it in my memory.

"Damn," I groaned, rolling to the side to snatch my phone from the nightstand. I winced as the screen flashed to life, blinding me for a second before my eyes could adjust.

I sent a text and forced myself out of bed.

Rook: Chapel.

Her reply came as I finished tugging on my jeans and a pair of socks.

4

Unknown Number: Meet you there in fifteen.

I shook my head with a smirk, tucking my hard on into the waistband of my jeans with a grunt as I threw on a t-shirt and ran my hands through my hair to force it back into shape.

A shower might've been nice, but fuck it. Mrs. June wouldn't mind.

I paused in the hallway as I left my room, my eyes still burning from the light.

With two fingers, I tried the handle to the room where Grey laid Ava Jade to rest last night. It was locked tight. Listening, I could hear the faint sound of her even breathing inside.

Grey bounded up the stairs at the end of the hall, pausing when he saw me outside of her door.

I pointed toward the locked door, lifting a brow to ask the question without speaking.

He sighed, coming to snatch me from the hallway and drag me down the stairs with him.

I glanced back, my throat suddenly dry, before the door was out of view and we emerged into the kitchen.

"Let her sleep," Grey said. "I checked on her half an hour ago, and she didn't even stir. She's exhausted."

"We're leaving her here?"

"The door's locked," Corvus said, entering through the other side of the kitchen and prying the fridge door open to grab a Gatorade. "Grey'll come back and get her at lunch."

I laughed, shaking my head at him as I ran my thumb over my lower lip, smudging out a smirk.

"And if she wakes before then?" I asked.

Corvus whirled, pulling the bottle from his lips to swipe the back of his hand over the shine there. "Then she'll know her place."

5

I shook my head, biting my lip ring to keep from smiling. That would only make him even more grouchy than he already was, and I wasn't in the mood to poke the beast today. Maybe later.

"She won't wake up," Grey assured me. "She was dead to the world when I checked in. Twenty bucks says when I come back to get her at lunch she's still a corpse."

My lips pressed into a tight line.

"Your funeral," I muttered, brushing past Grey to grab myself a bottle of water from the still ajar fridge. "Are we leaving or what? I have someplace to be."

She rushed through the chapel doors like a thief in the night, spinning rapidly to ease the large wooden pane closed behind her, wincing as the lock caught with an audible *click*.

"Caroline," I greeted her, leaning against the back pew with a grin.

Her brows lowered as she turned and took me in, confused by the state of my clothes and something on my neck. Dirt, I assumed from the gritty feel of it. From digging the Ace's grave last night.

"Problem?" I asked her.

She hurriedly shook her head, wetting her lips as she walked over to me. Hips swaying, cheeks flaring pink beneath her makeup.

Mrs. June reached for me, going for a kiss, but my stomach twisted, and I stopped her, my fingers rough around her throat. I shook my head.

"No," I said on a breathy growl. "Kneel."

Her eyes lit with her smile as she dropped to her knees, thin fingers unbuttoning my jeans as she wetted her lips again.

I moved my hand to her head, messing up her prim little blonde bun as she freed my cock from my jeans. I

6

tipped my head back as she took me into her mouth, waiting for the *need* to take me.

Her tongue lapped at my flaccid cock and she added a hand to pump its base when that didn't return it to the rock-hard state it'd been in earlier.

She did that thing I liked with my balls, and redoubled her efforts with her tongue, pumping double time with her fist now.

My patience waned, and I snatched up a fistful of her hair and thrust my cock deep into her mouth, making her choke on it.

She gagged and moaned, happy to open wide and let me do as I wanted.

Except...this wasn't it.

The image of Ava Jade passed through the fog of my thoughts like a ghost and I grimaced, sneering as Mrs. June struggled to breathe. Then a more vivid image. The image of her beneath me, pressed between my thighs and the pavement on fight night when I held her down. The look in her eyes.

The panic.

"*Fuck*," I hissed, grinding my teeth as I pulled out of Caroline's popping lips.

She stared up at me, her eyes wet with tears from choking, her mascara smudged and running down her left cheek.

A week ago, I'd have fucked her throat raw.

A week ago, I'd have gotten hard at the mere sight of her teary eyes and smudged mascara.

A week ago, I wasn't being haunted by Ava Jade Mason.

"Wh-what is it?" Caroline asked, breathless. "Do you want my ass? You can——"

"Get out."

7

Her face broke. "What?"

"Get the fuck out."

She didn't move so I bent, batting her hand away from my still limp dick, snatching her by the throat in the process to force her to stand. She made a shrill little sound and pulled back, clawing at my hand and wrist as she tried to step away. "But——" she croaked, her words cutting off as I squeezed.

My monster reared its ugly head, solidifying my body, widening my stance. The *thump thump* of it echoed in the empty chasm of my chest.

"*Caroline*," I warned, throwing her away, making her choke and cough from the pressure on her windpipe. She gasped, catching her breath as she spun unsteadily on her heels to leave. She didn't look back.

I wiped a palm over my jaw as the chapel door fell closed behind her.

I tugged my jeans up and forced the monster back into its cage with a nip of whiskey from the flask in my back pocket.

This was a fucking problem.

Whiskey might do the bare minimum to tame my beast.

I lit up a cigarette and inhaled deeply, blowing smoke toward the altar.

Cigarettes might help take the edge off.

But sex…

It was an equally important remedy to the growing dark within.

Damn.

I smirked at the ridiculousness of it. At the ridiculousness of *her* and what she was doing to us all.

Score one for the ghost.

Zero for the Crows.

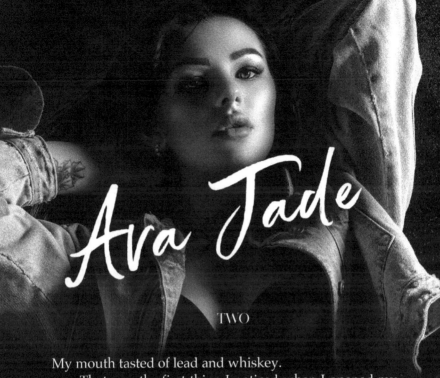

Ava Jade

TWO

My mouth tasted of lead and whiskey.

That was the first thing I noticed when I opened my eyes Tuesday morning. The second was the locked door.

Really?

A locked door.

What did they think this was, amateur hour?

I rolled my eyes after trying the handle for a second time, my fingers sleep numbed and body heavy with the after effects of Rook's whiskey and lingering dread. I'd let Grey lead me to this spare room sometime in the early hours of the morning. I'd been in a daze, still reeling from everything that'd happened, and everything that *would* happen now that I'd been forcibly enrolled in the trials.

"*Hey,*" I hollered through the wooden pane, the sound hoarse, vocal cords demanding coffee before they'd function properly. I pounded a closed fist on the wood, shouting a second time. "Grey?"

I listened carefully, closing my eyes to await the sound of footsteps, but none came. The only sounds in the Crow's Nest were the ominous noises houses made when nobody was home. The whir and *shhh* of the air conditioning. The scratch of branches on window panes. The creak and groan of flexing floorboards.

Speaking of, there were no windows in this closet of a fucking room.

For all I knew it *was* a closet. One they'd converted to a ten by ten atrocity of a guest bedroom. With a lumpy single pushed against the wall and a wobbly nightstand and not much else. It was clean though, not a speck of dust in the air or coating any surface.

Honestly, it was more than I'd had in Lennox, but I'd gotten used to the grandeur of my shared suite with Becca back at Briar Hall. And that shower…

Mmmm, I could use one of those right about now. I could feel dirt under my fingernails. Forest debris in my hair. Stale sweat making my skin tacky.

"Either you open this door, or I'll open it my damn self," I tried one last time, tipping my head to the side for a stretch as I rolled my shoulders back and inhaled deeply to force my heavy limbs to wake.

"Fine," I growled. "Have it your way."

I had my blades on me still, but nothing small enough to try to pick the fucking thing, and it was an exterior lock. The kind with a key. Installed with the key side in. A new one by the look of it. I had to wonder if they'd somehow managed to install it while I was asleep. I couldn't remember noticing hardware that strong on the way in, and I would've noticed. At least, that's what I'm telling myself.

I was a real wreck last night. Apparently, I also hadn't noticed the lack of alternate exits in the room.

These Crows were going to be the death of me.

At least falling asleep in my clothes also meant passing the fuck out in my shoes. The runners wouldn't get the job done as well as if I'd worn my shit stomping boots, but they'd do.

I limbered up, stretching my quads and calves and rolling my ankles.

I just needed the right amount of pressure in the right place and…

My heel connected with the door, an inch too high, but still it rattled, the metal lock bits beginning to come apart. If this was an exterior door, I might've been fucked, but lucky me, it was the bustable interior wooden kind.

The second kick ricocheted up my leg and I grimaced, cursing each one of the vultures for each subsequent kick.

"Fuck."

"You."

"All."

The metal lock *pinged* as it hit the floor and the door fell open, busted up into a mess of chewed wood around the lock and hanging on now by only one hinge.

"Bastards," I heaved, catching my breath as I strolled out. I went to the window down the hall, clutching the sill to peer out onto the gravel drive. The Rover was nowhere in sight.

What day was it again?

Tuesday.

Right.

Still morning by the look of it. Had they really locked me in a room with no fucking bathroom and gone to class?

They told me they had to keep an eye on me. I remembered that part of the conversation. Something about Diesel making me their responsibility, and then there was the part about him not trusting me. And why should he? I wouldn't trust me, either.

I found my way back down to the living room, scanning the low coffee table and couch until I spotted my phone. I jammed the side button, but the screen stayed dark. Dead.

Figures.

Briefly, I thought about tearing a few gashes in the expensive looking sofa before deciding they weren't worth the trouble of honing my blades later. But I couldn't let them get away with locking me up, they had to know I was not some pet to be caged. No matter what they thought. No matter their orders.

It took me about ten minutes to find a Phillips head screwdriver tucked away in a small toolkit in the hall closet upstairs. It took me another fifteen to remove the door handles from every bedroom and bathroom door in the house and stuff them in a pillowcase to sling over my shoulder.

I couldn't help noticing the differences in their rooms, and my ability to tell whose was whose with barely a single glance.

That part surprised me, made something shimmy uncomfortably beneath my skin. I didn't want to know them, but there it was. Like it or not, they'd embedded themselves in my life. Made a home in my mind. Roosted in the cage of my bones.

Corvus': a neat, modern space with soft dark fabrics and espresso finished wood. Not a single item out of place. No personality, either. No posters on the walls. No books or CDs. Nothing that would tell me for certain it belonged to him other than its sterile, magazine page feel.

Grey's dead giveaway was his desk.

The rumpled bed could've been Rook's, but that desk, it was all Grey. A study lamp perched in one corner, school texts lined up neatly against the wall. Notepads galore, and...a drawing tablet. Unexpected, but also not surprising. I wondered if he were any good.

I couldn't see much of Rook's room. He had blackout curtains on the one window and barely a glint of natural light filtered into the space. The overhead light was burnt out, or perhaps purposefully removed from its socket in the ceiling. But I could smell him. Whiskey and tobacco and that musky man smell that did things to my insides. And I didn't need light to see what looked like empty cigarette packs, clothes, and bottles strewn over the floor and a fur blanket spilling off the side of a large bed. Fucking *fur*. Since this was Rook we were talking about, I had to wonder if it was real. Looked like it could've belonged to a black bear, maybe. Or a few black bears judging by the size.

Good luck sleeping in your dark cave without a door handle, asshole.

Good luck taking a shit, too.

I bounded down the stairs with my prizes, feeling lighter even with the five pounds of useless metal added to my frame. I strolled out the front door and spun, flipping the bird to the camera above the door before going around the Crow's Nest to the back. And then farther, through the sparse trees, up a small rock slope and to the edge of the cliffside to stare down to the rocky shore below.

Upending the pillowcase over the ledge, I watched with glee as the metal globes tumbled down like little bells, ringing against the rock until they finally laid to rest in the white-capped waves, burying themselves in the sand.

I sighed, looking toward the horizon as the sun peeked out from behind a hazy pink cloud, warming my

13

cheeks. For a minute I could almost pretend my whole life didn't just go to shit in the last twenty-four hours.

But the minute passed, and my victorious smile waned.

Fuck.

I turned and started a slow jog down past the Crow's Nest and into the trees, making my way to Briar Hall. My legs protested nearly every step, but I made it, slipping in unnoticed through the back door and up to my room.

For a heart stopping moment, I wasn't sure I had the key, but remembered I'd tucked it safely into that tiny, mostly-useless pocket on the inside of my pants.

"Becks?" I called, squinting to see the clock in the kitchen. It was past eleven. Not quite lunch yet, so she was still in chem, and I was supposed to be in AP math. I couldn't wait for the inevitable text from Aunt Humphrey after she got yet another call from the office to report my absence. Fucking *joy*.

Coffee would have to wait. A shower was absolutely mandatory before anything else. My sweat was sweating, and I had a sneaking suspicion that the sour smell clogging my nostrils was my own.

I plugged in my phone on the way, promising myself I'd figure out my life just as soon as I was caffeinated and didn't smell like a dead mule.

Corvus

THREE

"Which one is it?" Rook asked as we crested the top of the stairs, sending a trio of girls fleeing in the opposite direction, whispering as they went.

"That one," I growled, my back tensing with frustration as I jabbed a finger in the direction of her room. The silver number three marking the otherwise plain door.

Rook tried the handle. "Locked."

I banged on the wood twice, the thudding sound echoing back to us in the long hall of female dorms and apartments.

She didn't come.

I threw a fist through my hair, an audible growl vibrating in my throat. Christ, why couldn't she have stayed put? Grey was going to head over and let her out for lunch, escort her back to campus for the end of the day.

Fuck, it was his idea to leave her there in the first

place, to *let her sleep*. I only agreed once he changed the door handle and locked her in, and only because I doubted she would wake any time soon.

She was dead to the world when I looked in on her. Sprawled facedown with one leg hanging off the mattress, like she just flopped and didn't bother moving to get comfortable.

I'd kill to be able to sleep like that. Just once.

"Grey," I gritted out, stepping back so he could slip ahead. He dropped to his knee and pulled out his wallet, drawing two pins from one of the card slots to pick the lock.

He cracked it in less than fifteen seconds, and we were in.

Her shared apartment sprawled before us. A wide space that would've been bright with all the natural light from the long windows across the floor, if not for all the black sucking the life out of it. Black couches. Black tables. Black cabinets in the kitchen. Even black throw rugs under our feet.

"AJ?" Grey called, but I was already moving. I could hear the shower running in the room to the right, and I headed for the door, shouldering through into her bedroom. Her smell permeated the air, like citrus fruits and salty caramel, making my jaw tighten.

I shoved through the bathroom door just in time to see her arm snake out of the shower and her wild eyes shining through wet dark hair as she threw a blade at me with a shriek.

I only just managed to dodge it, stepping to the left as it embedded in the door where my fucking head was a spit second earlier. A goddamned kill shot.

"Fuck, Sparrow!" I cursed, staring between her and the blade.

"Fuck me?" she howled, stepping out of the shower ass naked and dripping wet, making my fury heat into something more potent. "Fuck *you!*"

She angrily ripped a towel from the hook to cover herself, and I opened my mouth to say something, but she looked at me like she might kill me if I dared. She didn't know how much I'd have liked to see her try.

Rook appeared at my back with Grey only a step behind him.

"Great, now it's a fucking party," she hissed, tucking the corner of her towel down between her perky little tits.

"Can we rewind?" Rook asked, biting his lip ring as his heavy-lidded eyes narrowed on her body. "I think I missed the show."

Ava Jade rolled her eyes. "I should carve each of your stupid eyes out," she said, but I could tell she was quickly losing steam. Exhaustion dragged down the corners of her eyes, fucking with the usually bright and tawny color of her skin.

I couldn't help noticing the bruises.

And the scars...

Her short towel did almost nothing to hide them. Perfect little lines of white raised skin in neat rows on her upper thighs.

Self-inflicted.

My upper lip twitched up into a scowl, wanting a villain to blame. A face to smash. A life to end for her suffering.

I stopped myself. Cut off the thoughts with clenched teeth.

"I can't believe you locked me in that tiny ass room," she said, shoving a heavy mass of wet hair away from her face as she approached us. Seeming to be completely unbothered that I'd seen every inch of her naked body.

17

"*Uh*, move or I'll move you," she sneered at me, shouldering past us all and into her bedroom.

"I mean, what the fuck did you think I was going to do? Stay there like a good little bitch? Maybe chew your furniture a little if I got hungry? Piss on the floor? Wag my little tail when you got home?"

Rook snorted.

"I was going to come get you at lunch," Grey said in defense, and she whirled on him with a glare fit to smite him to ashes. I didn't know how I didn't see it in her from the start.

Her power.

It would have to be tamed if we were going to get her through this alive.

I pinched the bridge of my nose as Rook settled in to lean against the wall, loosely crossing his arms over his chest as she rummaged for clothes in the closet. He watched her like a starved lion before a feast. Transfixed. Like when he finally bent for the kill, he might not stop at blood and bone, but go for her heart, too. Her soul. I'd never seen that kind of obsession in him before, not even in his drug days, and it made my own blood chill to ice in my veins.

The edge of a dark duffle bag poked out from behind a stack of haphazardly folded jeans and I snatched it, shoving it at Grey. "Pack her a bag. We're taking her back to the Nest."

Her back stiffened, but she didn't turn as she strolled to the edge of her bed, dropping her towel to give us an unobstructed view of her ass.

Jesus fucking Christ.

"I had a really good shower think after my rude awakening this morning…"

My cock thickened as she bent to tug on a thong and

18

then a pair of jeans, jumping on the spot to hitch them up over her peachy ass. The searing urge to string her up and fuck her until she screamed herself hoarse made my muscles bunch and my erection push insistently down into the leg of my jeans.

"I decided the whole thing is a hard pass. I'm not doing it."

"Doing what?" I asked through gritted teeth as she pulled a fitted tank over her head, going braless beneath the thin navy fabric.

"The trials," she retorted, shooting me a raised brow glare over her shoulder. "I'm not interested in being inducted into your fucking cult."

"Cult?" Rook asked, squinting then nodding as though he might agree with the assessment.

"Sect," she tried again, rolling the word around in her mouth. "Whatever the fuck you call a group of sinners dressed as Saints."

"It's too late for that, AJ," Grey said, perching on the edge of her desk. The growing light of the day deepened the shadows beneath his eyes. Our roles reversed for the moment. He didn't sleep last night either. I heard him pacing in his bedroom. Rifling through pages until long past dawn. "We've been over this."

Did she really think this was optional? The frustration heating my blood made me unsteady on my feet, and I had to grit my teeth to keep my frame from wavering. Last night wasn't the only one I hadn't slept through. It'd been days. My bones were heavy with fatigue, muscles strained from overuse without rest.

"It's already begun," I intoned, my voice flat. Dead. "Your first trial could be today. We won't be in on all of them. They can happen anytime. Any place."

"Yeah. Yeah. And anyone or anything is fair game. If

19

I don't comply, I die. If I fail, I die. And if I somehow make it through the whole fucked up thing alive, I'll be in so deep that your dear ol' dad will own my ass for the rest of my life. *I remember.*"

"You should be grateful, Sparrow. If Grey hadn't done what he did, you'd be six feet under.."

"Ha!" She sneered, her face contorting with rage as she stepped up to me, jabbing two fingers into my chest, poking the beast within. "If *I* hadn't done what *I* did, it would be *your ass* buried six feet under."

A muscle in my jaw ticked, and she must've seen something in my stare because she backed off a step, dropping her arm with a grimace.

"There's no way out of this," Rook said, joining the conversation with a cavalier shrug.

Ava Jade clamped her mouth shut, and I knew she was already thinking of ways she might do just that. Though I doubted she was about to share any of them with the group.

"Aves?" Becca called from outside the room, the front door of the apartment sweeping closed behind her with a click. "You in here?"

Ava Jade tipped her head up to the ceiling with a sigh and closed her eyes before tossing her towel toward the bathroom floor and leaving the room.

"Babe, where *were* you? I texted, but you didn't…"

Rebecca Hart's words trailed off into shocked silence as we followed Ava Jade from her bedroom.

"Sorry, Becks," Ava Jade said, her frustration clearly evident in her voice. "I got *held up*."

She sent a pointed glare in our direction as she pilfered through the coffee on the counter, trying to dump way too much espresso into the portafilter.

"Um," Rebecca said, swallowing as she glanced

between us and her roommate, making her way carefully toward the kitchen. "Here," she offered, gingerly taking the portafilter out of Ava Jade's shaking hands. "Let me do it."

She stooped to whisper something to Ava Jade, who gave her head a miniscule shake.

"Apologies for the intrusion, *Becks*," I said. "We've just come to collect Ava Jade, and then we'll be on our way."

Her mouth opened in a little 'o' of surprise as the color leached from her face. She didn't respond to me, instead looking to her roommate for confirmation.

Ava Jade leaned heavily against the counter with a soft groan, watching the espresso drip steadily from the portafilter into a bowl-shaped mug.

"Grey," I growled, and he turned, heading back into her bedroom to begin packing the duffle still clenched in his fist.

"Aves?" Rebecca asked, her panicked whisper meant only for my Sparrow. "Are you really going with them?"

"*No*," she replied, locking eyes with me across the room. "I'm not."

"Yes," I argued, taking another step toward the kitchen. "You are."

Becca turned off the steamer wand and slammed the metal jug of hot milk down atop the marbled counter top, making some slosh out the top as she spun to face us.

"Look, I don't know what the fuck you're doing here," she said, her dark eyes alight with fear and the misplaced desire to protect her friend. "But if Ava Jade says she isn't going with you, then she *isn't going with you.* You should leave."

I lifted a brow, trying to reconcile this Becca with the one I thought I had pegged as a docile non-threat.

When I glanced at Ava Jade, she was staring at me, doing an analysis of her own.

"It's okay, Becca," she decided, reaching out to squeeze her roommate's arm. To reassure her. "Corvus knows I'm not going with him. He's smart enough to know that no matter how many times he drags me back to the Crow's Nest that I'll just keep escaping. And that I might just decide to slit a few throats on my way out next time."

"*Mmmm*," Rook moaned almost inaudibly.

Heat rushed across the back of my neck at her defiance, making my hands curl and stiffen, my jaw clench.

Touché, little Sparrow.

Becca nodded to her roommate, busying herself pouring the frothed milk into the cup with the espresso before handing it over to Ava Jade, who looked like she might come on the spot at the first sip. A curl of wicked jealousy wrapped its green fingers around my stomach.

She peered at me over the brim of her cup, waiting for me to play the next card.

"Aww, let her stay," Rook said, sauntering toward the kitchen. He cut in between Ava Jade and Becca, scooping a mug from the top of the espresso machine with his pinkie. He held the mug out to Becca with a grin, ignoring Ava Jade completely. "Can I get one of those, love?"

Flustered, Rebecca cleared her throat and took the proffered cup with a little nod, setting to work making another latte.

I sent Rook a pointed glare, telling him without the need for words that we'd talk about his idiocy later.

"*Fine*," I said just as Grey exited Sparrow's bedroom with a duffle full of clothes, my skin practically fucking *itching* with irritation. If she kept pushing me, I was going to blow.

How did she *do* that?

Nothing affected me like this.

I made sure of it.

Always calm.

Always level headed.

Except with her.

"She stays," I announced, turning my attention back to Sparrow, fixing her with a hard stare. "But one of us stays with you. One of us is with you at all times."

She paused, her latte frozen in mid-air with a grimace.

I drew my phone from my pocket and thumbed in her number, my angry strokes messing it up twice before I got it right. It was one of the first things I memorized from her file.

I sent her Rook, Grey, and myself as contacts via text. "I just sent you all of our numbers. If I text you, you reply. If I call, *you answer.*"

Her expression soured.

"And if I don't?"

My spine tingled.

"If you don't, I'll drag your ass back to the Nest and design you your very own fucking prison cell," I warned, the image of her locked behind iron bars, chained, and as naked as she'd been only minutes ago made my cock thicken once more.

"Don't think I won't do it," I added. "Nothing would make me happier."

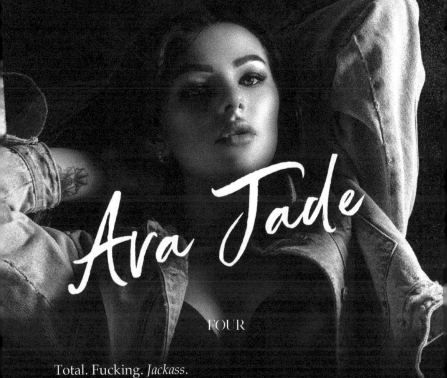

Ava Jade

FOUR

Total. Fucking. *Jackass*.

I grumbled wordlessly to myself through the last two classes of the day, barely able to focus on anything at all. At least fifty times the thought crossed my mind to just take off.

But even in the two classes I didn't share with any of the Crows, their authority was ever present.

I didn't doubt if I stepped one foot out the door of the classroom that somebody would be sending Corvus my movements. I'd already caught two seniors watching me. Guys who looked like they might be on their way to roles in the gang for themselves someday, if they made it through the trials.

If Diesel even deemed them worthy enough to take them.

I could get away though. I knew I could.

But did I want to?

Did I want to risk having to spend the rest of my life, or at the very least, the next several years running? Constantly checking the rearview? Only to possibly be dead before I could even hit legal drinking age?

Fuck. That.

They said there was no way out of this for me, but I knew of at least one. If I took them all down, then they couldn't own me. I could trade their secrets for my freedom. Ruin them from the inside.

I had one card left to play, and it was nestled safely behind a wooden board in a dark and cobweb infested nook in my closet. Officer Vick would be happy to help me if I decided to take him up on his offer.

My phone buzzed audibly in my pocket a few minutes before the end of the last class of the day, and I clenched my teeth, glancing up from my blank worksheets to the teacher.

Mr. William's gaze met mine for an instant before he looked away, ignoring the sound.

Huh.

I drew out my phone in full view, curious now.

A text flashed over the screen.

Dick Face: Grey will be outside your class waiting for you. Don't make this hard.

I rolled my eyes, not bothering to reply before slipping the phone back into my pocket.

Mr. William met my gaze again, his lips pursing before he went back to reading his book.

Not a coincidence then.

He really wasn't going to take my phone or even reprimand me.

Perks of forced proximity with the infamous Crows.

I'd take it.

I'd take it all.

I stuffed my blank pages in the textbook as the bell rang and made a beeline for the door, eager to get back to my room before Grey could escort me there. I didn't need to cement it in people's minds that they owned me. Corvus already did a good job of making them all think that without my help.

"AJ," Grey said as I breezed through the door, making me grind to a halt, a tremor of annoyance zipping down my arms, making my fists clench.

"Oh good," I said on a breath, not letting my frustration show. "You're here. Right on schedule. We're going for a run."

"What?"

"*A. Run,*" I enunciated, giving him a dubious look. "You know, like walking but faster."

"I'm starving. I thought maybe we could—"

"You thought wrong. We'll eat after. Hope you have some better shoes with you."

I glanced down at his brown leather boots, the tongue flapping out, laces loose. He'd never be able to keep up in those. Not that I cared. I needed to run. Now. Before I exploded with all this pent-up energy and rage. If Grey didn't want to be in the blast radius, then he'd better shut up and go along with it.

Grey opened his mouth to argue, but shut it again instead, pressing his lips together as he swept a sarcastic arm toward the hall. "Fine. Let's go for a run. Lead the way."

We didn't speak as I led him back to my shared apartment, changed and laced up my runners. Not even as we walked back down through the halls and out to the back gardens toward the trailhead at the back of campus, our shoes scuffing along tile and stone and eventually grass.

27

A little tremor of unease skated down my back, remembering the ominous messages from my would-be stalker still taking up space on my phone's hard drive. I hadn't run this path in weeks, but now, with Grey to accompany me, I supposed it was safer.

Perks.

I stuffed my earbuds in my ears just as he opened his mouth to say something. I pointed at them with a false apology curling my lips into a frown. "Sorry. Can't hear you," I told him as I hit play and broke into a jog, the crisp air in the shade of the matured trees already working small miracles on my nerves.

He kept pace easier than I thought he would in those boots. Laced up tight like he wore them now, I supposed they weren't completely useless.

I kept my eyes ahead after that, trying my best to ignore the fact that he was there as I let the exertion, the wind, and the smells of the forest swallow me up.

The sounds of Lola Blanc's Angry Too blared in my ears, distracting enough to keep my mind from wandering to bleaker territory again.

A smile curled my lips when I remembered that at any minute, Rook and Corvus could be noticing their missing door handles. I held onto that little joyous tidbit, letting it propel me onward. I thought for sure they'd have gotten a notification from the camera when I left earlier. Actually, they might've. It was probably why they came looking for me, but they didn't know that the pillowcase slung over my shoulder contained nearly every door handle in their entire house.

"AJ," Grey said some time later, his voice barely audible above the song in my ears.

Maybe if I didn't answer him he would shut up and stop ruining this for me. He better not be tired already. I was nowhere near finished.

"*AJ!*"

Fuck.

Moment ruined.

I stopped, tearing an earbud from my ear, heaving as sweat trickled down my back. "*What*?"

"Look, can we just…" Grey trailed off, a bit breathless, his dark green t-shirt stained darker from sweat around the neckline. His face pinched.

"Who is that?" he asked, gesturing to the earbud pinched between my fingers and the sounds of Primal Ethos' *Anthem of the Broken* blaring through it.

I rolled my eyes. *Of course* he wouldn't know who Primal Ethos is. He probably only listened to top 40 songs and whatever was playing on Virgin radio like his vapid bitch of an ex-girlfriend or ex-fuckbuddy or whatever she was.

My stomach soured, and I cursed myself for the wave of jealousy that sank deep into the marrow of my bones.

"You wouldn't know it," I barked, sniffling as I caught my breath, bouncing on foot to foot so I wouldn't ruin my runner's high. "That would require you to have actual taste in music."

His eyes widened, lips parting on a reply that he didn't bother speaking.

"What do you want, Winters?" I asked after another beat of silence. "You're kind of ruining my high right now."

He jerked his head back toward the path. "Come on, we can talk and jog."

I growled, pissed that he fucked with my high, but was happy to start moving again at least. Grudgingly, I popped out my other earbud and tucked both of them into the pocket of my running shorts.

"I wanted to apologize," he said, head bent to the earth, his jaw taut.

This surprised me enough that my own jaw clenched in response. I didn't want to hear this. I didn't want an apology. I wanted my goddamned freedom back.

If I didn't hold onto my anger, I would have nothing left to shield me, and I was going to need one heck of a shield for what was to come.

"For what?" I demanded. "For taking my freedom? For trying to own me? For locking me in that——"

"For all of it," he interrupted, his brows drawing together as he looked up at me.

I looked away. "You're not sorry," I muttered. "Your 'apology' isn't for me. It's for you. To assuage your guilt. Own your shit, Grey."

"That's not—"

"It doesn't matter. What's done is done."

"AJ..."

"Just stop, okay?" I stopped dead on the trail, forcing him to stop with me. "I don't care if you're sorry. Sorry doesn't fucking help me."

A muscle in his temple twitched and the sky above us rumbled, accentuating my anger. Beneath the shade of the trees, I hadn't noticed how the sky had begun to darken. Storm clouds rolled overhead, casting Thorn Valley in a mottled darkness.

"Besides," I continued, sighing, my runner's high officially dead now. "I have a feeling it wasn't you who locked me in that fucking room."

He winced.

"Your brother has a control problem."

He pressed his lips together.

"Or more like an *asshole* problem," I muttered, more to myself than to Grey.

30

He brushed a hand through his damp blond hair. "You just don't know him like we do," he said, his voice softer now. "He comes across like a controlling asshole, and, well, he sort of is, I guess, but he's also fiercely protective of us. He's—"

"I don't care," I cut him off, spinning on my heel to start the slow walk back toward Briar Hall, smelling rain in the air.

"Wait," Grey started, snatching my wrist and pulling me to a stop. "Just give him a chance. Get to know him. I know he wants to get to know you."

I laughed, a loud, howling thing.

"The bastard lost my blade," I started, tugging my wrist away, but moving closer, letting him see the resolve in my eyes. "Which he still hasn't replaced, by the way. He tried to blackmail me. Tried to own me. And that's not even including the fact that he's unbearably controlling *and* a rude dickface. I don't give a fuck if he wants to know me. I don't want to know *him*."

It was a lie, I realized as the final words fell full of venom from my lips, and that only made me even more furious than I already was.

I threw my hands up, exasperated.

"It wasn't just him," Grey said quietly after a moment. "We...Rook and me, we did a lot of those things too."

He was right, of course. The blame wasn't all on Corvus, but for some reason he was the easiest one to hate, and I wasn't ready to let go of that.

I tipped my head back, breathing deeply to soothe the waking darkness within. "You know what, let's just get back."

My phone buzzed audibly in my pocket, and I clenched my teeth. "Speak of the devil," I snarled, anticipating another message from Corvus. Furious that I would have to be dealing with his bullshit text messages, and no doubt phone calls, for my foreseeable future.

But it wasn't him.

Unknown: What a mess you've made, Ava Jade. I thought you were smarter than this.

My breath caught in my throat and immediately my head snapped up, scanning the forest on all sides, but there was nothing. Nothing save for overgrown weeds and trees.

My phone buzzed again in my hand.

Unknown: First the blond one. I knew that was just a mistake. But then you let that asshole touch you behind the curtain, and you even looked like you enjoyed it. Disgusting. And now you're right where Diesel wants you and you have no one to blame but yourself.

"What is it?" Grey asked, moving closer.

I stepped back, turning away from him as another two messages popped up onto the screen.

Unknown: You're just confused, I know, but that's no excuse.

Unknown: Don't worry, my love, I'll help you...but if you let them touch you again, I'll have no choice but to punish you.

Got you, you fucking ASSHOLE.

It was him. It was him *all along.* Taunting me. Teasing me. Trying to scare me.

The bastard.

No one knew we were behind that curtain on fight night. *No one* would've been able to see us. The slit in the edge of the curtain was tiny. There was no way...

It was Corvus.

Had been from the start.

"I'm going to kill him," I deadpanned, taking off at a

sprint into the trees, carving a path directly toward the Crow's Nest with Grey lagging behind, shouting for me to wait. To tell him what was going on.

Distantly, I heard a grunt as he fell. Good. Now there was no chance he would catch up.

The darkness I'd been working to suppress came rushing back, gushing up from deep within like a geyser.

From the start, I had a feeling it was him. I should have trusted my gut. Now there was no doubt.

It was funny how even though this wasn't the regular route I took to the Crow's Nest, I still knew exactly where I was going. Its location was anchored in my memory, a magnet to my compass. It drew me in as though I'd been going there my entire life.

My focus narrowed and the sound of Grey in the forest fell away, moving to nothing but a distant drone in my ears.

I couldn't believe Corvus' nerve.

This was a whole new low, even for Corvus. I understood icing me out. I could even understand trying to control me and attack me when he thought I was a threat. But this was just cruel. What was the purpose of it?

What was he trying to pull here? Did he want me to run? Was he trying to scare me away? So that Diesel would kill me? That way he wouldn't have to get his hands dirty himself.

That had to be it. I could see no other reason why he would do this. Unless he just got a kick out of making girls feel uncomfortable. Which, from what I knew of him, was entirely possible.

Either way, he wasn't going to get away with it. And if Rook and Grey were in on it with him they would go down, too. But something told me they weren't. This had Corvus written all over it. My chest began to ache around the same time the burn in my legs rose to an all-time high.

Until I was just an inferno of aching, burning fury.

The truth of it stung like a betrayal. But that was ridiculous, how could I feel betrayed if there was never trust to begin with?

I burst through the trees onto the gravel drive leading up to the Crow's Nest.

The front door stood ajar, and the Rover was parked in the driveway, the back hatch lifted to reveal several grocery bags and a flat of bottled water. It looked like they'd just returned home.

Corvus appeared in the doorway, exiting the house to retrieve the last of the groceries from the Rover.

I saw red.

My hands trembled as I stormed toward him.

"Motherfucker."

His distant gaze found me, brows drawing together. His lips parted, caught off guard to see me.

"Sparrow?"

I rushed him. Surprise registered in his icy blue eyes, one second too late.

I shoved him back, with my phone still clutched in my fist, the other slapping flat against his wide chest.

He stumbled back three steps, lip twisting into a sneer.

"What the fuck is your problem?" I demanded.

"AJ!" Grey shouted, breathless as he jogged up the drive.

I ignored him.

A shadow moved behind Corvus inside of the Nest, and Rook appeared in the hall, casually leaning against the wall as though there wasn't a seething dragon in his doorway.

"Suppose we have you to thank for our new open-

34

door policy?" he asked with a crooked smile.

"What?" Corvus snapped at him, gaze jarring between Rook's unruffled posture and my flaring nostrils, his own frustration rising to meet mine.

Triumph at my success with my little doorknob trick would have to wait. I had more pressing matters to attend to.

"How long have you been stalking me, asshole?"

Corvus feigned confusion.

That's when it clicked.

A long fucking time.

The stalker saw me that night on the train tracks. The stalker knew my darkest, dirtiest secret.

Corvus knew what I did that night.

Shit.

No, no, no.

"I'll ask you again," Corvus said, inhaling deeply to rein in his control. "What in the actual fuck are you talking about?"

Cold dread filled my veins, dousing the fire that burned there only a moment before. I didn't realize I was still gripping my phone in my hand until Grey snatched it away.

"Don't!"

The fire roared back in an instant, and I launched myself at Grey to get it back.

"Hold her," Grey growled, and Corvus was able to get his arms around my middle, fastening me to him as though we were welded together with steel.

"What the fuck," I gritted out, writhing. "Let go!"

"What are you doing?" Rook asked Grey so calmly that it just infuriated me even more.

"It was something on her phone," Grey mused. "She read something and then just took off like a bat out of hell."

"Shit," he cursed. "It's locked. What's your password?"

I continued struggling against Corvus' hold, but the way he had my arms tight against my sides, getting free was proving to be a chore and a fucking half. The muscles in my biceps and forearms flared from the effort while he grunted through my attempts at escape, his scent overwhelming my senses, playing tricks on my mind.

"Fuck you!" I spat at Grey. "I'm not telling you shit."

"*Sparrow...*" Corvus warned, his breath hot against my ear.

Fine. They wanted to play it like that? They could have it their way.

I stomped as hard as I could on Corvus' instep. When his hold loosened, I swung my leg forward and launched my heel back into his kneecap.

His hold on me broke enough for me to squirm free as he dropped to his good knee on the gravel drive.

He cursed loud and long, thick fingers reaching to try to grab me again, but it was too late. I was already on top of Grey, fighting to get my phone out of his grasp.

I didn't want to hurt him, well at least not that much, so I took him down gently. My version of gently.

My phone knocked from his hand as he fell. The wind gushed out through his lips from the impact with the gravel. I snatched my phone and stood, glaring at all of them. At Corvus on his knees. At Grey on his back. At Rook leaning against the door jamb with a prideful smirk on his mouth.

Smart fucker, not joining the fray. I wouldn't have gone easy on him, and I doubt he'd have gone easy on me, either. It would've been glorious.

A lot of that hot, angry wind in my sails died down as

the realization of what Corvus knew truly sank in. I was still pissed, but also very wary of him telling the others… That was, if they didn't already know.

"AJ, can we stop for a second?" Grey asked, a note of impatience in his tone as he got to his feet and brushed the gravel dust off of his ass. "Could you just tell us what's going on?"

I pointed an accusing finger at Corvus, my chest heaving.

"Why don't you ask him?"

Grey's eyes slipped to his adoptive brother.

"Don't fucking look at me," he said, raising his arm in a shrug. "I have no idea. Maybe it's that time of the month."

Fucking prick.

I chuckled darkly to myself, the sound bordering on mania as the muscles in my jaw tightened again. I hadn't really realized how stressed and creeped out the messages had been making me with everything else that'd been happening, but now, at least, it was over.

With fingers rigor mortis stiff, I jabbed the phone screen until one of the newest messages from the unknown number appeared. The one detailing what Corvus and I did behind that curtain on fight night. I closed the small gap between us just as he finished getting to his feet, barely able to put any weight on his right leg.

I thrust the phone out, forcing him to look.

"So, you're telling me this *wasn't* you?"

Corvus' nostrils flared, his face growing red as he squinted to read the message on the screen. Leaning in, his sneer turned quickly to a frown.

"Sparrow, I didn't send that."

"Oh, and I suppose you didn't send any of the others, either?"

"Others? How many messages like this do you have?"

Concern pinched the skin between his eyes, and the muscles around his mouth. It certainly added to the effect of his claimed innocence. I had to say, I almost believed him.

"You're so full of shit."

"Ava Jade," Corvus pressed, straightening to his full height, and for some reason, the look on his face combined with the succinct way he spoke my name gave me pause. "I did *not* send that."

Rook, curious now, moved from his leaning stance against the door jamb to stand next to Corvus. "What is it?"

"But…" I trailed off, not breaking eye contact with Corvus even as my own began to burn from not blinking. There was no lie in his stare. He was either a *damn* good liar, or he wasn't lying to me at all. "It has to be you."

He shook his head once.

"Corv doesn't lie," Grey affirmed for his brother. "He owns his shit. If he does something, he does it with purpose. Without apology."

Corv gave Grey a grateful nod, and I could see it.

It made sense.

If it were him, he wouldn't have lied about it. He would have given me that infuriating smirk of his with a satisfied *gotcha* gleam in his bright eyes.

"Let me see the other messages," Corvus said, not a request, but a demand.

I faltered back a step, swallowing hard. "No," I muttered, blinking as I tucked my phone back away in my pocket. "No. It's nothing."

I cursed myself for not deleting all the other messages sooner. The one about what I'd done at the train tracks, especially. Now this stalker's words felt as though they were burning a hole in my pocket.

My relief at knowing this wasn't Corvus after all was overshadowed by a whole new brand of dread.

This person, whoever they were, had been watching me more closely than I'd thought. They were there, somehow, on fight night, and less than twenty-four hours ago, at that yard out behind the abandoned building.

The worst part was, I hadn't sensed it. If I had a tail, I should've noticed by now. *Why* hadn't I noticed?

Oh, yeah, probably because I've been fucking distracted by three *vultures* bent on making my life hell since the moment I got here.

Maybe Corvus wasn't Mr. *Unknown Number*, but it was his fucking fault regardless.

"It's *not* nothing, let me see," Corvus continued.

"AJ, just give him the phone."

"Just forget it," I snapped, promising myself I'd delete every single message from this asshole as soon as I got back to Briar Hall and had a moment alone.

"I told Becca about fight night. I forgot. It was probably her being stupid," I lied.

"What about fight night?" Rook asked, his teeth slipping across the silver loop of his lip ring.

Shit. Okay. *Just shut up, Ava Jade.*

By the way Corvus was eyeing Grey from his toes all the way up to his *blond* hair, I knew he was piecing that part of the message together right at this very moment.

This was *not* what I was after when I came here.

Steeling myself, I clenched my teeth and spun on my heel, snatching Grey's wrist as I went. "Come on, I'm hungry. Let's get out of here."

Grey shrugged at his brothers, and I caught Rook saluting him from the corner of my eye before we began

39

the slow walk back down the hill.

"Want to tell me what that was about?" Grey hedged, a dark aura around him, shadowing his light.

Behind us, I heard Corvus ask what Rook was saying about an open-door policy and stiffened.

"Keep up," I told Grey, releasing him. I picked up my pace, pushing my aching legs into a quick jog to escape before the nuclear fallout hit.

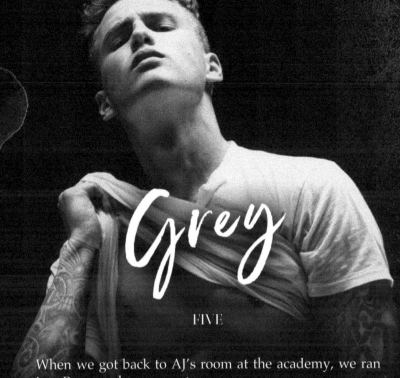

Grey

FIVE

When we got back to AJ's room at the academy, we ran into Becca on her way out.

I'd been about to ask her more about what happened back at the Nest, but the appearance of her friend silenced me for the moment. I may not have been as perceptive as the others, but I got the sense AJ wasn't telling us everything. She was downplaying the message, or *messages*, since she said there were others.

Guilt lingered long after the short-lived altercation with Corvus. I shouldn't have taken her phone, or told Corvus to hold her while I tried to read the messages.

But...

The distress, *the fury* in her eyes when she read whatever was on her phone was too much to ignore. I needed to know what it was. What could possibly drive her to that level of anger that quickly. I wanted to crush it. Shatter it. Burn it to ashes.

I wanted to ask her to tell me, now that the others weren't with us, what it was that she'd read. Of course, I could ask Corvus, but from the way he was looking at me before we left, I got the sense that I'd done something to piss him off.

He was already on edge. Best to leave him alone until he managed some shut eye. But they weren't letting this go, either. My phone buzzed nonstop the whole run back to the academy, and I knew it was them.

"Oh, hey girl!" Becca trilled uneasily, glancing between us as we nearly bumped into her leaving their shared apartment.

"Hey," AJ grumbled, pasting on the ghost of a smile for her friend.

"I was just on my way out," Becca continued, jabbing a thumb back toward the door. "But," she paused, eyes slipping toward me. "I can stay if you want me to."

AJ waved her off, kicking her shoes off to step farther into the living room. "Nah. I'm good. You go ahead."

"When will you be back?" I asked, earning myself a confused look from Becca and a pointed glare from AJ, who paused on the threshold to the kitchen.

AJ's nose wrinkled. "Leave her alone, Grey."

"I just want to know when to expect her back," I explained, not allowing AJ to overrule me on this. She didn't understand the stakes here. What exactly was going to be happening to her over the next sixty days. Her trials could happen anywhere, at any time. Someone entering the flat could just as easily be a member of the Saints, come to attack her in bed. Testing her ability to react in the heat of the moment.

If I heard an intruder in the night, I could at least give her a few seconds head start. Wake her up. Tell her to be ready for attack. And maybe not to kill whoever it was.

They were prepared for that, though. I'd have killed the one who surprise attacked me during my trials if he wasn't wearing a vest and tactical gear.

"Um," Becca replied, uncomfortable now. "I don't know—"

"You don't have to answer that," AJ told her friend.

"It's fine," Becca replied with a little wave of her hand.

"I don't know exactly when," she told me. "But it'll be late. Midnight, maybe. One, the latest."

I cocked my head at her. I hadn't expected that response. That was late. Really late. Where was she going?

Not my business.

"Thanks," I said with a tip of my head. "I have your number. I'll text you so you have mine. If you wouldn't mind texting before you get back, that would be great."

"You have my number?" she asked, surprise paling her salon-quality tan.

"Have a good night," I replied, my words punctuated by a loud groan from AJ in the kitchen, followed by muttered curses as she began messing with pots and pans in the cabinet.

"Uh, yeah," Becca replied, in a bit of a daze. "You, too."

She left without another word, and I leaned over to lock the door behind her, bending to unlace my boots.

A *snap* preceded a light sting on my forehead, and I jerked my head up, finding an elastic on the floor by my feet and AJ shooting mental daggers at me from the kitchen. "Don't harass my friend or the next thing I launch in your direction won't be as nice."

The cast iron pan clutched loosely in her hand accentuated her point. I sighed.

"It's for your own good," I tried, seeing that I was

43

going to get nowhere with her tonight. Not while she was riled up and still on edge about whatever was happening on her phone.

"*It's for your own good,*" she mocked, turning on the gas burner and dropping the heavy pan onto it with a loud clamor. "If you're eating here, then you can at least help me cook. Get over here and peel the onions."

It was going to be a long night.

My hip bone and shoulder ached, pressed against her bedroom floor.

I shifted, trying to get comfortable with only one pillow to work with and no blanket.

I explained after dinner how I'd need to sleep in her room. Diesel's orders meant as little separation from her as possible. If I slept in the living room, she could easily slip out her bedroom window without me noticing. I checked it out earlier, it wouldn't be all that difficult to climb down.

As it was, with me on the floor between her bed and the window, escape using that route wouldn't be possible. She could sneak out the front door, but I was a light sleeper. Unless she was ninja quiet, I'd hear her.

Not like I was getting any sleep, anyway. Though, neither was she.

She tossed and turned in her bed two and a half feet up and five feet away from me. Restless. Sighing heavily every few minutes.

I had no doubt it was my doing. The fact that I was here, in her personal space. Corvus was the same way. The only time he ever slept was alone in his room with the door both locked and deadbolted. His phone right beside his head. The light from his studio closet left on in case he needed to see anything when he woke.

I wondered if she was thinking of earlier, when I

made her sit in her bathroom with me while I showered off the sweat from our run. I thought she might turn away. Not look as I stripped down and stepped into the glass encased shower, but she didn't.

She folded her arms over her chest and stared openly, her expression betraying nothing as she watched me step inside and then wash myself meticulously from top to bottom.

It was almost impossible not to be turned on with her watching me like that, even if it was a cold kind of stare. A stare that said, *you don't affect me,* even though the slight squeeze of her thighs betrayed the feeling she concealed beneath her mask.

Ava Jade groaned slightly before sitting up in bed. I listened as she sighed again, checking my phone for the time.

It was just past eleven, and there were already several more messages waiting on there from the guys in the group chat.

Corvus: Did she tell you anything more?

Corvus: If she's not going to fess up, can we hack into her phone? We need to see what else she's hiding from us. Those messages seemed threatening. I think she's lying about it being Becca.

Rook: Agreed. Something's off. I don't like it.

Angling my phone so she couldn't see, I typed out a quick reply, knowing neither of my brothers would sleep until I did. Ava Jade shut down my questions all night about the texts she claimed were from Becca, making me even more on edge. It took all the restraint I had to let it go, but only because I knew we'd find out whether she wanted to tell us or not.

Grey: I'll look into it. Shouldn't be too hard.

Corvus' reply was immediate.

Corvus: Good.

Ava Jade rose from her bed and padded to the door, stepping out into the living room, and even as tired as I was, I was grateful to have to get up off the solid floor.

Corv liked his bed hard, the mattress so over-firm it was uncomfortable even to sit on. But not me. I liked a good soft bed. Pillowtop. Plush. More like Rook's, though fur and Egyptian cotton weren't really my thing.

I'd take either over this, though. This floor was going to leave me with goddamned bruises.

I stretched out the kinks in my bones and went to the door, squinting out into the moonlit space. AJ was in the sunken area by the couches, searching beneath the coffee table for something. When she didn't find it, she huffed, moving onto the fireplace mantle and eventually the little cabinet beneath it. Getting more and more annoyed as she searched.

What was she looking for?

AJ paused as she pulled something forward from the back of the cabinet, tilting the box-like shape toward the light.

She pressed a button on it and it whirred to life as she leaned back, grabbing something from the top of the coffee table.

The television mounted above the slim fireplace flicked on, the blue light expanding until it coated the room with its eerie glow, making AJ reel back for a moment from its brightness.

It was clear what she was doing when she changed the input and drew what was unmistakably a controller from the back of the cabinet. She wiped the dust off the controller with her shirt and then toggled to the downloaded games as the console finished coming to life.

She chose a first-person shooter. A zombie game I

46

hadn't heard of. There weren't a wide array of choices. She wasn't half bad, either. It took her a few rounds, a few virtual deaths, before she hit her stride, cutting down zombies and their offspring with ease, zooming through challenges and levels.

Her hair kept falling in her face as she played, and she roughly threw it back between zombie kills. The urge to hold it back for her, to pull it up into a ponytail out of her way gripped me, and I frowned.

It was an odd thought. What did I care if her hair was getting in her eyes?

Sitting how she was, cross legged on the floor, backlit in blue, she looked like my own personal poltergeist. Disturbing my routines, throwing my life into chaos.

And yet, just like before, I couldn't say I wanted her gone.

Or that I wished she never came here.

On the contrary, I wanted her more.

Even knowing what she was trying to do to us before the night at the warehouse didn't change anything. If I was in her shoes, I'd have done the same. Hell, I might've done worse.

The strap of her shirt slipped off her right shoulder, and she flicked her hair back again, sweeping it to the side, away from her slender neck. So fucking beautiful.

My cock thickened in my boxers, and I pawed it, trying to readjust.

I did say I wanted to talk to her, but maybe talking wasn't going to fix anything. Apologizing to her with words for earlier wouldn't mean shit. But maybe I could show her in other ways.

I was thinking with my cock again, a flaw Corvus constantly reminded me I needed to fix, but right now, I didn't give a flying fuck if this was a good idea. Or if she'd stab me for trying.

"I know you're there," she said quietly, her attention still focused wholly on the game. Her neck craned upward to see it. "I'm not going anywhere so you can just go back to sleep."

"I wasn't sleeping," I replied, my voice huskier than intended.

Her shoulders gave a slight shudder that I took to mean I was on the right track, my erection pressing harder against the front of my boxers now, but it wasn't me who'd be getting his rocks off.

Not yet, anyway, this was an apology after all.

I knelt behind her, and she faltered, getting attacked by a zombie, her health depleting a little before her virtual avatar managed to fend him off.

"What are you doing?" she asked, a note of impatience in her tone as she jammed the attack button on the controller, grunting as she took down another three of them on screen.

I leaned in, inhaling her scent, my nose brushing along the soft skin just below her right ear. "Apologizing," I replied.

AJ shied away as though I'd tickled her, and I wondered if she was ticklish. Something to explore another time. I slipped a hand around her middle, caressing her ribs before my fingers splayed over her belly.

She let me, at least at first.

The controller went lax in her hands, a horde of zombies taking advantage of her distraction, and she grabbed my hand, stopping its downward trajectory.

"Just let me touch you," I crooned, and her grip on me held for another few seconds until it relented.

"Why should I?"

"Call it an apology. You know, since *words won't help.*

48

I thought this might."

She hesitated another second, the muscles in her arms swelling as she clutched the controller tight and then set it down.

"No," I blurted. "Keep playing."

"What?"

"Bet you can't keep focus," I taunted, making it a game. A challenge.

I got the feeling she didn't back down from those often.

I swore I could almost hear her smirking from my position behind her as she took the controller up again just in time for another zombie to attack. I placed my hand back on her stomach, and she let out a small gasp as I dipped it below the waistband of her little pajama shorts.

"Focus," I reminded her as my fingers brushed her clit, making her hips buck forward slightly, pressing her sweet cunt into my fingers, aching for more. I rested my chin on her shoulder, sitting with my legs pressed against her, wrapping her in my scent. Marking her as mine.

I shivered internally, her need making my own soar. My cock ached in my boxers, throbbing in time with my pulse as I began a slow circular motion with my fingers, light and teasing.

She made a small moaning sound, and I clenched my teeth to keep myself from jumping her right there on the floor. From tossing the controller out of her grasp and forcing her onto her back.

No. This was about her. Not me.

Not today.

I pushed through her slick folds, finding the heat of her center as I slid in first with one finger, then with two.

Her shots on screen went wide, and she stopped altogether as I added my thumb to the mix, rubbing her clit as I fucked her with my fingers.

"Uh, Uh," I warned with a tight smile on my lips, pressing them lightly against her neck. My cock ached inside the confines of my boxers. I slowed, almost stopping, and she continued playing. Redoubling her efforts to focus on the game. "You stop, I stop," I murmured in her ear, licking the fingers of my other hand before wrapping it around her to join the first below the waistband of her shorts.

I rubbed her clit mercilessly with one hand while I pumped my fingers in and out with the other, gaining speed. But it wasn't enough. I wanted more. I wanted her screaming.

I wanted her to shatter with my name on her lips.

AJ let out a small whine as I withdrew both my hands and moved to kneel. I grabbed her waist, lifting and moving her until she was seated on the edge of the coffee table.

My knees brushed the soft rug as I found my place in front of her and looped my fingers into the waistband of her shorts to tug them off. She obliged, wiggling her hips with a knot between her brows as she continued her game.

She opened her mouth to speak, but I hushed her. "This means nothing," I said for her, an echo of our last encounter in the bathroom. It was written all over her expression: how much she wanted this, *needed* the release, and how much she hated that she wanted it.

I hated wanting her, too. Or at least, I did.

Before.

Now?

I didn't think there was anything I could hate about her. Not even if I fucking tried.

I pried her legs apart and buried my face in her pussy before she could change her mind and push me away. Her sweet heat coated my tongue and *fuck* she tasted so. damn. good.

Her thighs squeezed, muscles clenching from the attack of my tongue, little gasping moans stuttering from her lips.

I was good at this, I knew. She got a taste in the bathroom, but today she would get the full experience.

With one hand clenching her hip to hold her in place, I slid the other between her legs, slipping it beneath my chin to join my tongue. I pushed inside, never ceasing the quick flicking motions with my tongue even as I began viciously finger fucking her.

AJ moved, squirming from the pleasure. You'd almost think she was trying to get away with how much she squirmed, but my bruising grip on her waist held her steady. Forced her to feel *everything*.

She stopped fighting a minute later, instead, grinding herself against me. AJ fucked my face like a woman starved, and I ate up every fucking second of it. Increasing the pace with my fingers to match her. We moved together, every thrust of her hips, every flick of my tongue, every stroke of my fingers, perfectly in sync until the controller clattered to the floor, and her fingers dove into my hair, gripping tighteningly, holding me there with a shout as she came on my lips.

I continued through her orgasm, forcing it to lengthen, making her shudder and twitch, trying to pull away, but I didn't let her. Not until the violent pull of her fingers in my hair began to soften and eventually to cease.

Only then did I stop, staring up at her with her wetness gleaming on my lips. She looked down at me with something I couldn't identify in her eyes. Heat, but not hatred. The knot never left the space between her brows, not even when she slumped back onto the coffee table, hands going to her chest as it heaved. Utterly spent.

I got uncomfortably to my feet with a grimace, my cock so disgustingly sensitized that even the brush of it against my boxers was like the phantom stroke of her fingers.

Her eyes were heavy-lidded, face flushed and slack.

She was so tired.

"Come on," I whispered, stooping to lift her from the table, slipping my forearms beneath her knees and around her shoulders.

She didn't protest as I carried her back to bed, setting her onto the soft mattress and drawing the blanket up to her chest.

"Sleep," I ordered, and her eyes shuttered despite her efforts to keep them trained on me.

She was uncomfortable, but maybe it wasn't because of me after all. Maybe it was because she knew as well as I did that someone could come in here for her first trial any minute. Or maybe it was something else I wasn't even aware of.

"I'll keep watch if you like," I added on a whim, and she looked at me strangely. Pained almost.

Her gaze flitted to the other side of the bed and for a heart-stopping moment I thought she might draw back the covers, invite me to sleep there with her on the bed. But then she turned away, drawing her knees to her chest without a word.

For a girl who always had something to say, her silence was disconcerting. I didn't know what it meant. While I cleaned up the evidence of what we'd done in the living room, I tried to analyze it, wishing I could be as perceptive as my brothers.

A key slipped into a lock as I shut off the TV and grabbed AJ's wet shorts from the floor. I froze, rushing to the edge of the fireplace as the intruder pushed inside.

I'd be damned if I was going to let him ruin her sleep. After how hard I worked to send her off.

I stepped into the wide entry, making my shoulders wide and thick as I lifted my head. "Not tonight, asshole. *Leave.*"

"*Um,*" squeaked a very female voice. "I just want to go to bed."

The small pod light in the entry flicked on, and I reeled back at its brightness, taking in all six feet of Rebecca Hart in a pair of strappy black heels, her hair in disarray.

Her wide eyes zeroed in on AJ's shorts in my hand, and the erection next to them.

My face heated as I covered it with the shorts, clearing my throat.

"Shit," I muttered, trying to keep my voice low so I wouldn't wake AJ. "Sorry, Becca."

"I texted," she said, defending herself. "Just like you asked."

Right. Except I left my phone in AJ's room.

"All good," I replied, already moving away. "My bad."

"Who…" Becca trailed off, her brows drawn. "Who did you think I was?"

Again, my bad. Obviously, AJ hadn't told her about the trials. She *should* tell her. Everyone was fair game after all, but it wasn't my place to do it for her.

"No one," I told her. "Don't worry about it."

I jabbed a thumb back in the direction of AJ's room. "I should probably…"

Becca's brown eyes flitted down to my erection and then away. "Yeah. You two have fun. 'Night."

AJ was going to kill me.

I paused after only a step, a prickle crawling over the back of my neck. "Actually," I said as I turned back to face her, keeping my voice as low as I could. "If I ask you something, could you keep it between us?"

Becca's gaze slid to her friend's bedroom door and back to me again, narrowing. Her jaw clamping tight.

"It's important," I urged.

Grudgingly, she pursed her lips. "Depends what it is."

I stifled the urge to shout, remembering AJ's twisted face in the woods.

"Did you text AJ earlier today? A little while after last period?"

She frowned. "Why?"

"Answer the question."

Her throat bobbed. "No," she finally said after a few beats of tense silence. "No, I didn't text her."

Fuck.

"Thanks. That's all I needed to know."

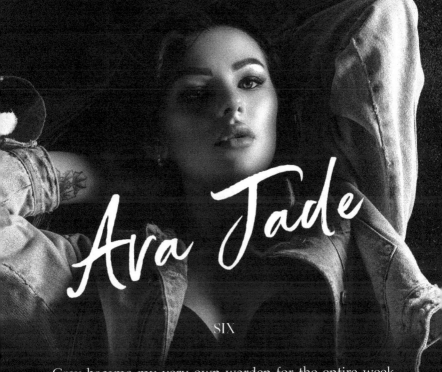

Ava Jade

Grey became my very own warden for the entire week. Nobody said it, but I suspected it was because Corvus was too angry to be around me for any length of time, and they didn't trust Rook not to eat me.

That was the vibe I got, easily surmised from the fact that Corvus hadn't spoken to me since Tuesday night over the phone, and when Rook offered to take over for Grey yesterday after class, Corvus and Grey replied a resounding *no* at the exact same time.

Rook shrugged it off with a roll of his eyes and a wink in my direction, but something told me it bothered him more than he was letting on.

"So, what now?" I asked after last period on Friday, barely looking up to check if Grey was waiting outside of class as I exited, heading for my room. His distinct footfalls padded along beside me. I'd grown accustomed to them over the last few days.

"Corv said we had…."

The hairs along the back of my neck pricked as the elevator down the hall pinged dully, the doors sliding open. Grey's sentence trailed off as his brothers exited, scattering the students that still lingered in the corridor.

"We have a pick up out of town," Corvus announced.

Grey stiffened. "*All* of us?" he asked. "What about her?"

He jabbed a thumb in my direction, and I tried not to let the heat of my anger rise. I hated when they talked about me like I wasn't even here. Like I was cargo. An obstacle. Like I didn't have a choice.

Corvus' cold blue eyes slid to me and then away. "She's with us. Diesel wants all three of us on the job."

"And he wants us to bring her?" Grey challenged, a doubtful note of sarcasm in his tone.

Corvus visibly tensed, annoyance in the knot between his brows. "He offered for us to drop her off at Sanctum with him," he all but growled, watching Grey carefully for his reaction.

"That's what I thought," he continued. "So, she's with us. When we're close, we'll blindfold her. And she can wait in the car."

"Could you all stop talking about me like I'm not right fucking here?"

"Problem, Sparrow?"

"Yeah, actually. I have plans tonight."

"Cancel them," Corvus bit out, a muscle flexing in his jaw. "And in the future you might want to check with me first before making *plans*."

"Asshole."

Rook laughed, his teeth pulling lightly on his lip ring as he watched me. "Come on, Ghost," he said. "I'll buy you an ice cream."

Ghost?

Corvus turned to raise a brow at him but said nothing.

"Better be one hell of an ice cream," I sighed. "I'm missing movie night for this shit."

"Trust me," Rook replied, a gleam in his dark eyes. "It'll be worth it."

I drew out my phone and ignored the newest text from Aunt Humphrey while thumbing a quick text to Becca, telling her I was sorry but I didn't know when I'd be back.

I could put my foot down. Refuse to go. But I figured that was exactly what Corvus wanted. He'd fucking love that. An opportunity to flex his control muscles. To try to throw me over his shoulder again, kicking and screaming through the halls of the academy as he dragged me to their car.

I wouldn't give it to him.

Besides, this was exactly the sort of intel I'd need to be able to bring them down. And ice cream was just the cherry on top of the pie.

Corvus jammed the elevator button again and stepped in as the doors re-opened, Rook following, and Grey ushering me in behind them.

"Get those handles replaced?" I asked innocently, breaking the silence on the slow descent to the main floor, basking in my triumph for the first time. God, it felt good.

The air in the elevator seemed to heat in the split second before Corvus replied.

"No," he growled. "They were *imports*."

"We have another two weeks of our new open-door policy before they'll arrive," Rook put in, looking nearly as smug as I felt, until his dark gaze fell back to Corvus and his smirk faded.

"Too bad," I sighed, turning back to face the doors, injecting some drama into the words.

The *ping* of the elevator rang like a dinner bell in the hot silence, and I was dragged backward as the door opened, the fist in the back of my shirt tossing me against the wall. The air knocked from my lungs as Corvus pressed me there, his forearm a bar against my throat. But I was ready for him this time, my blade pressed firmly against his side, just below the ribs, angled up.

Unbothered by the blade, he pressed against my throat, his blue eyes burning with the heat of a thousand suns. The red veins bright as fresh blood against the whites.

"You think this is fucking funny?" he demanded. "*Hmm?*"

"Actually, yeah," I spat back, my voice strained from his arm. "I do."

Corvus choked on a reply as Grey gripped him by the shoulder and hauled him back with a grunt.

"*Stop.*" Grey's voice resounded in the elevator.

"Just stop," he repeated as I gasped for a full breath, still keeping a wary eye on Corvus. Grey was giving his brother the same look, though his was tainted with worry and something else I couldn't name. I got the feeling Corvus didn't often show his anger in a physical way. He reserved that level of animosity just for me. "When was the last time you slept?"

"Don't fucking start," Corvus sneered. "You try sleeping with no goddamned door handle, see how you like it."

"Right, because *the floor* is so much more comfortable."

Corvus glanced between Grey and me, his right brow lowering in question. He hadn't expected that. Did he really think I was letting Grey cuddle up to me every night? Even after his *apology* Tuesday night, I wasn't about to go soft. It was a release I needed, and I could already feel that pressure building again, but it didn't change anything.

They were still my enemies.

"Want to trade?" Grey pressed, challenging his brother. "I'll take no door handle over rock solid floor any fucking day."

Rook raised his hand, a sly smirk tugging up one corner of his mouth. "I'll trade," he crooned, eyeing me up and down. The path of his eyes leaving a scorching heat everywhere it touched, making my insides squeeze. "Anytime."

Corvus scrubbed a shaky palm over his face as he sighed. "Fuck it," he said finally, dropping his head as he shook it, inhaling deeply. It was as though I wasn't even there anymore and I realized he'd just gone back to ignoring me. Pretending I wasn't there was easier than admitting I was getting to him. That I was *always* getting to him.

Under his skin.

Into his head.

I could see it.

And I fucking reveled in it.

"Let's go get this pick up handled. The sooner it's over the sooner she's out of my sight."

My chest squeezed, and I swallowed hard to squelch the unwelcome sensation, strutting from the elevator as though I didn't have a care in the world when the doors opened.

"Sounds peachy to me."

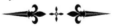

I thought I had some idea where we were headed, at least for the first hour of the drive. But now, closing in on two hours of driving, I needed to admit I had no fucking clue where we were going. The fact they hadn't even blindfolded me yet told me there was still a decent amount of ground to cover. So much for making it back in time for late night movies with Becca.

I grumbled wordlessly to myself, almost as loud as the growling in my belly, as I checked the map app on my phone again. Still heading south. We were basically in the middle of butt fuck nowhere. This county road seemed to lead to some tiny place called Eugine, but as far as I knew there was no Saint presence this far away from Thorn Valley. And I'd been doing my research, a lot of it.

Grey's gaze flicked to me in the rearview, his reflected eyes falling to the device in my hand before flitting away again. It wasn't the first time I'd caught him watching me, or rather, watching my phone, and my reaction to what I'm looking at on its screen.

He wasn't sold on the idea that my little outburst earlier in the week was nothing. I didn't think any of them were, but Grey seemed the most suspicious. The others, at least at the surface level, seemed keen to just let the whole thing drop.

I thought I'd better send a quick reply to Becca's earlier texts since they'd likely be taking my phone and putting it into airplane mode around the same time they blindfolded me.

Becca: Hey girl, where are you?

Becca: What time are you coming back later?

Ava Jade: Not sure and not sure. Sorry. I'll let you know when we're on our way, though.

Another text pinged through before I could repocket my phone.

Becca: Are all the guys with you?
Ava Jade: Yeah. Why? Everything okay?

She took so long to reply this time that I almost called her, wondering why she'd want to know where they all were. If she was in some sort of trouble. Diesel-sized trouble. I wouldn't put it past him to use her against me in the trials, but if he did, it would be a massive mistake.

My finger hovered over the dial button when her reply came in.

Becca: Everything's fine! Sorry, I just got a call from my beau. I'm off to see him. Don't wait up for me, k?
Ava Jade: Have fun!

Rook shifted, stretching his leg out further as he lounged in the back seat next to me. A frown turned down the edges of his mouth as he, too, stared at the device in my hands. I shut it off and cleared my throat, pocketing it with a sigh.

I'd deleted every trace of the so-called stalker from it, but I knew there were ways to recover those messages. Grey seemed like the type to know exactly how to do that, so I needed to make sure I didn't give him an opportunity to. I slept with it under my pillow all week, refusing to give him any opportunity to snatch it from my bedside table.

Other than that first night, I'd barely slept more than an hour at a time, every time he shifted against the hard floor, sighing, I woke, ready to smother him with a pillow in sleepless frustration. It was a wonder he still drew breath.

"How much longer?" I asked, speaking over the low hum of the radio for the first time.

"As long as it takes," Corvus grumbled in reply from the seat in front of me, his elbow resting on the window's ledge, his thick fingers propping up his heavy head at his

61

temple.

I rolled my eyes and caught him giving me a spiteful look in the side view mirror. To which I flipped him the bird and he looked away, appearing bored, but the vein throbbing thickly in his neck told a different story.

"I'm fucking starved," Rook groused, sliding his tongue over his lower lip. "Let's stop for food, yeah?"

"No," Corvus deadpanned.

My stomach rumbled at the mention of food, and Rook shot me a smirk.

"Awe, come on, man. I promised the girl an ice cream."

He winked at me and *dammit* if my toes didn't curl.

"I don't care."

"It's five now," Grey put in. "By the time we get back, it'll be past eight. We should eat."

Rook reached a tatted hand around the headrest to squeeze his brother's shoulder with a triumphant grin. "Majority rules," he said, smug as fuck.

"Fine. But make it quick."

"There's a diner up ahead," Rook said, his teeth spinning the lip ring at the edge of his mouth. "Stop there."

Corvus made a disgruntled sound and sank lower in his seat, bloodshot blue eyes fixed on the horizon.

The diner came into view as we crested the top of a low hill. A short, squat building that looked like it hadn't been renovated whatsoever since the eighties. Only three cars were parked in the front lot and through the fogged glass windows, I could only see a handful of people seated at purple pleather coated booths.

I'd eaten at worse. Dad always joked I had an iron gut. Forged on trailer park water supply and fifty cent street hotdogs for dinner. I could eat whatever the hell I wanted here and be fine tomorrow, but these guys?

I doubted they could say the same.

"Pull around back," Rook directed as Grey slowed, the Rover's tires moving from uneven pavement to the dirt and gravel drive of the diner.

Grey cast Rook a look in the rearview, but did as his brother asked, driving us around to the back of the building to park beside a rusted old black van I assumed belonged to the owner or an employee.

"Who's going in?" Grey asked. "We should grab some shit to go. I want to be back before dark."

Rook nodded, his glimmering gaze hedging in my direction.

"We'll send her," he decided, still turning his lip ring.

"I'll take their fattest burger," he told me, licking his lips. "With fries and a shake. Chocolate."

"Oh, so now I'm your fucking butler, too?"

"She's not going in alone," Corvus huffed, as though he was explaining something for the tenth time to a bunch of dimwits. It wasn't lost on his brothers, either.

Grey's jaw tensed as he shut off the ignition. "Where the fuck is she going to go?" he asked, and it was odd seeing this side to him. Ever since that night out at the warehouse, something in Grey has shifted. Hardened. He wasn't who I originally thought he was.

Not their weakest link. Not by a longshot.

Though that's what he'd have you think.

Corvus lifted his head from resting on his knuckles to give Grey an appraising look.

"She's not to be out of our sight."

"There's nothing for miles," Rook chimed in. "She could run as far as she wanted in any direction and we'd find her in half a minute."

He wasn't wrong. The terrain here was desert-like. A

flat expanse of hard packed, hot dirt with the odd shrub or stunted tree jutting up from the cracked earth. Nowhere to hide. Nowhere to run to.

Corv's jaw flexed, but he didn't reply.

Guess that meant I was playing servant.

Though the prospect of being alone without any of them to shadow me, for even five minutes, felt like anything but a punishment.

Grey removed his seatbelt with a sigh. "I'll go with her."

"You won't," Rook snapped, cutting his brother a meaningful look before his expression levelled back out. "She's got this. What'll it be, Brother? Clubhouse?"

Grey's brows lowered, his lips pressing together as he considered his brother.

Was I missing something?

"Yeah," Grey replied. "With fries and gravy."

"Corv?" Rook asked, expectant.

"Not hungry."

"He'll have whatever looks the least greasy."

"I said I'm not fucking hungry."

"Ignore him. He'll be less of a hangry grump once I've stuffed dinner down his throat."

I bit back a laugh as Corvus growled quietly to himself, his jaw grinding.

I slipped out the door, but Rook stopped me. His rough fingers slipping around my wrist, making me shudder internally. "Don't forget your ice cream, Ghost."

He slipped a small wad of bills into my hand and released me. "Oh, and I'll be needing you to leave your phone with me."

A bolt of ice struck low in my gut. "Why? I probably don't even have service here."

A lie. I did have service, and I fully intended to make

a call while I was alone inside. I needed a better bug. The one I'd planted in the knotted wood beneath the kitchen window at the Nest was a fucking dud. It barely lasted more than twenty-four hours after the second charge. Useless. I needed the good shit. The kind Kit's contact could get for me. If I made it worth his while, I was willing to bet I could even get him to drive it out to me at Briar Hall.

Rook's devilish grin told me he knew exactly what I'd been plotting. Or at least, that I'd been plotting *something*.

He held his hand outstretched, the tough leather of his palm flat and expectant.

My jaw clenched as I slid the phone from my pocket and dropped it into his hand.

"Fine."

He closed his fingers around it and nodded. I reassured myself that there was nothing they could do with it here in the middle of nowhere, without a computer and the proper cords to bypass my password and hack into the device's backup drives.

My call to Kit would have to wait. At least for now.

I shut the door behind me, maybe a little too forcefully, as I could feel Corvus' eyes burning a hole into the back of my skull as I stalked around the building towards the front entrance. The smells of greasy bacon and home cooked chicken soup drew me in, and my stomach twinged in hollow discomfort.

I should've eaten more at lunch, but Becca had about a million questions and I wound up leaving with my plate still half full. A waste of perfectly good food. Enough to have fed Mom, Dad, and me once upon a time.

I wanted to tell her the truth of everything that was going on, but wasn't sure what exactly the rules were. Not that I was averse to breaking them...more like I just didn't want to deal with Corvus' bullshit if I did.

The bell atop the yellowed glass door jingled as I stepped into the diner, the humidity kicked up a notch from the dry heat outside. I inhaled deeply, reveling in the greasy scent. I wondered if I could eat a burger fast enough to keep my ice cream from melting.

Sounded like my kind of challenge.

I ignored dirty looks from an older couple seated in a booth to my right and approached the counter, sliding between two tall pleather coated bar stools to flag down the waitress at the other end.

She caught sight of me and gave an apologetic smile to the man she was working down at the end. He looked like he was about a minute away from asking her to marry him. And from the look on her face as she turned away from him, she knew it, too.

If he looked beyond the pound of makeup on her face and her big tits, he'd have noticed the slight swell of her belly beneath her apron. The way her pupils were more dilated than they had any right to be given the lighting.

She had a nice body, I'd give her that. But in less than, maybe about six months, she'd lose the belly and trade it for the babe growing inside. If she had her way, though, she'd be one baby daddy richer, too.

Poor bastard.

Men could be such idiots. Only seeing what we wanted them too. Not bothering to scratch any deeper than the surface. I wished the three bozos out back were as stupid as the man in the plaid shirt at the other end of the counter.

"Can I get you somethin', hon?" The waitress asked as she walked up, her shuffling steps giving away sore feet.

"Yeah. I need a few things to go."

"You need a menu?"

I shook my head as she dipping her fingers into the apron of her faded pink uniform and drew out a notepad and a pen. "Name?"

"Evangeline." The response came automatically, my nom de guerre rolling from my lips almost easier than my own. Another thing dad taught me. If they don't need to know your name, don't give it to them. Everybody could be a mark someday. Give nothing. Take it all.

"Pretty. What'll it be, then?"

"A clubhouse sandwich with fries and gravy."

She nodded.

"Two of whatever your best burgers are, with fries and one chocolate milkshake. A salad. Don't care what kind. And an ice cream, what flavors do you have?"

The bell jingled behind me, and I didn't have to turn to know it was Rook. His footfalls gave him away, and I cringed inwardly at how I'd somehow already memorized the sound of each of them. Their mannerisms. Fuck, they even breathed differently.

Like air wasn't a necessary thing for them. Like it was lucky to enter their lungs at all.

I rolled my eyes. They couldn't leave me alone for even five fucking minutes.

The waitress lifted her head from jotting down my order. "We have chocolate, strawberry, and va—"

Her words choked off, eyes widening at Rook just behind me with a gasp.

Yeah...he had that effect.

A startled cry from one of the patrons by the door sank into the pit of my stomach.

Maybe it wasn't Rook, maybe it was...

I carefully ran my fingers down the side of my leg, ready to make a grab for my blade.

Before I could whirl on him, he had me.

The barrel of a gun pressed to my temple. His gloved hand snaked around my waist, securing me to him, enveloping me in the scent of him.

Rook.

What the actual fuck?

"Everyone down on the ground, hands behind your head," he shouted. "Now!"

His warped image reflected back to me in the old mirror backing on the other side of the counter. Unmistakable eyes, even distorted, but the rest of his face was concealed beneath a black ski mask.

A muted shot hissed in my ear, and I snapped my head up to see he'd fired a round into the kitchen, a silencer on the barrel of his gun. It wasn't a kill shot, but a warning that had the knife brandishing cook with the Kurt Russell moustache dropping his knife and raising his hands in defeat.

"Any other heroes want to take their chances?" Rook hissed, and I could hear the smile in his words.

The gun pressed back to my temple, and I realized what was happening and had to keep the smile off my face, wear a stricken look of horror instead.

It was a con.

A motherfucking con.

Adrenaline flooded my veins, making my fingers twitch and my breaths come heavy. My face heated, and my vision swam. It probably only added to the effect of *armed robber takes hostage.*

"No," I cried. "No, please! *Please* don't kill me."

It was easy to summon the tears, they were always there, held back by the force of a strong dam I'd had in place since I was barely a teenager. They poured freely now, streaking down my face.

68

Rook stuffed a wad of white cloth into my hand, and I took it, hands shaking.

"Open it," he ordered me, and I clumsily found the opening to the pillow case.

He gave my waist a little squeeze that I felt all the way to my greedy little cunt.

Fuck.

"You," he hissed, momentarily training his weapon on the waitress lying on the ground muttering prayers to herself. "Get up."

She tripped as she stood, stumbling into the counter.

"Just do what he says, Cher," her plaid wearing hero called from where he lay face down on the dirty linoleum flooring next to his stool. "It's okay, doll. Everything's gonna be—"

"Oh, shut the fuck up," Rook groaned as Cher stood. "Fill it," he ordered her, the cold steel barrel back at my temple.

When she hesitated, he cocked it back and I felt the *click* all the way to the marrow of my bones. Like a current of electricity plugged straight into my flesh. I gripped the countertop, a hard breath gushed past my lips at the sensation of being *alive*.

Curiously, I peered toward the gun. Not many handguns needed manual cocking. I was no expert, preferring my blades, but Dad showed me a thing or two.

It was a Browning Hi Power. Semi-automatic. A sleek black number with a worn mahogany grip. He held it like an extension of his arm.

Why was that so damned *hot*?

Cher hurriedly emptied the register, pulling out wads of fives and tens and a few twenties. Nothing to get excited about, but right now, I didn't care, this was the most fun I'd had in *ages*.

I forced a whimper as she cautiously stretched her arms over the counter and dropped the bills into the pillowcase.

"You want the money out of the safe, too?" she asked, her voice a meek whine.

Was this bitch serious?

I hear the cook curse to himself in the kitchen and Cher realized her mistake, going whiter than the pillowcase between my fists.

"How very accommodating," Rook replied, tugging me closer to him, letting me feel the slight bulge of his erection against my lower back.

I pushed against it, biting my lip, making him grunt and pull back.

"Hey!" he shouted, spinning us both around to face the man who'd been in the booth by the door. The one with his cell phone in his hand. "*Uh, uh, uh,*" Rook cooed and roughly shoved me over to the man, forcing me to my knees at his side. He snatched a fistful of my hair, pulling until my scalp stung and I shivered.

"In the bag, *hero*," he said through gritted teeth, and I opened the bag for the man to drop his phone inside to join the cash. He wasn't giving me any dirty looks now, was he?

Dick.

"You too," Rook ordered his wife. "Your phone. In the bag. Everyone! Phones out, lay them beside you. *Now!*"

I feigned injury as Rook dragged me to my feet and forced me around the diner, collecting phones from the floor. "I'm sorry," I whimpered as I took each one, depositing them into the bag until we got back to the counter.

"Get his phone," Rook growled at Cher, gesturing to

70

the cook in the kitchen with his gun while I took Cher's phone from the counter and dropped it in with the others.

"I don't have a phone," the cook lobbied through the pass-through window.

Cher's breath caught, giving away his lie.

Rook's rough fingers moved from my hair to my throat, the leather of his gloves flexing as he squeezed. I made a show of choking, letting my eyes bug out of my head.

"P-please," I begged.

"Do you want her blood on your hands?" Rook bellowed, his voice ringing out in the diner. "Hmm?"

"All right, *all right!*" the cook said, his hands raising palms out in a stop gesture.

I gasped for breath as Rook loosened his grip on my throat but kept his fingers there, brushing the sensitive skin on the side of my neck.

The cook reached very slowly into the front pocket of his stained apron and tossed the phone through the pass.

Cher grabbed it a second after it clattered to the floor and thrust it at me.

"Now, how's about we open that safe you mentioned, Cher?"

She sent an apologetic look to the red-faced cook before dropping to her knees and opening a small cabinet beneath the register. The telltale tinkling sound of a dial being turned gave me goosebumps.

Cher came up with an armful of cash. Stacks of bills elasticized together with little receipts at the tops of each one that denoted the amounts contained within each stack. My blood buzzed with a euphoria bordering on madness as she shakily stuffed them into the heavy bag clenched between my hands.

"Th-that's everything," Cher told Rook. "Now...now

just let the girl go and—"

"An ice cream cone," interrupted Rook. "With all the flavors. Pile it high."

Her brows drew together.

"Did I fucking stutter?"

She jumped and sped into action, rushing down to the end of the counter to scoop ice cream onto a waffle cone.

Butterflies.

This psycho just gave me butterflies.

My thighs squeezed and he must've sensed where my mind went because he let his fingers slip lower, brushing down my collarbone, and lower some more until they caressed the tops of my breasts.

A soft moan escaped my lips just before Cher rushed back with a monster ice cream in her hand.

"Be a good girl and grab that for me, would you, love?"

I closed the sack of money and phones into one fist and took the ice cream with the other.

"Everybody stays down until that clock over there strikes six. If you get up, you die. If you call the police, *she* dies."

"The girl!" The cook called from the kitchen as Rook began dragging me backward to the door. "You said you'd let her go."

"Did I?" Rook asked. "*Hmm*. Don't think I did."

"Please!" I begged. "Please let me go!"

"If these good people here forget what they saw, you'll get your freedom."

"Please," I croaked, my plea meant for the patrons in the diner now as Rook hauled me out the door and around the side of the building.

Once we were out of sight of the windows, his arm around me dropped and I let out a small laugh, unable to hold it in for another second.

"That was the most—"

He ripped his mask off with one hand as he shoved me with the other, my back hitting the rough wall behind us. His lips parted as he stared openly at me, his dark eyes darting between my light ones. Trying to find something in their depths.

"Rook?"

I barely got his name out before he stole it from my lips with a brutal kiss that tore through every inch of my body like a shockwave. I gasped against his mouth as a sensation that bordered on pain twisted like a knife in my belly. The butterflies there turning to iron, their edges sharper than honed steel.

Rook's tongue slipped between my lips, and I let him take me. Lost in the feel of him as his hands gripped me roughly, fingers pushing into flesh like hot branding irons.

When his lips left mine, I blinked through a dizzy haze, unable to breathe.

His fingers gripped my chin, forcing my eyes to meet his. "You did good, Ghost."

"What?" I breathed, struggling to focus.

"You just passed your first trial."

Corvus

"Is that…?" Grey trailed off as Rook emerged into the back lot of the diner, dragging Ava Jade along by her wrist. Both of them grinning like fools as ice cream dripped down Ava Jade's fingers, all the way down to her elbow, and a heavy sack swayed in Rook's fist.

They rushed for the Rover, faces flushed and eyes bright.

Fuck.

"Start the car!" Rook called before they were even inside, hurriedly tearing open the back door to help Ava Jade into the backseat before slipping in himself.

"I said *go*, man," he repeated, giving Grey's arm a shove. "Unless you want us all to be ID'd and arrested."

Sparrow laughed, leaning back in her seat with stars in her eyes as she caught her breath. I'd never seen her like that, and something within me pulled, straining against the confines I'd set for myself as a boy.

"What the fuck did you do?" I growled as Grey started the ignition.

"Forward, brother," Rook said when Grey tried to put the Rover in reverse.

"But—"

"Just do it, we don't need them seeing the Rover."

Grey muttered something to himself but did what Rook demanded, driving over the cement barrier and out onto the hard-packed dirt of the desert terrain. He'd find a way to avoid the road for as long as he could before slipping back onto it.

"What. Did. You. Do?" I asked again, whirling in my seat as the Rover bumped over uneven ground.

Rook leaned back and wrapped an arm around my Sparrow, smiling down at her in a way that made my teeth clench. She leaned into him, wiping away a tear from the force of her laughter. "Fuck," she said on a breath. "That was fun."

"Our little misfit here just passed her first trial," Rook said with a lopsided grin, and I frowned.

"What the fuck did you just say?"

"Diesel was busy," Rook explained with a shrug. "He said I should devise something for her first trial until he could get around to having something set up."

His words were like a punch to the gut.

Diesel had asked *Rook* for help with her trials, but he didn't even *tell* me. He always told me.

He never kept me in the dark.

He wouldn't—

He would, I realized, the knots in my stomach tightening for an entirely different reason now.

Damn.

Diesel asked Rook *specifically* to facilitate her first trial because he thought Rook would scare her off. He'd be the

76

most likely to. And the least likely of the three of us to care what happened to her.

Except Diesel was wrong.

About Rook.

About Ava Jade.

He was wrong about a lot of things.

He didn't know that Billy the Butcher's blood was on her hands. Grey had filled us in on the footage he found on her phone. Footage he'd erased from the drive for good. She'd been there, watching us, and not only had she done nothing to try to stop us from giving Billy his warning, she'd decided that wasn't good enough.

She'd not only hidden quietly as we tortured him, but also finished him off after we left. Even *I* still didn't know what to make of that. My controlling nature told me she should be punished for her insubordination. We had a system. A way of doing things, and she was upsetting that. Fucking it up beyond repair.

And my inquisitiveness had me begging the question of whether it was the first time she'd killed. I didn't think it was. She wasn't haunted by it. I'd seen her the very next day, and she'd looked rested. Happy, even.

Like Rook after a kill. As though something inside of her had been sated.

She'd surprised us in every possible way. She *continued* to surprise us. She would continue to surprise Diesel, too, until she would win him over. I was sure of it. So long as she lived long enough.

"We should dump the phones," Sparrow said, licking around the base of the ice cream cone to clean up the drips of vanilla in a way that drove me absolutely mad.

I shook my head, the situation coming back into focus as Grey drove over a deep hole in the terrain and I bounced in my seat, hitting my head on the roof with a curse.

"Phones?"

"We took their phones," Sparrow explained. "We should dump them before we get too far away so they can't trace our route."

I narrowed my gaze on Rook, who shrugged.

"You held up the diner?" I asked redundantly. "With *her*?"

"You should've seen her, man." He bit his lip ring as he gazed down at her eating her ice cream, happier than a pig in shit. "She didn't know shit, but when I put the gun to her head, she played them all like fiddles. Could've had a career as an actress. I'd watch that movie on repeat."

She let out a little giggle, still high from the job, her pupils wide and dark.

"You put a fucking gun to her head?" Grey demanded, making Sparrow squint at the back of his head in the front seat while Rook began picking cell phones out of a bag of cash and tossing them out the rear window, unperturbed.

"She's still alive, isn't she?" Rook asked with a raised brow and Grey shook his head, his jaw flexing from what I could see of his side profile.

My face heated with rage, and I turned back around to face the moving landscape around us, trying to maintain a sense of calm. "It was stupid to organize it alone," I deadpanned. "You should've come to me. What if you missed something?"

"I didn't."

"What if—"

"I know how to run a fucking job, Corv. There's no CCTV out there. We parked around the back. No one saw the Rover. No one saw my face. My hands. No tatts. We took the phones. No prints. *It's fine*."

"They saw *her*," I corrected him.

"They saw the face of a victim. A hostage."

"And when the hostage is never freed? When *the hostage* never goes to the police? When does your *hostage* start looking like an *accomplice*?"

And there it was. The hooked bait.

It was half the point of the trials, wasn't it? They saw her face. But as long as she did what she was told and didn't betray the Saints, we'd back her. She'd always have a solid alibi. She'd have access to the best lawyers money could buy. She'd stand before a judge who'd already been paid handsomely for the outcome of her trial.

So long as she was *one of us*.

Ava Jade put her face to the hot, dusted wind blowing in through her window and smiled, not giving two shits about the argument going on right next to her. I doubted she was even listening.

Rook, ignoring my comment, rifled through the bills in the bag before pulling out two large stacks and dropping them into Ava Jade's lap. She startled. Looking down at the cash and back up to Rook.

"Your cut," he explained, winking at her. "You earned it."

The way she smiled at him…

She'd never smiled at me like that. Never smiled at me *at all*.

"You still owe me," she replied, smug as she licked her ice cream. "I bet seven grand on you."

"A solid investment. Too bad you lost it on your second gamble, Ghost."

She pursed her lips, but even that couldn't hide the smile still trying to weasel its way onto her lips. I got the feeling I was missing some private joke between them and jealousy roiled in the pit of my stomach.

I turned around at the same time Rook reached forward and jammed the auxiliary button, connecting his phone to the car's speakers. The beginning notes of Queen's *We Are the Champions* played low before he reached forward again to crank it louder. I watched in the mirrors as he sang along, putting his arm back around Ava Jade. Rook rocked her side to side as the main chorus played, until she sang with him.

He gave Grey a shove in the front seat. Then kicked the back of the seat until Grey sang with them too, driving us off the uneven desert terrain and back onto a side road, leading to our next destination.

"Come on, Corv," Rook called over the music between verses. *"We are the champions—"*

"We are the champions," Sparrow and Grey echoed. The dark cloud that'd been hanging over Grey for days seemed to lift, his eyes brightening as he gave himself over to a second hand high.

So easy for him to forget his burdens. To shuck off the weight of his reality.

I wished it were even half as easy for me.

Rook

EIGHT

The moon cast an eerie glow over the road as we veered off the highway and entered Thorn Valley at half past nine.

Ava Jade still munched on cold, stale fries from our fast food stop two hours before. She seemed determined to finish every last one even though she'd been full after just the enormous double decker burger she ordered.

She sighed as she ate the last one and set the paper container back into the bag at her feet, setting a hand on her stomach. She cooperated well with the pick up after our little stunt at the diner, seeming almost eager as I drew out the blindfold and wrapped it around her eyes, pulling it tight to her head.

I doubted it would do much to dull how lethal she was, but it did the job of hiding the location of the pick up and our arms dealer's faces from view.

My Ghost checked her phone again, flicking through

notifications with a frown. I caught Rebecca Hart's name before she flicked that one away too with another heavy sigh.

Tricking her felt wrong.

My brothers didn't seem particularly at peace with it, either, but we all agreed it was necessary. After Grey told us Becca had nothing to do with the texts that had Ava Jade wound up tighter than a top, we agreed on the need to know who *did*.

It was always the plan to stop. Always the plan to have Ava Jade leave the Rover and leave her phone behind.

Grey was ready with his laptop—the software he'd need loaded up and primed for use—along with a micro-usb cord to connect it all together. It was all beneath the passenger seat.

It would take him some time to decrypt the deleted messages recovered from her phone's drive, but he had what he needed now so it was only a matter of time.

She didn't know it yet, but whoever was trying to fuck with her was a dead man walking. No one fucked with the Crows. *No one* fucked with our girl.

I winced as my lip ring tore through skin, the coppery tang of blood filling my mouth. I hadn't noticed I was biting on it.

"Think you can still get a movie in?" Grey broke the silence, turning down The Edge as he drove off the main road and up towards Briar Hall.

Ava Jade shrugged. "Maybe. But Becca went out since I wasn't coming, so…"

She shrugged again.

My phone buzzed in my pocket at the same time Grey's chimed and Corvus' chirped. It meant only one of two things and my blood sang in hopes of one over the other.

Please be Julia.

Diesel: Corv, I need you. Grey, Alicia needs help with the month end shit from September. Go give her a hand before she has a fucking aneurism.

It was sent through our group chat, and I jammed the side button on my phone after reading it in disappointment. Would've been fun to take my Ghost to a strike two.

Ooooo, or a strike three.

I wondered if she would join me in the shed like Corvus. Watching over my shoulder as I worked.

I peered at her from the corner of my eye, trying to judge if she'd stay or if she'd run. If it would make her sick...or if she'd want to help.

The prospect of the latter made my cock harden in my jeans and I rolled my hips, savoring in the pleasure that image brought.

"Dies needs us," Corvus said from the front.

Grey shifted. "For what?"

"The books, for you," he replied. "That new one he hired is useless."

Grey didn't disagree. "What does he want you guys for?"

Corv shook his head. "Just me, and I'm not sure why."

Corvus thumbed out a message to Diesel and my phone buzzed again as it was received in the group chat.

Ava Jade, no longer staring out the window, sat up straighter in her seat.

"Should we bring her to Sanctum with us?" Grey asked and I snorted, rolling down the window to rest my arm on it, feeling the cool breeze on my neck as I dug deep into my pocket for the cigarettes there, lighting one up.

"He doesn't need me," I said, ashing my smoke out the window as they shared a look.

"I don't want her near Dies. Not right now," Corvus said to Grey. I might as well have not even bothered speaking. Not that I cared.

"Can't Rook come stay with me at Briar Hall tonight?" Ava Jade asked, and I tipped my head to one side, considering her in the moonlight. It was a simple enough question, but not one I'd ever expect her to ask.

She watched me string up Billy. Watched me beat him. Carve him up.

She was there the night outside the shed with Frank, too. Grey hadn't admitted it, but he didn't have to. Corvus and I both knew where he got that too-perfect cut on his arm. We knew who'd given it to him. Who was watching from the shadows as we unloaded poor Frank, stinking of piss and stale beer, and dragged him to my shed.

She knew what I was, and still she asked the question.

Her sea-glass eyes found mine in the dark, and in them, I saw a resolve few of the strongest men I knew possessed.

My Ghost wanted to know if she could handle me alone.

Maybe almost as much as I wanted to know it.

"Nah," I said, my lips turning up of their own accord. "Come back to the Nest with me. Have a drink. One of the others will drive you back to the Hall later."

"Why?"

"Do you have whiskey in your room?"

She shook her head.

"I do."

She pursed her lips as though to say *can't argue with that*, giving a small one shoulder shrug. "Okay, but I'm not sleeping in that closet of a room. Either you drive me back later or I'll walk back myself."

"It's settled then. I'll keep an eye on her. It'll be fun, won't it, Ghost?"

Grey's hand tensed on the wheel, and Corvus chewed on my words, his jaw grinding through the side view mirror as I finished my smoke.

Ava Jade gave a low chuckle, settling back into her seat as Grey drove us past the turn off to Briar Hall and around to the road running parallel to its grounds, around and up the mountainside.

The five-minute drive was tense, but when we got to the Nest, that tension broke as Ava Jade hopped out of the Rover. Like she was going to visit an old friend, not off to spend a few hours with a man who'd lost count of how many other men he'd killed.

This girl…

I shook my head as I stepped out of the Rover. The things I wanted to do to her. What would it take to make her scream? To make her beg?

Would she ever?

Or would she die silently? Resolute in her desire to not give in?

Mmmm…

Fuck.

"Rook," Grey called from his window, and I paused as Ava Jade went up to the front door.

"Yeah, Brother?"

He struggled with what to say, but I saw the truth of what he wished he could say written all over his face. *Don't hurt her.*

No. Worse than that.

If you hurt her, you'll be hurting me.

It stung.

Just as much as the watchful stare of Corvus from the

opposite seat. A warning stare.

Where was the trust?

I'd admit I hadn't earned it, at least not in this respect, but still.

She was taking the trials. A Saint to be. A Crow in girl's clothing.

We didn't kill our own.

They should've known better.

They should've known *me* better.

I hurt women, sure, but only the ones who wanted to be hurt. They knew the risk. They *liked* the risk. Just because that one almost bled out last year didn't mean I would push it that far with Ava Jade. I wouldn't.

Would I?

I pasted on a smirk. "Don't worry, Brother," I crooned. "Her pretty face will be just as you left it when you get home."

...though I couldn't say the same for her pussy.

He nodded, his throat bobbing as he shifted gears into reverse and turned the Rover 'round. I watched the red taillights bob over the gravel drive for a moment before looking away.

Ava Jade waited in the doorway, her arms crossed over her chest. She lifted a brow. "What was that about?"

I stalked toward her, and she shifted to one side, letting me pass to unlock the front door. At least she'd left that handle and the one to the back door alone. I stepped inside, and she followed, kicking off her shoes and trailing me into the kitchen.

"I asked you a question," she pressed as I pulled two glasses down from a cupboard and poured two whiskeys, one shorter than the other. She took the fuller one before I could hand her the one with less and I smirked.

Too slow...

"My brothers worry too much."

"About you?"

"About other things."

"Should *I* be worried?" she asked, leaning against the counter by the stove to sip her whiskey, her lips tightening in a slight grimace at the taste, though it didn't stop her from taking another sip. A larger one.

I didn't answer her, downing my whiskey in one gulp to pour another.

She took my non-reply for what it was: the uncertain truth.

I couldn't tell her one way or the other if she should be worried. Tonight? No.

In the future? Possibly.

There were too many factors.

Too many nights I didn't remember, where I woke up covered in red.

But that was before I got clean. Now, I remembered my kills. Now, I have more control.

More than my brothers thought I had.

"They should trust you more," she said after a few minutes spent in easy silence, sipping whiskey. "You're family. Their brother. Family means trust. Or, at least it should."

Her face darkened and I felt something in me darken at the sight. Sea-glass eyes fell to the floor, shifting as her fingers clenched her glass a little tighter than they had a moment before that.

"Who hurt you?" I asked, the words evicted from the dark place inside. The decision to speak them wholly unconscious.

Ava Jade looked up, her lips parted, then closed. She cleared her throat. "No one."

She kicked at the floor and then grinned. "Do you

want to fuck with them?"

"What? Who?"

Her eyes lit with mischief, and I licked my lips.

"The others. They don't trust you like they should. I say we fuck with them. Tit for tat."

She watched my tongue travel along my lower lip, her breathing growing heavier as she shifted her feet.

How could I say no to that? How could I ever say no to her?

I grinned.

"What did you have in mind?"

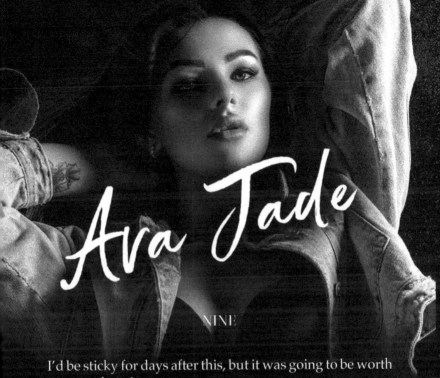

Ava Jade

I'd be sticky for days after this, but it was going to be worth it to see their faces.

"Hurry up," I urged Rook, they could be back any minute.

He ladled more of the red liquid from the metal mixing bowl onto my stomach, letting it drip and puddle on the kitchen floor.

"Does it look real?" I asked, trying to arrange my limbs in an unnatural way. The way I'd have fallen if I was a hundred and twenty pounds of *dead* Ava Jade.

"*Shit*," Rook hissed, stepping back to admire our handiwork. He bit his lip ring, sucking a noisy breath in through his teeth. This was turning him on, I could see it in his dark eyes.

It'd been easy to mix up a couple liters of fake blood. You only needed a few household ingredients. Hell, we had all those ingredients back at the trailer and that was saying something since our cupboards were chronically empty. But with corn syrup as the main ingredient, it was going to take some elbow grease and a full bottle's worth of shampoo to get it all out of my hair and off my skin.

Worth it.

Unless they killed Rook, but I was banking on that not happening. They'd probably say something like *I knew this would happen,* or *I told you so,* and then offer to help get rid of my body.

That's when I'd jump up and shout *surprise motherfuckers,* and hopefully scare the ever-loving shit out of them.

Solid plan.

Definitely a solid plan.

Rook sloshed more blood to the floor and nodded to himself. "You're a masterpiece," he said.

I smiled. "Hurry, let me see before they get back. Take a picture."

I put on my dead girl face and held my breath while Rook took out his phone and snapped a picture, kneeling in the fake blood afterward to let me see.

Damn.

"It looks so real," I said on a laugh. Getting my skin to look so pale hadn't been easy, but the darker reddish-purple circles around my eyes weren't faked. They were *au naturel,* courtesy of Diesel's watchdog order. Sleeping with another person in my room didn't bode well for comfort.

The blood though...it was looking super realistic. Pooled on my belly until it was dark, concealing the fact that there wasn't actually a wound there. Spilling over onto the floor, pooling around my 'corpse' until it soaked into the edges of my dark hair, fanned out over the floor.

One of my blades on the floor next to me, just out of

reach of my bloodied fingertips.

So fucking dramatic.

Tires over gravel had Rook pocketing his phone. "That's them. They're back."

"Go!" I hissed. "Like we planned. You come in from the other room when they get to the kitchen."

Rook's lips pressed into a smile as he shook his head. "This is so fucking cruel."

"They deserve it," I whispered, hearing a car door open outside. "Now get the fuck out of here."

He lifted a hand to scratch the back of his neck, the first and only sign that he might've thought this wasn't as good of an idea as I did.

He'd see. It was a *great* idea.

I owed Corvus a mountain of vengeance after the way he'd been treating me. I was only just getting started.

I took a few slow, shallow breaths as the front door opened, willing my body into stillness. *I am dead.*

I am dead.

Dead girls don't breathe.

Dead girls don't move.

My body grew heavier, each limb forced into a state of relaxation. Limp. Numb. I got ready to only permit myself the shallowest, tiniest of breaths.

"I need a real bed," I heard Grey mutter from the doorway, continuing their muffled conversation from outside. "I have bruises on top of bruises from that floor."

"So buy a mattress."

A pause.

Clearly Grey hadn't considered that as an option.

Corvus sighed. "Fine. I'll stay at Briar Hall with her tonight. Tomorrow we'll go get a fucking cot or some shit. Sound good?"

"Yeah. Thanks, man."

"I still say it'd be easier to chain her up here."

Grey chuckled and a wicked sense of satisfaction raced through me.

My blood sang with anticipation, making it almost impossible to stay still as their footfalls echoed down the hall, coming closer.

Oh my god.

This was going to be fucking *priceless*.

They entered the kitchen.

Don't breathe.

"Good luck with tha—"

Grey's words abruptly cut off, along with the sound of their footsteps.

"*AJ...*" Grey's voice was no more than a whisper. A rough exhalation of air.

He flew into action a split second later. Uncoordinated footfalls pounding on the floor as he rushed to me.

"AJ!"

I could sense him at my side, my heart pounding so loudly in my ears it was a wonder he couldn't hear it as his hands hovered over me, brushing over the surface of my skin, my clothing, as though he were too afraid to touch me.

A playful whistled tune drifted into the room, along with the sound of crinkling plastic as Rook dragged a tarp into the kitchen as we planned.

But, unlike we planned, his whistled song paused. So did the sound of the tarp dragging over the tile floor. It took everything within me not to open my eyes and see what made him stop.

"Corvus..." Rook trailed off, his brother's name on his lips almost a question. Confusion evident in his tone.

"*What...*" Corvus snarled, trailing off as he struggled

92

to inhale. *"What did you do?"*

"Come on, man, she was a liability and you know it."

"What the fuck did you do!"

Something crashed and there were five stomping steps that shook the ground as Corvus went after Rook.

Another crash, the sound of something raining down onto the plastic tarp.

"Stop!" Grey called, his voice sounding oddly broken, pitched all wrong. But he didn't go to help Rook or to stop Corvus; he stayed with me, his hands less fluttering now, but insistent as they struggled through the sticky blood to find the hollow under my chin, searching for a pulse as he twined the fingers of his other hand through mine, squeezing tight.

This...this wasn't funny anymore.

Rook coughed as a loud *thud* resounded in the kitchen. The cough turning into a laugh. The fucker knew this would happen. He was probably banking on it. I doubted he was even fighting back. Reveling in the pain like I once did.

Another thud, and I shuddered. This wasn't what I wanted.

"She was one of us!" Corvus roared, and I heard Rook struggle for breath.

Enough.

Grey found my pulse.

"She's still alive," he called, but Corvus was beyond hearing him.

I squinted an eye open, wincing at the sight of his face, drained of color, frantic. "Gotcha?" I said, biting my lip to draw attention away from the feeling squirming around in my gut.

He fell back, blinking like he was seeing me for the first time. The reality of the situation slowly registering as

93

Corvus threw Rook against a wall at the other end of the kitchen.

"Christ," Grey said on a breath, scrambling to his feet, slipping on the blood. He caught himself on the kitchen island, getting his footing as he called to his brothers.

"Corv, stop!"

Corvus' hands were around Rook's throat. His back tight and biceps flexed to bursting.

Grey grabbed hold of him. "I said stop!"

But Corvus flung him off, blind to everything but his target.

Shit.

"It was a joke," I blurted, standing. "Corvus."

No response and Rook's face was turning a scary shade of red, though it didn't diminish the gleam in his eyes. Just like I thought, he wasn't even fighting back, not really. He held Corvus' arms, staring his brother square in the face. Daring him to finish what he started. His lip dribbled blood. A fresh shiner swelling on the edge of his left brow.

It hurt to watch.

I closed the gap, batting Grey's hands away when he tried to stop me from advancing. "*Corvus,*" I hissed.

I put my hand on his arm near the wrist, gripping him. Forcing him to *see* me.

He flinched, his burning stare finding me through his rage. His pinched face twitched, a knot breaking and reforming between his brows as his bright blue eyes flickered with recognition.

"Let him go."

His hands loosened, and Rook choked for air, bending over to hack until he could breathe again.

"You could've killed him," I said, the words venomous. Not how I intended them.

94

"Sparrow?"

His fingers brushed my cheek, and I pulled back, flushing hot.

"It was a joke," I repeated, angry, though I couldn't peg the reason why. "Just a stupid fucking joke."

I licked my fingers violently to prove the point. "See? Corn syrup."

His lips parted on a breath, a vein throbbing at his temple when he clenched his jaw again. "*A joke?*"

"Yeah."

"You think this was fucking *funny*?"

He shook his head before shoving past me, the smack of his firm body into my shoulder sending me back a step. I felt the hit all the way down to the pit of my stomach. It festered there, the ache spreading to my chest.

The front door slammed a second later. Then another door. The garage outside.

We all listened to the backdrop of Rook's strained breaths as an engine started. A motorcycle. And then he was gone. The whine of the engine and exhaust loud as he sped away from the Nest.

Rook found his way to the sink, hunched, running the water cold and cupping it into his mouth with his hand to spit reddish water down the drain. He swiped the back of his hand over his mouth when he finished, reaching for the whiskey on the counter to take a swig.

Grey's hands balled to clenched fists at his sides, his expression darkening by the second.

"Grey?" I hedged. "I didn't mean—"

"I need a minute," he interrupted, walking away before I could finish as he left too. Following Corvus' path out the door, to the Rover, and away down the road.

I pressed a hand to my stomach, hating the guilt that I felt lying heavily there. "That was way less funny than I thought it would be," I muttered.

Rook shrugged, setting the whiskey aside. "I thought it was pretty funny."

"You're an idiot."

"So I've been told."

He laughed and winced, coughing.

"You're hurt."

He licked the blood from his lip and looked away.

I went to him, lifting the edge of his shirt to see his chest. He lifted a brow, but didn't stop me as I ran my fingers over his tan, muscled abdomen. Over the tattoo on his hip and up higher, to the rapidly darkening bruise on his ribs. I pressed gently over each rib until he hissed at my touch at the fifth one up.

"It might be broken."

"Wouldn't be the first time."

I cocked my head at him. "Do you often try to kill each other?"

"Brothers. It's what we do. He wouldn't have killed me. He'd miss me too much."

"Sure as hell looked like he was doing his best to," I scoffed.

"You don't know him like we do."

A silence stretched between us as I continued to lightly trace the edge of the tattoo curving over his hip bone and disappearing into the low-riding waist of his dark denim jeans.

"What happened to you?" I asked, truly curious. Needing to know what forged him. If he was born or made.

I liked to think I was born good. Happy. Healthy. Without even a touch of madness.

I also hated to think that, because it would mean that the darkness took root later. After mom did what she did.

After that man bled out near the train tracks in Lennox. It would mean that I *let it* take root.

Did Rook's darkness bury itself deep inside him after a trauma? Or was it there all along? Was mine?

Did our darkness lurk deep inside since we took our first breaths? Waiting for us to give into it...

"I'll show you mine if you show me yours," he said in a whisper.

I swallowed hard.

"The person who hurt you..." Rook trailed off, catching my hand as it traced a path across his lower abdomen, trapping it in his iron grip. Making me look at him. Making me remember the man by the train tracks. The weight of him pressed against my body, holding me down. The feel of him between my legs. Of his blood spraying over my face and bare chest. "What was their name?

I shook my head. "It doesn't matter."

"It does."

"It doesn't matter because he's dead."

He didn't seem surprised. A bit disappointed, maybe, like he was sad he wouldn't get the chance to play with whoever it was in his torture shed.

It really was a shame. I'd have liked to watch.

"You?" he asked simply, and ice bloomed behind my breast. A cold sweat slicked my chest and forehead. I'd never told anyone since the day it happened and that old fear came rushing back. The image of a cell, cold, with iron bars and a toilet in the corner flashed over my eyelids as I shuddered, closing my eyes.

But the man on the tracks wasn't the only man I'd killed now. There was Billy, too. You could even say I had a hand in the death of the Ace at the warehouse. And I didn't lose any sleep over them like I did that first kill.

I was smarter, more careful.

And they deserved it.

I nodded.

I placed the hand not clutched in Rook's tattooed fingers to his stomach again, slipping my hand along bumps of muscle to his back, finding the puckered ridge of a burn hidden beneath his ink. "And the one who did this?"

He didn't move as I fingered one scar, then another, staring at me like he was looking for something he couldn't easily find. "Barbequed."

A smile found its way to my lips, and his brows furrowed at my reaction.

"Good."

Rook jerked forward, taking me by the throat to pin me against the center island. The hard marble countertop slammed into the base of my spine, and I gasped, kicking up a heel to snatch a blade. He could've, but he didn't try to stop me as I drew it and pressed it between us, to the zipper of his jeans.

His hold on my throat didn't waver.

"Tell me to let go," he challenged, leaning in until his warm breath was a promise on my lips. His own upper lip raising in a silent snarl. He squeezed, and I moaned.

I fucking *moaned* as he leaned in ever closer, a knowing smirk on his lips.

"Go ahead and cut me, Ghost. Leave your mark. I will."

"You can try," I croaked before thrusting my arm upward, taking him by surprise. His hold on my throat was broken, and I ducked low, rolling out of his reach, my blade drawn as I fixed my stance, a thrill going through me.

He ran his tongue over his teeth like a wolf might

right before a kill and my breathing hitched.

"Will you kill me?" I asked seriously, the ache between my thighs begging to be quelled in the way I thought only this Crow could quench it.

"Want to find out?"

My nostrils flared.

Did I?

I saw the madness in him almost from the start, but it was a familiar thing. An intelligent sort of insanity. Others didn't trust him. Thought he had no self-control. I was willing to bet it was the complete opposite. He had all the control in the world, he just decided to let it go sometimes.

Was I willing to stake my life on it?

Rook darted forward, and I parried to the right, going around the kitchen island to put it between us, stepping carefully to avoid the tacky smears of fake blood on the floor.

He watched me with the eyes of a predator, still, and calm. Waiting for his opening.

I shook my head, laughing to myself. At the idiocy of tempting the devil.

But that was exactly what I was going to do.

From the first moment I saw him, I wanted him. He was the forbidden fruit and I was fucking *starving*.

"Fuck it," I muttered, ditching my blade. Letting it join its cousin on the floor as I leapt over the kitchen island, tackling Rook until *he* smashed into the countertop. He took me like he was the one who was starving. Defiling my mouth with his wicked tongue.

A low sound in his throat made my knees quake as he took a fistful of my sticky hair and held me there, stealing all the air from my lungs. Bruising my lips with his kiss. His lip ring cutting into me until I tasted blood.

His hard cock pressed insistently against my belly,

and I reached my fingers between us to stroke it through his jeans, making him groan. Little hard nubs ribbed his cock, and he shuddered as my fingers brushed over each one. His teeth found my lower lip to bite down hard, the pain adding to the eruption of sensations making my body shudder and shake.

I unbuttoned his jeans, rushing to lower the zipper. Wanting to see what I could feel through his jeans. To free it.

Rook's cock sprang free, nudging against my palm. Hot and thick and harder than steel. Lined with a row of frenum piercings running up the base like a ladder. I counted eleven. Eleven to form Jacob's Ladder. I'd always wanted to be fucked by a pierced cock, and I licked my lips at the sight of him. I jerked him hard, making him thrust forward at my pull.

He laughed, hot against my mouth. "You want to play rough, Ghost?"

His fist in my hair pulled down, forcing me to my knees. "We can play rough."

I knew what he meant to do. To force his way past my lips, but I was already two steps ahead of him, taking him deep into my mouth, making him curse.

I took him deeper still, wanting to feel him at the back of my throat. The laddered piercing ran over my tongue, pushing back until I choked. Rook stared down at me incredulously as I opened my mouth wide for him, holding him there until I could hardly breathe.

"*Fuck…*"

I wanted him. I wanted him so fucking badly it hurt.

I needed him to show me his darkness, because then maybe…

Maybe I could show him mine.

He pulled back after another second and I gasped for

100

air.

"Fuck my mouth," I demanded. "Don't hold back."

Fear flickered over his features, gone so quickly I questioned whether I saw it at all as he slammed back into my mouth, using his fist in my hair to hold my lips around the base of his cock.

And then he did what I asked.

He fucked my tight little throat until it burned, until I was gasping and tears burned in my eyes. Until my panties were ruined from my own wetness. My cunt throbbing with a vicious ache, demanding to be touched.

I reached my hand down, fumbling to get my fingers below the waistband of my pants as Rook continued to pound into my mouth, low, rough grunts falling from his lips.

"No," he growled, popping out from between my lips, leaving me gasping. He had me by the throat again, and I was beyond fighting him, giving myself over to whatever he wanted. Happy to *not* be in control for once. Even if it meant my end.

My back found the countertop of the center island. The air knocked from my lungs as Rook dragged me to its edge, releasing my throat to tear my pants off.

They were still hanging uselessly from one leg when he pushed between them and slid two fingers against my wet heat, making me startle with a sudden cry at the violent sensation.

My back arched, and I pushed closer to him, aching for him to take me.

A tug on my ankle and I realized he'd taken my last blade from its sheath there. I bucked again as he laid the flat edge of it against my stomach, cold and hard.

I watched as he traced a line with it downward, turning it slowly to its freshly honed edge.

He watched me carefully while he moved the blade, biting his lip ring, breathing hard.

His cock was almost level with my opening, jutting out from him, throbbing in time with his heartbeat. The little silver balls catching the light. Menacing and glorious and *all fucking mine.*

"Do it," I told him. "Do it all."

He flicked the blade just below my hip bone, and I sucked in a breath as the fresh cut met the air. He bared his teeth, sucking in breath through them as his muscles bunched. Watching transfixed as the warmth spilled down my hip, rolling onto the counter.

It was shallow. I cut *myself* deeper than that.

"More," I hissed, the feeling of being *alive,* of *feeling* awakening something inside I thought long dead. "*More.*"

This time when he pressed the knife to my flesh on the opposite side of my hip, I pushed into the blade, my eyes rolling back at the sweet, *sweet* release of the pain.

Rook drew back and the blade slipped out, leaving a fresh trail of red over the counter. He blinked, snapping out of whatever held him hostage and threw the blade, embedding it in a cupboard. It was a good throw, and I squinted at him.

"You aren't the only one who knows how to use a blade, Ghost."

He grinned, rough fingers curving around my thighs, lips glistening as he watched the streams of crimson flow out of the wounds like ribbons wrapping around my hips and waist.

He pulled at the same time he thrusted, seating himself inside me to the hilt in one movement.

I lurched as he hit something deep inside me, whimpering as he settled himself there. There was no time to adjust to his size before he was edging out, his Jacob's

Ladder rubbing in the most delicious way before he thrust again. Harder. His thighs slapped noisily against the counter. My body heaved against the cool marble.

I cried out, and he tipped his head back, his jaw taut as he released sounds of his own ecstasy.

"Fuck, you're so wet for me," he groaned as he thrust again, the pain pleasure mix of his fucking already sending me dangerously close to the edge.

"Rook!" I blurted on his next thrust, baring my teeth at his bruising force.

"Does it hurt?" he asked, never ceasing.

"Yes."

"Do you like it?"

He doubled his speed until I bounced on the countertop, his fingers digging deep into the meaty flesh of my thighs as he fucked me.

"*Yes*," I moaned, biting down on my lip to keep from screaming as my orgasm built.

He changed the angle, pitching himself forward, and I screamed at the loss of the build he'd been laying stroke by stroke. But then his fingers left my thigh to wrap around my throat and my eyes flew open to meet his.

When his other hand grabbed my aching clit, I arched again, unable to scream this time for the dam blocking my air supply. He pinched it hard, and I buckled, then he soothed the ache with gentler circular movements, never changing the pace of his cock between my legs.

"Holy fuck," I whimpered when his grip on my throat loosened just long enough for me to draw a breath.

He began to slow, and I growled. "If you stop, I'll kill you."

He smiled, bending to take a nipple into his mouth through my shirt, I clutched his head with a crow of surprise when he bit down, my fingers tangling in his hair, gripping so tightly I'd be shocked if I didn't rip a bunch out.

"*Oh god,*" I said on a breath, feeling my climax build.

Rook, sensing it, re-tightened his grip on my throat, rolling my nipple between his teeth, forcing me to jump from that ledge.

He grunted, pained and shuddering, coming to his own release, and it was that knowledge that broke me. I came hard on his cock, gripping him like he was the only life raft in a turbulent sea. Stars burst against the back of my eyelids as I struggled for breath.

He pumped his last with a feral sound stealing from his lips. When his hand around my throat opened, I cried out, shouting as the orgasm continued to tear through me, making my muscles tighten and spasm, legs shaking, cunt throbbing.

Rook remained there, seated inside me, lightly flicking my swollen clit to keep the orgasm rolling even when I tried to fight him off, tried to squirm away, unable to take any more.

His cock slid out, hands dragging down my body until he was upright again, breathing heavily.

The front door burst open, and I pulled my knees in, rolling from the countertop to snatch a blade from the floor as Grey raced into the kitchen, wild eyed.

I made my gaping mouth shut, staring like a kid caught with his hand in the cookie jar.

Rook leaned back against the counter by the sink, wholly unbothered. His cock still hard but softening slowly.

It took Grey a moment to realize there was no threat. The grip on the gun in his right hand loosened as he swallowed, replacing it into the back of his jeans.

"If you'd gotten back just a little sooner, you could've

joined us," Rook said, bending to grab his pack of cigarettes from the floor, tugging one out to put it between his lips.

Grey frowned.

"You know how Corvus feels about smoking in the house," Grey said, his shoulders tensing as he waltzed through the kitchen past us to the stairs. "Go outside."

"Grey," I hedged and he paused on the landing, his knuckles going white from their grip on the banister.

"Stay here tonight," he said without turning. "If you don't want to sleep in the spare room, I'm sure *Rook* won't mind sharing his bed."

With that, he left us, ascending the stairs. His footfalls echoed in the silence, but there came no slammed door. Just the faint tap of wood on wood. Of a door closing without a handle to keep it properly shut.

I winced, dropping my head with a sigh.

"Want a dart?" Rook offered, and I turned to find him lighting the cigarette between his lips while holding another out to me.

I stole the one from his lips instead, inhaling the tarry smoke and exhaling it on a sigh. I wasn't a smoker, but there was something about a good smoke after a good fuck.

I took another drag before passing it back. "You held back," I accused him. I felt almost cheated. The truth was, I could tell he was holding back *a lot*. The fact that he *could* hold back boded well for my survival, but I'd told him not to. I wanted it all. Every dark, depraved part, but he'd denied me that. Why?

The smug look dropped from his face. "I…"

"You what?"

He jerked his head to the stairs. "Come on, Ghost. You need bandages—and a shower."

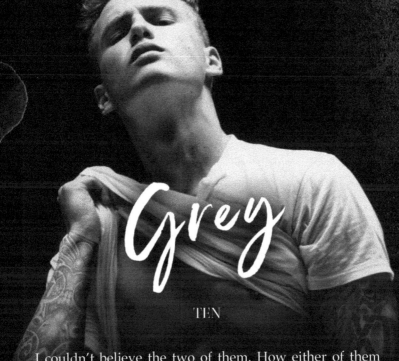

Grey

TEN

I couldn't believe the two of them. How either of them thought for a second that their little prank would be funny was beyond my fucking ability to understand. What I felt in that horrible moment when I saw her there on the floor, pale and bloodied and still…

It was unlike anything I'd ever felt before.

The *loss*.

The terror.

The fucking pain.

All felt through a sieve of numbness. Like I was in a nightmare. Like it wasn't real. Couldn't be real. Like I was beside myself, not really inside the cage of my bones anymore, but forced to bear witness as a phantom bystander. Able to feel all the pain, but unable to do anything to make it stop.

A prank.

A fucking prank.

More like a slap in the face, but maybe one I deserved for not trusting my brother. He'd crawled and clawed his way to the man he was now since Barrettes Home for Boys and since the years we don't talk about that came after.

My bicep ached and burned as I lifted the dumbbell for the last rep of the set, grimacing as I lowered it down to the ground for a moment before switching sides. Across the home gym we built into half the garage last year, Rook pummeled a heavy bag, dancing around it like there wasn't anyone or anything else in the room.

I gritted my teeth as I began reps on the left side, watching his lithe body strike blow after blow, ducking low, keeping his face protected.

Funnily enough, their *prank* wasn't what kept me up half the night.

I truly didn't know whether I wanted to punch him in the face or pat him on the back. I'd been vacillating between the two since I walked in on them last night in the kitchen.

As if my brother knew exactly where my head was, hadn't spoken to me at all since he came in to train twenty minutes ago. He just gave me a nod and went about his business. Patiently waiting for me to make up my mind between that punch or that pat. Happy to accept whatever I decided on.

She's good for him, the logical part of my mind argued. I'd already noticed some positive changes in him over the past few weeks. The itch he usually had by now wasn't nearly as prominent. He was drinking a bit less. He seemed *happy*. And not *I-just-killed-someone* happy, but actually happy. Rook never trained in the mornings, either. He reserved mornings for late wake-ups, spiked OJ, and the inevitable shouting from Corv for him to move his ass.

108

I wanted to be happy for him, but there was the other part of me—the one that whispered through clenched teeth *she's mine*.

I had her first, after all.

She liked me best, didn't she?

But didn't she also like Rook? And even on some level, Corvus, too?

We'd shared before. Once or twice. But those girls didn't matter. Not like AJ.

Inside the Nest, I heard heavy footsteps thudding down stairs and sighed, letting the dumbbell back down to the mat for a stretch and a break before my next set. Whatever he was coming to say, I didn't want a dumbbell in my hand when he said it. As it was right now, I was liable to throw it at him.

He came home in the early hours of the morning, not bothering to be quiet as he parked his Ducati and entered the house. He spent the hours leading to dawn pacing his room or rifling through the kitchen. I was having a hard enough time sleeping as it was *without* his noise keeping me up.

Corvus stepped through the open door to the garage, his back raised and jawline tense. "Why aren't you watching her?" he demanded of Rook, his bloodshot blue eyes laser focused on my brother.

Rook fell back a step, wiping the sweat from his upper lip before lowering his wrapped fists. He pointed two fingers at himself. "Me?"

Corvus' brows lowered, his cheekbones flaring.

"She's asleep," Rook defended. "Besides man, she ain't going anywhere."

"If she does, it's on *you* to explain that shit to Dies."

"Fine."

But Corvus wasn't finished, his shoulders shook so

slightly that if you didn't know him well enough to know the signs of his anger, you'd never notice. And right now, Corvus was furious, and he had something else to say.

"Fine," he growled. "Maybe you want to explain to me why she's naked in your bed, then?"...so I guessed we weren't going to be talking about their little prank last night then.

Rook raised a dark brow at him. "You're smart enough to figure that one out."

His nostrils flared for a moment before he turned his rage on me. "And you?" he pressed. "You've fucked her too, haven't you? And don't fucking lie to me."

I lengthened my spine, standing to place the dumbbell back onto the rack with a sigh.

"I did," I admitted, my tone filled with more animosity than I intended. I never lied to him. I never lied to either of them. Except for her. To protect her.

When I turned around, crossing my arms as I leaned against the half rack, he was still watching me. That animalistic gleam in his eyes told me he was on the very precipice of his control. I'd never seen him this bad this often. Maybe he was right. AJ was a threat. She might just be the death of us.

But oh what a sweet death it would be.

As I began to come up with ways I might restrain him if he actually went feral, something in his stare changed and the muscles near his cheekbones twitched as he began to calm and eventually to sag, sighing heavily.

He wiped a palm over his mouth, partially covering a shaky breath.

"I don't get it," he said finally, no longer looking at either of us, but searching the mats at his feet instead, like they might hold an answer he was seeking. "Why…" he started but stopped.

"Why not you?" Rook supplied, and I squinted at him, confused.

That wasn't what I thought Corvus was getting at, but I could see it now. The tightness between his eyes. The set of his shoulders. He was angry, yes, but he was fucking *jealous*, too.

When Corvus didn't reply, giving away the truth, Rook stopped the heavy bag from swinging gently back and forth and began unwrapping his hands, squatting to sit on a low weight-lifting bench. "Because you're a complete and utter dick."

I cleared my throat to cover a laugh. "He's right," I agreed. "And a controlling asshole to boot."

"When it comes to Ava Jade, at least," Rook added, and I snorted.

"Name someone he's *not* a controlling dickhead with?"

"Don't fucking push me right now," Corvus warned and, rolling his shoulders back. "I'm only like that with her because she—"

"She likes to push your buttons?" Rook interrupted with a mischievous smirk.

"Because she refuses to be controlled?" I added.

"Oh!" Rook blurted. "I know, because you want her all to yourself and you can't stand the thought of her wanting us more than she wants you. Is that it?"

I grimaced.

"Low blow, brother," I leaked out through another grimace.

Corvus' face reddened for a second before the blood drained back out.

"I already want to skin you alive for that fucking shit you pulled last night, Rook. *Don't. Push. Me.*"

He pinched the bridge of his nose. "It's not because of

that," he said. "Not *just* that, anyway. It's…"

"Because you care about her?"

I could see it now and wasn't sure how I hadn't seen it clearly before. Corvus cared about Ava Jade. Similar to how he cared about us. It wasn't just control for the sake of control. He didn't give a flying fuck what happened to any other girl, or many of Diesel's men. He didn't try to control *them* because he didn't care about them.

He was a controlling prick with us because he cared. He demanded a reply when he texted because he cared. He wouldn't let Ava Jade out of our sight for the same reason. I doubted it had anything to do with Diesel's orders at all.

He just didn't understand her—the things she needed. What she would and wouldn't tolerate or understand. She didn't know him. How could she when he was always so busy erecting walls to cage himself in?

"Admitting it doesn't make you weak," I continued. "We all care about her."

Corvus opened his mouth with a rebuttal, but I shut him up with a glare. "Don't lie to me," I said, turning his own words against him. "Lie to yourself if you want, but don't lie to us."

"If you were right, which I'm not saying you are…" He trailed off, and I caught Rook rolling his eyes when Corv wasn't looking. "How would I…*you know*…make it up to her?"

"Stop being such a dick, for starters," Rook put in, going back to the heavy bag bare-fisted for another few hits.

"You could try giving her some trust. Some freedom." His upper lip curled.

"Or…you could try flowers?"

He blinked at me like I just said the stupidest thing in

the world. "All right, yeah, that won't work for AJ." I thought about it. "You owe her a blade, don't you?"

"I say get her a flamethrower," Rook grunted between hits.

"You're *not* getting a flamethrower," I told him.

"It's not for me, it's for her," he argued, pausing.

"Sure it is."

"You really think I can fix this?" Corvus asked, stopping my and Rook's little sidebar stone dead. "She hates me."

I shook my head. "Not as much as you think she does."

"She's one of us," Rook said to Corvus, his heaving breaths evening out as he sniffed and reached for his water bottle. He fixed Corvus with a hard stare as he took a swig and set the bottle back down, his stare never wavering. "You said so yourself last night. Remember?"

"I didn—"

"*You did*," Rook barked. "She's a Crow and you know it. She belongs to *us*...and we belong to her. The sooner you both stop fighting it, the sooner we can all be exactly what we're meant to."

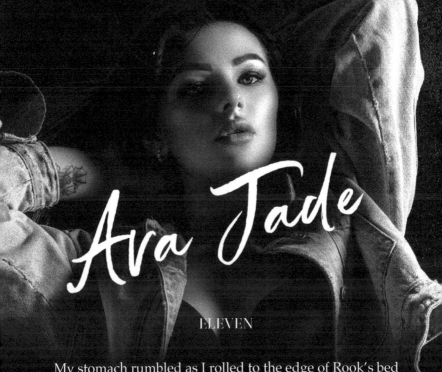

Ava Jade

ELEVEN

My stomach rumbled as I rolled to the edge of Rook's bed and forced myself to sit up with a sigh. I glanced back at the disheveled fur covers and silky black sheets and pillows, but he wasn't there. My thighs clenched, cunt aching as I recalled vivid images of him between my thighs last night. Of his thick, warm cock in my mouth.

I traced the line of the small two inch cut running crossways below my hip bone, and shivered, all my little hairs standing on end.

I shifted against the soft sheets and searched the floor for my clothes, but couldn't find them even with the light from the hall filtering in through the half open door.

The smell of cooking bacon that woke me made my mouth water as I stole a swath of black fabric from the floor. It appeared to be a top sheet that I'm assuming a housekeeper put on his bed only for him to kick-off the first night it was there.

A house full of boys didn't stay this clean without a little help, though in all the times I'd spied on them here or listened in, I'd never heard or seen a cleaning person anywhere near the Nest.

I folded the sheet lengthwise and wrapped it around my back, crossing the ends in front to tie at the back of my neck. It was the ugliest toga you ever did see, but it was soft as fuck and would have to do for now. I'd go down naked to get the bacon if I had to, but the morning brought with it a chill and the makeshift dress did just enough to stave it off.

The Nest grew warmer the further outside of Rook's den I got, and I wondered if he kept it purposefully colder in there than the rest of the house. If he actually slept with those heavy furs covering him all night, he must've because there was no way I could sleep beneath them without sweating my ass off otherwise. And I had slept beneath them, like a fucking baby.

The best sleep I'd had in weeks.

I couldn't even remember the feel of him lying next to me, which made me question whether he even had slept next to me. Or if after I slipped into his bed, still damp from the shower, and he laid the heavy covers on me, he'd just left?

I followed my nose down the stairs, salivating as the smell of breakfast grew stronger with each step. I paused on the landing, finding Corvus swirling and tossing a pan of small-cut potatoes shimmering with oil.

He expertly switched between three different pans and checked the bacon in the oven, pulling it out to place it atop a cooling rack on the counter.

His back stiffened slightly before he turned, feeling my eyes on him maybe. His lips parted as they took in the swath of silky black fabric covering my naked body, before

116

he turned back, the tension never leaving his shoulders.

"Morning," he said curtly.

"Uh...morning."

I went to the sink, searching through the cupboards for a cup to fill with water before planting myself at a stool at the kitchen island, the furthest one from Corvus.

"Hungry?"

"Starving."

I peered around the edge of the doorway leading to the living room, but couldn't see the others. Where did they go?

"*So*," I said, playing with the condensation on my glass. "You're not still angry about last night, then?"

A derisive laugh told me everything I needed to know, but he replied anyway. "Oh, I'm angry, but I told Rook I'd skin him alive if he ever pulled something like that again."

I pursed my lips, noticing for the first time how *clean* the kitchen was. I'd passed the fuck out after my shower so who...

"Did you..." I trailed off. "Did you clean up the, *um*, the mess?"

"Fuck no. It was spotless by the time I got back."

Rook, then. I smirked. I owed him one for that.

"You don't give him enough credit, you know. He isn't the loose cannon you think he is."

"You don't know him that well."

"*...well enough*," I muttered to myself, squirming in my seat right next to the spot on the kitchen island where we'd...

Best not to think about it or I'd sully his pretty sheets.

Corvus grunted, going back to focusing on the stove. He flipped the eggs before taking down two plates and beginning to fill them with crisp bacon, sautéed spinach, hash browns, and eggs. Maybe the others weren't here, then, or maybe it was presumptive of me to assume I was going to be offered a hot breakfast.

Once he'd finished arranging everything how he wanted it, he turned, pushing a plate down the length of the marble counter to me.

I must've had a look on my face because he frowned. "Thought you said you were hungry?"

"I am," I admitted, swallowing to clear my mouth of saliva.

"Eat," he ordered. "You've dropped at least five pounds in the last week. You need to keep your strength."

I ignored the way it sounded like a command because in truth, I planned to fucking annihilate everything on this plate and lick it clean. Even the spinach, and I didn't even like spinach. But he did something to it to make it smell like green gold.

The eggs were perfectly cooked. Buttery soft with slightly runny yolks. The toast was some freshly baked ancient grain blend that tasted like it came straight from 1892.

Unable to help myself, I moaned as I bit into a piece of bacon and caught Corvus watching me as he stood at the other end of the counter, eating his own breakfast slowly. The tiniest smirk tugged at the edge of his lips, and I schooled my face back to its usual hostile wariness, making myself slow down so my stomach wouldn't be aching when I was finished.

I couldn't remember the last time someone made me a meal. I must've been very young. A child.

"So, who's with me today?" I asked when I was nearing the end of my breakfast, resisting the tempting urge to run my fingers over the juices on my plate and lick them clean. I didn't want to give him any more satisfaction than I already had. That prank last night was far less than he deserved after all the shit he'd pulled over the past weeks.

"I have an essay to write and want to change my clothes. I need a run, too."

Corvus mulled over my request, chewing his food painfully slow as he considered.

I jumped as a man's garbled electronic voice screeched from the front entryway.

"*Door!*" It yelled. "*Door!*"

"Is that your fucking doorbell sound?" I asked, my heart pounding.

He was really smirking now, and trying to hide it.

"Rook chose it," he said by way of explanation before leaving the kitchen to answer it, wiping his hands on the tea towel slung over his shoulder.

I took the opportunity while he left the room to hop down and grab two more pieces of bacon from the tray on the counter, stuffing them quickly in my mouth before going to sit back down and chew furiously, eyes rolling at how good it tasted.

He must have done something to it to make it taste so good.

I overheard a muffled conversation at the door and let myself relax. I half expected it to be an intruder. Maybe my would-be stalker. Or a Saint come to give me another trial.

The door shut and Corvus came back into the kitchen just as I finished swallowing the wad of bacon in my mouth.

"What was that about?"

That's when I noticed the long, slim black box in his hand. I lifted a brow at it.

"It's, *uh*...It's for you actually."

What the fuck did he just say?

119

Corvus repositioned himself, leaning against the counter near his half-eaten meal and slid the box down the length of the marble countertop, making me have to stop it from careening off the edge.

The box knocked against my palm and something inside of it shifted. Something heavier than anything that size ought to be.

"I'm good," I replied tensely. "Whatever it is, I don't want it."

"You'll want this one. Besides. It's not a gift, so don't look so damn uncomfortable."

Was it that obvious?

"It's payment for what's owed."

I held the box between my fingertips, a muscle beneath my eye twitching.

"Go on," Corvus prodded. "Open it."

I sighed but did as he asked, lifting the top off the box...and gasped.

"You like it?"

It was a blade. Similar to mine, black with gleaming metal edges honed to perfection. Though that's where the similarities ended. A silver crow in flight emblazoned the tang, etched into the black coated metal so that it gleamed silver in the light. A tiny blue gemstone set into the place where it's eye ought to be.

I didn't have to ask to know it was a sapphire.

"I know it isn't the same, but..."

I lifted the blade out of the box, carefully running a finger along its edge. Turning it in my palm to feel the even weight distribution. Finding the crow's wings wrapped all the way around the tang to the other side.

It was beautiful craftsmanship.

But what did it mean?

An unnamed emotion roiled in my gut like a

tightening fist. Was he trying to tell me I, too, was a Crow?

Or was this meant to assert that I belonged to them. A weapon to be honed in their image, to be wielded once Diesel owned me.

I clenched my teeth at the warring possibilities. Trying to pretend I hated both of those options, but the hopeful ache in my gut told me the truth my rational mind tried to deny.

I set the blade back into the box and glanced up, finding no evidence of either in Corvus' stony blue eyes.

"Do you like it?"

I swallowed hard before replying, to ensure my voice came out without any indication of what was going on within. "It'll do."

He nodded.

I cleared my throat. "So, about who's supposed to be watching me today—"

"Go whenever you like. I'll come get you later."

I cocked my head at him.

"I have some things to take care of here and Dies needs the others tonight. If you wouldn't mind." He gritted his teeth and I wondered how hard it was to *ask* me something rather than demand it, "could you stay here one more night? There's a loft above the garage you can use. It's furnished and has windows and doors that I promise won't be locked when you wake up. *Or* you can have any bed in the house you want. No one will be using them tonight."

This was...weird.

I opened my mouth to reply but shut it again. I wanted to argue for the sake of arguing. I liked the way his face soured when I told him no, but this was different.

He was giving me something. Trust. My freedom, even if it was for just a few hours. In return he asked for a small favor. In all honesty, I'd sleep just as shittily no matter where I laid my head tonight anyway.

"Fine," I replied. "Just tonight."

The ghost of a smile brushed over his lips before it was gone, and he nodded. "Good. I'll text you when I'm on my way."

"Okay," I said, jumping from the stool and remembering what I was wearing. I wouldn't be running anywhere in a fucking sheet.

"You wouldn't happen to know where my clothes are, would you."

He jerked his head toward the entryway. "They're washed and in the dryer. The laundry room is through the door at the end of the hall, but I guess you already knew that since you removed the handle."

I bit my tongue, rushing from the kitchen to go and get my fresh clothes before I said something that might ruin my chances at a few hours of freedom.

My spine went ramrod straight as I walked into the laundry room, finding my phone sitting atop the dryer. *Fuck.*

What was wrong with me?

A good prank and some good dick and I lost all fucking sense.

This was *not* me.

I'd told myself this once, and I'd keep saying it; these Crows were *literally* going to be the death of me one day. At least as long as they lived.

I snatched my phone and checked for any messages they might've somehow read. I had three missed messages, but I'd changed my settings so the lock screen wouldn't show message previews anymore, only the sender.

One message was from my Aunt Humphrey, another

was from Kit. The last said only *unknown*.

I stiffened, leaning back against the wall as I unlocked it and thumbed over to read them.

I scrolled to the one I dreaded the most first, reading only the first line of text before I swiped to delete the message without reading the rest.

Unknown: I warned you…

Whoever it was could *warn* me all they liked. Whenever they wanted to stop talking shit and *do* something, I'd be ready for them. Come at me, fucker. I dare you.

Next on the list of messages I least wanted to read. Dear ol' Aunt Humphrey.

Aunt Humphrey: If you don't return my calls, I'll have no choice but to revoke my offer. How you expect to finish the year with the grades necessary to get into a half decent college is beyond me. You have to actually attend class for—

I stopped reading. That was enough of that.

Kit: Dom's worried about you. If you aren't going to call me back, you should at least call her. I miss you.

I ignored Kit's message and thumbed over to my previous conversation with Dom, typing out a quick apology.

Ava Jade: Sorry girl. I'll try to call this week. Shit's been crazy. I'm fine so don't worry, k?

I was a terrible fucking friend.

I dressed quickly, rushing to my five seconds of freedom. I peered into the kitchen to tell Corvus I was leaving, but he wasn't there anymore when I walked past.

"Bye, dickface," I muttered quietly to myself as I tugged on my shoes and went to slip my newest blade into the sheath on my ankle, but thought better of it, deciding to keep it on me instead.

My skin prickled as I stepped outside into the growing warmth of the early afternoon, and I scanned the trees surrounding the Nest as I stretched for my run. Searching for anything out of place. Eyes that shouldn't be there.

There was someone watching me, that much was certain, but were they watching me right now? Were they out there at this very minute, waiting for an opportunity to pounce?

Did they see what Rook and I did last night? I glanced back, seeing through the window to the kitchen beyond it. A clear and unobstructed view of the kitchen island.

I shivered.

"Fuck this," I hissed. If whoever it was wanted to attack me, let them. I had a new blade to break in, and I'd pledged to carve out their eyeballs. I couldn't do that if I was hiding inside, now could I?

No music for my run today. I needed all my senses keen and sharp. Just in case.

A small pang surprised me as the unconscious thought that I wished Grey was running with me crossed my mind.

I shook it away and started at a slow pace down the gravel drive, picking up speed as the gravity of the hill pulled me down its slope. Soon, the wind whipped through my hair, lifting sweat slicked strands and cooling the sweat beginning to coat my chest.

But still my runner's high didn't come and my mood soured, hating a nameless faceless person. Hating Mr. Unknown for ruining the *one* thing I had that was mine.

In the distance, the sounds of the forest, my favorite sounds, became ominous things.

The snap of a twig could just as easily be a rabbit as it could be Mr. Unknown.

124

The rustle of leaves: a bird or a man?

It wasn't fear, not exactly, it was the same self-preservation *readiness* that always took over when there was a threat. When my adrenaline knocked at the thresholds of my veins, waiting to be released.

Like the world had gone from low-fi to high-def in the blink of an eye. Vision sharper. My ears picking up even the tiniest sounds. I couldn't enjoy the pounding of my feet on the earth or the sensation of flying as I soared over miles of woods and road. Not with this itching feeling scratching at the back of my skull.

"Fucking damnit," I groaned to myself through pants, slowing to a jog as I veered off the road and into the trees toward the trailhead at the back of Briar Hall. If I stuck to the road, I'd have to go all the way around. This way I could cut through and save myself fifteen minutes. I'd have loved to have those fifteen minutes before, but now? What was the point?

I jumped over a low red-berry bush and onto the trail, seeing the lit opening in the trees ahead that would put me out at the back gardens of the Academy.

I saw him before he even moved. A dark shape lurking in the shade behind an old redwood. My feet dug into the ground as he rounded the tree, and I readied my new blade to throw, cursing myself for not arming myself with one of my own blades. My aim may not be perfect with this one yet. We hadn't been properly acquainted. I held it up all the same, the dirt underfoot bunching under the sides of my sneakers as I slid to a stop.

"*Whoa,*" a familiar voice spoke, raising his hands to carefully peel back the hood of his dark windbreaker jacket, revealing his face.

"Officer Vick?"

"Put the knife down, girl."

Hesitantly, I lowered it, but didn't put it away or move any closer.

"You shouldn't be here."

He snorted derisively. "Do you know how hard it's been to get to you? You've been with at least one of them every bloody hour of the day and night."

My face pinched. "What do you want?"

"What do *I* want? I thought we wanted the same thing...you haven't called."

"Because I didn't have enough to give you yet."

Officer Vick narrowed his eyes on me, stuffing his fists into his windbreaker pockets. "It's true what I've heard then," he said, a look of disgust twisting his features. "You *are* taking the trials. They've turned you, haven't they?"

I frowned, a sneer curling my upper lip. "*Never.*"

He snorted and my face flushed hot, hands clenching.

"I didn't ask for this," I all but snapped. "It was the trials or death."

He cocked his head at me, interested now. "You saw something, didn't you? Something you shouldn't have. Tell me. Tell me and this can all be over."

My breath caught in my throat. The videos had been erased from my hard drive, but there was still a body. The body of a dead Ace in the ground out behind that old warehouse with one of Diesel's bullets in his skull. Would the body be enough?

"Would you need testimony?"

Officer Vick's hard look faltered, he hadn't expected that question. "Depends on what sort of evidence you've got."

"And if I didn't have any at all except my word and a body buried in the ground..."

He ground his teeth, considering the best way to

reply, and I knew already what his answer would be. If the court was going to be able to do anything with the evidence, my testimony would be paramount. And a trial could take weeks. Months, even. And no amount of police protection would be able to stop Diesel St. Crow from slitting my throat before it ever went as far as a conviction.

My stomach soured. Would the guys be implicated in that or just Diesel? Could I keep them out of it?

Did I want to?

"Like I said," I continued before Officer Vick could say a word, wanting to cut this conversation short before I said something I couldn't fucking take back. "I don't have enough yet."

"When?"

"I don't fucking know.

He nodded. "The trials can be quite…"

"I know."

"If you help us, there's a possibility we'd be able to offer immunity for any crimes committed in the process of obtaining the information we need."

"Gee, thanks."

Vick ran a hand through his short hair, glancing between me and the end of the trail a good twenty feet behind him. My chest grew cold at the idea of someone seeing us here, like this. Officer Vick and I out in the open.

"We really need—"

I held up a hand to stop him from pleading his case any more than he already had. "I'm *working* on it," I gritted out. "But you can't approach me again. *Ever*. If someone saw…"

I shuddered.

"But—"

"I can't give you anything if I'm dead."

I fixed him with a hard stare before starting back at a

slow jog. "*Move*," I growled and he stepped to the side as I pounded past him.

"We need you, Ava Jade," he called as I emerged from the path. "Don't disappoint me."

Corvus

There were a few things I was good at that didn't involve violence. Cooking being one of them.

I spooned the honey Dijon white-wine sauce over the roasted chicken and potatoes, laying small sprigs of thyme on each. I wrung my hands in the tea towel, sighing as I hesitated to bring Ava Jade's plate in to her.

The television in the living room remained quiet as she flicked through the options on one of the streaming services Grey had hooked up to the TV. She'd been trying to decide for nearly twenty minutes already. At this rate, I wasn't sure if she would find anything at all.

I set down the tea towel on the counter and scooped up the plates, bringing them to the living room. Breaking my own rules. We never ate in the living room. Dinners, at least when I made them, were eaten together at the kitchen island.

It wasn't the only rule I was going to have to bend if I

wanted Ava Jade to hold me in the same regard as she did my brothers. If I wanted her to stop hating me. *Did* I want her to stop hating me?

I shook my head, upper lip twitching at the idiocy of the internal question. *Of fucking course* I didn't want her to hate me. It was just easier that way...in the beginning.

"Hey," I said gruffly as I walked into the living room, the hot plates burning into my palms. "You hungry?"

She didn't turn from where she sat cross legged on the long couch to the right of the room, her side profile facing the television. Showing off the regal shape of her face. "I already ate dinner," she muttered, shifting on the cushion as she finally settled on something to watch. Cueing up a Marvel movie.

My grip on the plates tightened. "I didn't ask you that. I asked if you were hungry."

I couldn't help the tinge of acid in my voice and I cleared my throat to get rid of it, clamping down to get a hold on myself, purging myself of the angry thoughts vying for dominion in my mind.

She set the remote down on the table and peeked up at me, catching sight of the plates in my hands. Piled high with perfectly roasted chicken and potatoes and buttered carrots.

"Touché," she replied, the smallest smirk on her lips. "I'm always hungry."

"Just like Grey."

"Why is that?" she asked as I closed the distance between us and handed her a plate.

"You'll have to ask him. It's not my story to tell."

"What *is* your story then?" she pushed as I went to sit on the armchair across the coffee table from her. My back muscles tight and head heating as the hideous memories flooded my skull.

130

A small grumbling sound escaped my throat as I fought them back and my Sparrow frowned, dropping her head to her plate. "Sorry, not my business."

"No, it's not."

Fuck. There I went again, but I couldn't help it.

Appetite thoroughly ruined, I set my plate down on the coffee table and leaned back in the chair to watch the movie, attempting to clear the poison seeping in.

The *pop pop* of gunfire. The feel of their blood, hot at first, and then later, sticky and cold and stinking. The gore of it all. The numbness. The darkness. The whispers...

Not even Rook and Grey knew what led me to be brought in by the state, left with not a single blood relative to care for me. The only one who did was Diesel. I had a different name, then. Diesel wanted us to keep our surnames when he adopted us. Until we were adults, old enough to make the decision for ourselves. The St. Crow name was a dangerous one to call your own. He wanted us to be certain we wanted to wear it.

We all planned to take the name after graduation, becoming the Crows we've always been in practice on paper.

James wasn't my last name, though. It was my middle name. I'd never own to my true surname. Not ever. I couldn't *fucking* wait to change it. I begged Diesel when I was younger, but he told me it was important to remember where I came from. That I didn't have to use the name, but I had to bear it until I came of age.

I came of age last year and Grey suggested we all wait until graduation to make it official. What was another year after being forced to carry it for over ten?

I switched to watching my Sparrow when the movie did little to help distract me. Already over halfway through her meal, she closed her eyes briefly with every bite she took, unable to hide how much she enjoyed it.

Her cutting blue-gray eyes caught me staring and she pulled the fork from between her lips with a small blush. "Where did you learn to cook?"

"Diesel taught me some things," I replied, and she lowered her brows as though she hadn't been expecting that response.

"What? Does it surprise you that a gang leader would be a good cook?"

"Well, kind of, *yeah*."

I bit out a short laugh. "Well, he only got me started. Showed me some of the recipes his wife used to make before she passed. The rest I taught myself. I like food that tastes good."

"What happened to her?"

I resisted the urge to bark at her. The second-hand pain of her loss I'd had to feel from my surrogate father since the day he adopted me swelling in my chest.

"She died," I said simply, realizing how my fingers were curling into the armrest of the chair. I loosened them and coughed to clear my throat, lifting my plate again to try to force myself to eat. If I wasn't going to fucking sleep, I knew I needed to at least eat well.

"I gathered that," Sparrow murmured, but she didn't press the question.

I only knew the gist of it anyway, heard from the other Saints, but never from Diesel himself. He'd been injured in a shootout, hospitalized, and on the brink of death.

His wife, strongest woman I'd ever heard of, led the attack on the offending gang. She'd planned it expertly. Not a single Saint lost their life that night, but there was a reason you never heard the name *Viper* anywhere in Cali after that. She wiped them from the face of the earth.

Vengeance for her lover.

All the Vipers dead except for one.

The leader's son, hiding like a coward from the fight. It was his bullet that ended her once the fighting was through.

The Saints held him until Diesel was ready to deal with him himself. I shuddered to think what was done to him, but I know that if it were me, he'd have suffered for days before I allowed him to die. Weeks even.

I watched Ava Jade finish her meal and set the plate down, leaning back to drop a hand onto her belly. What would I do if someone took her from me?

She was *mine*.

Ours.

Grey needed to hurry up with decrypting those messages from her phone. Diesel needed him again tonight, to help with some tax shit that was past due. But Grey promised he'd be on it as soon as he was finished with that. Rook tagged along with him, happy to drink at Sanctum to allow me some time to try to repair what I had broken with Ava Jade.

She caught me watching her again and winced, shifting awkwardly. "Are you a good baker, too?" she asked, changing the subject.

"Why?"

She shrugged. "I like cake."

I snorted.

"I'm not bad," I told her. "It's Rook's birthday soon. He doesn't like to celebrate it, but I usually make a cake anyway. No candles or any of that shit. Just a big ass chocolate cake."

"Chocolate's my favorite, too."

"Of course it is."

She tipped her head to one side, considering me

133

before going back to watching her movie.

I half expected her to have fled when I went to pick her up a couple hours ago, but there she was at the door, ready to go when I knocked. If not a little grumpy. Rook had been right after all. She wasn't going anywhere.

She knew what running would get her.

I finished firing off an email to Max on my phone, getting last minute details sorted before the upcoming show. Later tonight, I'd have to finish the new song I was working on if I planned to unveil it in Lodi. And I needed the others to help me once I was through. Rook was mad good at syncing everything together for me and Grey was the only one I trusted to make the lyrics really *hit*.

Though showing them the song would mean admitting to them what I'd only just managed to admit to myself…

"So," I asked after Ava Jade clicked through to start another movie once the credits rolled on the first one. "Did you decide where you want to sleep?"

She shrugged. "I'm good here. I probably won't sleep anyway."

I snorted. *You and me both.*

My phone buzzed in my hand, and I looked down to see a reply from Max and a text from Grey.

Grey: How goes it? You kill each other yet?

I covertly snapped a pic of her across the room, illuminated only by the bluish light flickering out from the TV in the dark room. I sent it.

Corvus: Still alive.

Grey: Why are you sitting so far away? Go and sit with her.

My teeth clenched.

I glanced at the two empty cushions next to Ava Jade and pressed my lips into a tight line. My attention snagged on the outlet by the wall at one end of the couch, and the charger cord sticking out of it.

My phone still had twenty percent battery but it could use a charge.

Clearing my throat, I rose, crossing the room to fall casually into the cushion at the far end of the couch, reaching for the cord to plug in my phone.

Sparrow raised a brow at me as I settled the phone onto the armrest and turned back to the TV.

"Needs a charge," I explained, leaning back to watch the next Marvel movie in the queue.

Corvus: Anything from her phone yet?

Grey: I haven't had a chance. Diesel needs this done before the start of the business day tomorrow. I'm on it as soon as I'm done.

Corvus: This needs to take priority. I'm about three seconds from tying her up and forcing her to tell me herself.

Grey: Because that will get you all the brownie points...

Corvus: Fuck off. You know something isn't right about that shit. Becca said herself that she didn't send Ava Jade the messages. We made a deal. I play nice so long as you get us those messages so that we can see what the fuck is up for ourselves.

Grey: I know. Don't worry man, I'll get it done.

I clicked off the phone with a sigh and caught Ava Jade sneaking glances at me from the corner of her eye, curious about the rapid-fire text conversation I just had, but not curious enough to ask. Not enough to want to appear like she cared.

I wasn't sure how long we sat like that, quietly watching Marvel movies until my eyes burned like the fire of a thousand suns and the muscles around my right eye began to twitch. Until my Sparrow slumped over on the couch, curling herself up in a tight ball on the two cushions between me and the other end of the couch, doing her absolute best not to touch me.

It wasn't much longer until she fell asleep, though her face never completely softened. A tightness lingered around her eyes even though her breathing evened out and her mouth softened. Free of any of the sharp edges I was used to seeing.

Instinctively, I reached down to lightly brush a lock of hair from her cheek and she stirred, making a small sound of malcontent as she tried to stretch out her legs and was stopped by the arm of the sofa.

Without consciously thinking about it, I guided her to my lap, softly lifting her head as she did all the work of moving herself up with her feet braced and stretching against the armrest.

Her eyes fluttered open for a second and I held my breath, removing my hands from her shoulders, but she didn't fully wake, only enough to snuggle down, sighing as she fell back asleep.

Her hand brushed against my cock, and if she didn't stop nuzzling it, she was going to get a really rude awakening when it fully hardened. I gritted my teeth, multiplying math equations in my head until she settled and I could breathe again.

Extra carefully this time, I brushed her hair back, studying the curve of her face. She shivered at my touch. I tugged the throw blanket down from the top of the backrest and draped it over her, laying an arm over her shoulder to hold her there.

That tightness around her eyes loosened as she fell into a deeper state of sleep, her breaths coming slower. Her perfect lips parting just slightly. She really was the most beautiful girl I'd ever seen. I may not have thought so at first, but now...I couldn't imagine anyone I'd ever want more than I wanted her.

My chest tightened, and I ground my teeth against the ache. I already had too many people to keep alive, and I'd shatter if any of them were taken from me. I couldn't lose anyone else I cared about. I couldn't afford *to care* about anyone else.

I relaxed as the realization set in and a hopeless sort of wonder took hold.

It didn't matter.

It was too late.

She was already my Sparrow.

And I was already her Crow.

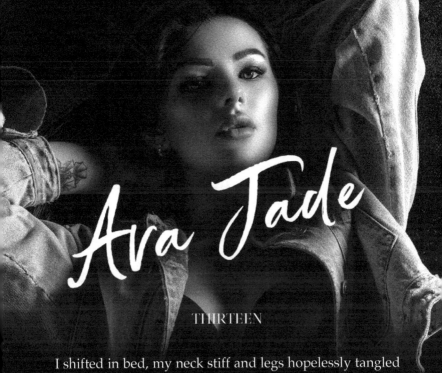

Ava Jade

THIRTEEN

I shifted in bed, my neck stiff and legs hopelessly tangled in blankets.

No. Not bed.

The leather creaked audibly beneath me. The denim under my cheek shifted as I stiffened.

I closed my eyes tightly, heat crawling into my cheeks as I very carefully lifted my head, turning just enough to see if my suspicions were correct.

Blinking to clear the sleep from my eyes, I peered up at him, ready with a snide comment o pounce from my lips about how he was the absolute worst pillow in the world.

But...I barely recognized him.

I sat up straighter, pushing the dark hair from my face.

Corvus was asleep. His body slouched low on the sofa, and his head was tipped back against the headrest, turned slightly to one side. His dirty blond hair sat in a mussed halo on his head, tipped forward to shadow one eye. Without his trademark sneer, he looked so different. He still had wicked cheekbones and a jawline sharper than a razor's edge, but now it didn't look ominous or threatening.

He looked like a Saint.

Or maybe an angel. He was only missing the wings.

Get it together, Ava Jade, I scolded myself internally, giving my head a little shake. It didn't matter what the dick looked like when he was sleeping. All that mattered was how he acted when he was awake.

A new blade and a couple meals weren't enough to fix anything. Though, I had to admit, if he kept feeding me, I might have to forgive him eventually. I'd gone through much worse than Corvus James to get a half decent meal and his were *divine*.

Careful, AJ, my smarter self warned. *You're getting too close to them.*

And I was. My walls were crumbling with each passing day since the start. I couldn't afford to let that happen. I needed to keep them at a distance. If I let them in too close, I was terrified I'd only want more. That I wouldn't be able to push them back out again.

It would only lead to pain in the end. When push came to shove, I knew where their true allegiances were. And I knew where I stood.

Carefully, without shifting the couch, I untangled myself from the navy throw blanket trapped in my legs and climbed from the couch, stretching until my spine and neck cracked. I winced at the ache in my neck, wondering how in the hell I'd managed to crawl into his fucking lap in the night. I hadn't even meant to fall asleep. Didn't think I would even if I tried to.

But there we both were, sleeping. Him, right next to

140

someone with enough blades to ensure maximum bleed out and me, on the lap of someone I vowed to loathe for all eternity.

Quite the fucking pair.

Yep, they would be the death of me for sure.

After one more stretch, I tiptoed from the living room, resolved to use the opportunity of being fully unsupervised in the Nest to have another good snoop around. If I'd been smart, I would've done it days ago when I broke out of the windowless closet room, but I'd had only vengeance on my mind that morning, and the haze of the whiskey from the night before.

Not a great combo for productivity.

The stairs creaked as I ascended and I paused, waiting to see if the noise woke Corvus, but after a few more seconds without the sound of him waking, I continued. I stuck to the outside bits of the stairs instead of the middle, spreading my weight to avoid any more unwanted noises.

I wasn't exactly sure what I was looking for, but I'd know when I found it. There had to be something here I could use as leverage. Or as proof of crimes that would see them all put behind bars. My stomach rebelled against the idea, and I pressed a palm to it, wincing.

May be wise to use the bathroom before Corvus woke up, too, since there was no door handle and I was pretty sure he'd stand in the open doorway while I peed out of spite. Ah well. Let him watch.

The first door belonged to Corvus' bedroom and it seemed as good a place as any to start. Perfect, actually. His offer for me to sleep in any room I liked had me thinking it was possible I wouldn't find a damn thing at all. If I was going to find something, I was willing to bet it'd be here, though. I would never have picked his room to sleep in, and he knew it.

141

I pushed the door open and stepped inside, finding it the exact same as the last time I'd seen it.

A bed, sleek with sheets and blankets pulled tight enough to bounce a coin off of, pushed against the far wall between two rectangular windows covered in modern blinds.

Against the wall to the right of me stood a tall mahogany dresser, it's top wiped clean of dust. The only thing marring its mirrored surface was a slender lamp that was really just a slim steel column with a light bar running up one side.

Aside from the night tables to either side of his bed, there was only a desk. Low and long, it dominated the space along the left wall. Three monitors perched on its surface along with some other equipment. A folding chair leaned against the desk, ready to be opened and used when needed. A temporary fix, I had to assume. It looked like our dining room chairs back in Lennox. The likes of Corvus James wouldn't be caught sitting on something so *cheap*. Not when the rest of his room screamed modern luxury.

I decided to start with the computer, walking over to tap on the keyboard, making it whir to life. I felt around under the monitors, searching for the volume buttons and finding them before the power on could make any sounds.

The password screen popped up and I cursed under my breath, but my attention snagged on several cords running along the floor below the desk. I cocked my head, following them to where they disappeared into the wall next to a closet door.

The fuck?

I took a breath. *Come on, baby. Give Mama something good.*

I opened the door with a flourish and stopped dead

at what I found in the dark room beyond.

My fingers slipped along the wall inside, searching for a switch. I found a dimmer instead and pushed it up, slowly illuminating the closet.

No. Not the closet.

The entire six by eight space had been gutted. The walls covered in dark bumpy soundproofing the whole way around. The cords jutted from the wall, snaking up a metal pole to the boxy microphone resting at its apex.

A barking laugh fell from my lips before I could squash it.

I had no fucking idea what I was expecting, but this sure as hell wasn't it.

Did Corvus fancy himself a rock star?

Or...*oh my fuck*...did he rap?

Pretend to be the next Slim Shady. Corvus James, *please stand up*.

I giggled to myself, unconsciously stepping into the closet to touch the mic, stepping up to it like Corvus must.

I bit my lower lip, finger on the switch to turn it on, a dark chasm opening in my gut. My heart thudded in my ribcage, and I swallowed past the wave of emotion threatening to drag me under.

I couldn't remember the last time I sang.

No. That wasn't true. I could remember. There was only one person I ever sang in front of. My dad. The last time I sang was four days before he was murdered. He played his guitar, and I sang one of his favorite songs. When I was finished, he smiled at me and set the guitar aside.

That night, he did what he always did. He gave my chin a squeeze before getting ready to leave. He kicked on his work boots and pulled on his navy-blue plaid sweater. He pocketed the money meant to pay the rent and

143

promised to be back soon. Further promising that *this time* he would win enough money to get us out of 'the hole.'

I didn't fight him on it. I knew from experience that it was no use and he would only go anyway. No matter what I said or did.

He said something different that night, though. He told me that if anything ever happened to him, that I should leave and never come back.

I didn't ask him why. I knew why. Even if he never told me himself.

You didn't teach your daughter how to throw knives and run jobs because you hang with the *right* sort of people. Good people. You taught your daughter those things and told her to run because you hang with the *wrong* sort of people.

I learned my lesson with mom. It was her debt that'd almost gotten me killed that night on the tracks. That's what that *filth* said.

Your junkie mom couldn't pay, so you'll *pay for her.*

I never did get the courage to ask her if she'd offered me up or if the slime ball of a man just decided to take what was owed in flesh instead of dollar bills.

She had her breakdown barely a week later and then she was gone. If I ever saw her again, I promised myself I would ask.

I hoped I never saw her again.

The mic felt cold against my fingers and when I slicked it on, the electronic hum of it filled the air, making the tiny hairs on my arms stand up.

Licking my lips, I shut the door, closing myself into the small soundproof box and cleared my throat. I belted a few notes; they were rough. Like I said, it'd been a while, but I'd never sung into a microphone before, and I liked how it made my voice sound. I went louder, testing the quality of the soundproofing, then stopped and opened the door quietly to listen for Corvus.

Nothing.

Huh. Not bad.

When I closed the door the second time, that same overwhelming feeling of grief took root in my stomach again. I caressed the mic in my palm and closed my eyes, taking a deep breath, remembering sitting with Dad on the ratty old rust orange sofa in our living room.

Remembering how he'd fallen into the seat next to me and dragged his guitar across his lap.

"Sing me a song, my girl," he'd said, plucking a few strings to let me know which one he wanted.

I'd rolled my eyes like he was the most annoying human being to ever walk the earth, but that was the furthest thing from the truth. I loved to sing, and I loved when he asked me to sing for him. It was one of the few things we ever did together that didn't involve sharp objects or criminal activity.

In the moments where I sang and he played his beat-up guitar, we were a normal family. A dad and his daughter, doing dad and daughter things.

My eyes burned as I began to hum the first few notes of his favorite song, but I couldn't do it. I couldn't sing that, not without him there to hear me. I would never sing that song again. The ache behind my breastbone waned as a more familiar emotion grew to replace it.

How could he leave me like that?

After everything he taught me, it was *him* who didn't know better.

I didn't care what I promised him anymore. I left Lennox like he asked, but I would go back...at least for a single purpose: to find whoever killed him and make sure they knew the real meaning of pain before they died.

It didn't matter that there was no evidence. There was always something. Whispers. People who knew. It was the Kings, it had to be. I just needed to figure out which one.

The silent promise made breathing easier. Became a balm for my broken soul.

And then I knew what I wanted to sing.

Primal Ethos' Anthem of the Broken filtered past my lips, quiet at first, no more than a whisper. I felt the lyrics in my bones, filling in the cracks and fissures, mending me as I let the song carry me away from all the dark awful things swirling just out of reach in my mind.

There was only me and this song. This moment and the words.

Knowing that there was at least one other person in this world who knew what it felt like to have this hollow pit inside, so deep there was no hope of it ever being filled, made me feel like I wasn't alone.

Somewhere out there, someone understood.

Someone had felt the betrayal. The loss. The heartache. The confusion. The fucking *pain* I'd felt, and they made this song.

My voice began to crack as the final lyric leaked out, my throat burning at the release and the acknowledgement I hadn't allowed myself since the day it happened.

He was really gone.

He wasn't coming back this time.

The dam I'd been struggling to hold up all these past weeks crumpled in an instant, and I wasn't fast enough to hold my breath before the waves of my anger and grief crashed over my head. Filled my lungs until I choked. Until I was so full of it that it leaked out, dripping down my face, onto the floor as I crouched, clutching my skull between my stiff hands.

I'd never sing for Dad again.

He'd never stumble home drunk off the rush of a win and declare it Ava Jade Day at five in the morning and demand that I get dressed because we were going for ice cream.

Not ever again.

It could have been only minutes, but it felt like hours as I cried for the first time in...I couldn't even remember how long. By the time the tears slowed and then stopped, my eyes burned and my nose was so stuffed up that I probably wouldn't breathe right for days. But I felt somehow better, like a weight had lifted from my chest and getting back to my feet felt just a little bit easier than before.

I switched off the microphone and used the hem of my shirt to dry away the tears still wet on my cheeks, and stepped out of the closet.

Corvus sat barely six feet away, folding chair facing the closet door. His body bent, elbows on knees, fingers pressed together in front of his lips like a prayer. His eyes, shadowed by the sweep of hair hanging low on his brow, found me from their darkness. His jaw twitched, clenching as he stared.

My stomach twisted.

"How much did you hear?" I demanded, my voice still half broken from crying.

He dropped his hands and looked away. "Enough."

I swiveled my head, finding the computer screens along the desk all powered on, a little red microphone light in the software he had open blinking instead of solid now that the mic was shut off.

My hands clenched to fists.

"You're an incredible singer," he said, meeting my spiteful stare again. "Has anyone ever told you that?"

147

"And you're a hateful prick," I hissed, hating how my lungs were constricting in my chest. How my stomach plummeted to my toes. "Has anyone ever told you that?"

He didn't reply. Didn't even look angry at my barb.

"What do you even use that room for anyway, *hmmm?* Fancy yourself a fucking rock god or some shit? Or does the sound of your own voice turn you on so much that you have to record—"

"I turned it off," he interrupted, completely ignoring every word I said. "When you started...I turned it off. I didn't listen."

"Oh, so I should thank you then?"

"Sparrow—"

"I'm not your fucking Sparrow!" I yelled, my nostrils flaring as a wicked heat sizzled up my spine.

He heard me. He heard me *break*. No one had ever...

No one would ever again.

I moved to storm past him, and he snatched my wrist. Unable to stop myself, I reflexively struck. The flat of my palm cracking loudly against his cheek.

He didn't let go. Even when it started to bloom red.

"You don't have to hide your pain from me."

My eyes burned anew, and I couldn't take it. I couldn't take any of this.

I ripped my arm out of his grasp and ran for the door, taking the stairs two at a time until I somehow got outside and the fresh air filled my aching lungs. I forced the tears to obey, swallowed them back down until I felt only heat and fury.

"*Ava Jade,*" Corvus called from inside the Nest, but I was already gone, running barefoot through the trees.

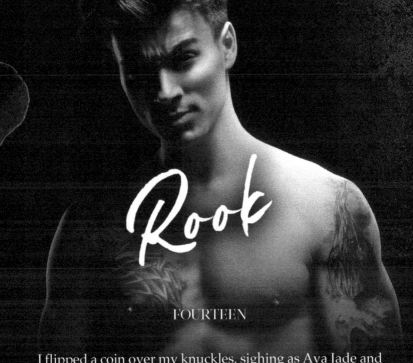

Rook

FOURTEEN

I flipped a coin over my knuckles, sighing as Ava Jade and Becca chatted in the living room while music played in the background from a Bluetooth speaker. I leaned against the black marble countertop, sipping the bourbon spiked coffee Becca made for me, glancing at my phone every few seconds.

It was getting late, but neither of them seemed ready to call it a night, happy to chat the night away and pretend I wasn't here at all.

Ava Jade had hardly spoken to me since Corvus dropped me at her door hours ago. She'd opened it, taken one look at me, and walked away, leaving the door open for me.

I was guessing it didn't go well between her and Corv. Judging by the light bruise on his cheek, she'd actually hit him. And somehow, he hadn't retaliated. Corvus was a monument to self-control, but you didn't touch him. You touched him and you died.

He let her hit him, and he did absolutely nothing.

I didn't know what to make of that.

But whatever he did had nothing to do with me. We'd had fun the other night, hadn't we? I knew I did.

My jaw clenched as I remembered the strain of touching her. The tremble in my fingers I hoped she hadn't noticed.

The aching need to choke her a little longer, to cut a little deeper, to fuck her raw...

Being unable to do it.

The idea of scaring her away from me—

Of going too far and—

I tapped my phone impatiently for the third time in as many minutes, distracting myself as the screen illuminated to show no new messages or missed calls. Grey offered to come and stay with Ghost tonight, but we needed those messages cracked *yesterday*.

We all wanted to think we were overreacting, but I think each of us knew that wasn't the case. I had a bad feeling. A hollow, ugly pit that'd been yawning open ever since that day she accused Corvus.

Something was very wrong, and we needed to know what it was.

If someone was threatening her...

I clutched the coin in my hand, a tremor racing down my spine, making my back heat.

They wouldn't be a *someone* when I was through with them. They'd be a nothing. A pile of ash at my feet.

Becca and Ava Jade turned to me, and I realized I'd begun tapping my foot, and stopped, polishing off my coffee and bourbon instead before swiping the back of my palm over my lips and refilling my mug from the flask in my back pocket.

"There's cola in the fridge," Becca offered. "If you want to mix that."

I shook my head. "Too sweet."

"Suit yourself."

They went back to talking about some event they were going to soon. Becca was asking Ava Jade if they'd have to bring one of her *shadows* with them because they only had two tickets. My Ghost said *fuck no*, but she was wrong if she thought Corvus was going to let her go anywhere, least of all out of fucking town to Lodi, without one of us with her.

It was cute that she thought she could get away with it, really.

"You want to tell me what's going on?" Becca asked in a hushed tone I wasn't meant to hear, her dark brown eyes slipping in my direction before falling back on her friend as she leaned in. "They haven't left you alone for weeks."

Ava Jade shrank back from her friend, the discomfort evident in the tightness around her eyes as she struggled with what to say. "Are *you* going to tell me what's going on?" she asked, replying to her friend's question with one of her own meant to divert the conversation back to safer waters.

I knew the tactic. Grey was a fan of that one.

"You've been here a lot lately," Ava Jade prodded. "You've only gone out, what, once or twice in the last week to see your..." she shimmied her shoulders. *"Friend."*

"He's just...been busy." Becca frowned, pushing her pin straight hair behind her ear. "Seriously though, Aves, why are they here? You know you can talk to me, right?" She lowered her voice, and I caught her brown eyes shifting to me in my periphery. "Maybe I can help you."

151

Shit. If she were dead set on staying here, Ghost really needed to come clean with her bestie. Before things got real fucking messy.

I busied myself on my phone, trying to give them a modicum of privacy to chat. Besides, I was wholly uninterested in anything Becca Hart naively thought she could do to help Ava Jade out of this inescapable situation or her sexual escapades with her booty call boyfriend for that matter.

Once upon a time I'd tried to get her into bed, but she didn't hold a candle to Ava Jade. No one did. She turned me down, anyway. Smart girl. The things I'd have done to that tight little body...

She never would have recovered.

I flicked over to the group chat with the guys and thumbed out a quick message.

Rook: What the fuck is taking so long?

His reply came after a minute.

Grey: I have them.

My teeth locked.

Grey: On the phone with Corv. One sec.

The fuck?

Rook: Three way me in.

My phone rang a second later and I picked it up, the mug in my hand clattering as I set it down harder than I meant to. I felt Ava Jade's and Becca's eyes follow me all the way into her bedroom.

"You there?" Grey asked.

"Yeah. Go."

I closed myself into the bathroom.

"It's worse than we thought."

"Fuck," Corvus hissed.

"Read them," I ordered. "Read them all."

Grey's voice wavered between a growl and a rasping

whisper as he read out a slew of text messages from Ava Jade's stalker.

That was exactly what this motherfucker was.

With each message he read aloud to us, the tension on the line grew, coiling just as tightly as the knot of wrath forming in my gut. My skin prickled with the urge to *kill kill kill*, but I had no outlet here. Nothing to crush or break or burn or bury.

I gripped the ledge of the counter, bending my head as I breathed hard in through my nose.

"What is he talking about? The train tracks? What does that mean?" Corvus roared down the line.

I had an idea, but it was Ghost's story to tell. Her choice who she told it to.

"And *the dark one*," Grey added. "That was sent on fight night. Whoever this is, they're talking about Rook."

"This ends now. Can we trace this guy?" Corvus asked.

I cared little about the threat to my life, but I knew my brothers wouldn't be taking it lightly.

What I was more concerned with was the threat to Ghost.

I'll have to punish you, this piece of shit said.

For being with us. For letting us touch her. Like she *belonged* to this...this coward who hid behind a set of electronic keys and the mask of being *unknown*.

"He sent most of them from different numbers. All burners. I can't get a trace on anything. That's why it took so long to get them decrypted in the first place."

"We need to talk to Ava Jade," I grunted down the line, that dark urge still souring in the pit of my stomach. Scratching at the back of my skull.

I twisted off the cap of my flask and drank deeply until the burn of the alcohol seared away some of the

153

darkness, numbing the places where it used to be.

"We need to lure this bastard out," I added as I set the flask down.

A pause before either of my brothers replied. A muscle beneath my eye twitched.

"He's right," Grey said. "She should've told us. Especially after whoever this is threatened Rook."

I could almost hear Corvus nodding on his end of the phone as he came up with a plan. "Tomorrow," he said. "Take her to the chapel instead of homeroom. We'll meet you there."

I wasn't able to hold back a growl. I wanted this handled *now*. I wanted blood *now*.

"Be cool." Grey spoke calmly, letting out a shaky sigh. "This guy, whoever he is, is clearly a coward. He's just talking. Threatening her. Trying to scare her. He hasn't actually *done* anything."

"You think he's all talk?" Corvus asked.

"Maybe."

What did it fucking matter? My vision darkened.

I heaved, my breaths coming heavier, making my voice come out a husky rasp. "I don't give a fuck! No one threatens our girl."

"No one threatens our girl," Grey agreed.

Corvus grunted his assent. "Grey, how soon can you finish up with that shit Diesel sent you to handle?"

"A few hours maybe. What about you? Didn't he need you to settle a dispute upstairs at Sanctum?"

"That's where I am now."

"And?"

"It's going to be a minute. Some fucker stiffed one of our girls and made off with an iPad. I'm tracking it down now, and then Tiny and I have to go handle it."

"Rook, can you make it until morning without saying

anything? If you confront her about it, she's going to lose her shit."

"What's the difference if she loses it here or in the chapel tomorrow?"

"Grey," Corvus supplied. "Grey is the difference."

It was clear it pained him to admit it, but he continued anyway. "She trusts him. You see how she is around him. Less on edge. Relaxed. He might be the only one of us that she won't stab first and ask questions later."

She would listen to me.

I didn't say it, because even though I thought it was true, I knew I wouldn't be able to speak calmly if she tried to deny the messages or continued trying to hide them or downplay them.

Grey could though.

"I can wait."

"Good," Corvus replied. "And Rook?"

"What?"

"I overheard Dies planning another trial for her earlier tonight when I was down at the pub."

"When?" Grey asked. "Which one?"

Corvus sighed. "Don't know. He stopped talking when he saw me. He seems determined to keep us out of it now that he has the time to administer the rest himself. Thought you should know in case it happens while you're with her."

"Don't kill anyone, man." Grey warned me. "It's not worth it."

"I know."

"Dies will shit a brick if you do, and she can handle herself."

"I said I *fucking know*."

"Sorry," Grey muttered.

"In the morning, then?" Corvus confirmed.

"Yeah," I said, and hung up, tossing my phone on the counter before I ran my palm down my face, trying to smooth away the angry lines I could still feel tight like pulled strings across my forehead and at the edges of my eyes.

Two soft knocks came at the door.

"Rook?" Ghost asked softly. "Everything okay?"

My chest ached.

Why did she think she had to endure this kind of shit alone when she had us? I wanted to throttle her and wrap her up in my arms at the same time. I could do neither.

Someone was threatening her, and she acted as though she wasn't bothered in the slightest when her reaction with Corvus proved that was anything but the truth. I pressed my palm to the door and sighed, the anger ebbing away almost as fast as it'd come. I winced at the loss of it, confused at how easily she could draw it out of me, like blood drawn from a wound.

What was this girl doing to me?

"Rook?" she hedged a second time, and I swallowed, pocketing my phone and the flask again before opening the door.

"What's up, Ghost?"

She studied my face, her cold gray-blue eyes darting back and forth between my dark ones. She'd find nothing there, though. I was a master at what Grey affectionately called *going dead eyed.*

Her brows pinched. "Who was that on the phone?"

"Corv and Grey," I replied. "Why?"

The knot between her brows smoothed out and she shrugged aloofly, like she didn't care. "No reason."

I cocked my head at her, my gaze snagging on the shape of her phone in her front pocket. Heat seared over my flesh, making it prickle as I wondered what other messages could be lingering there that she hadn't told us about. How much worse they could be than the ones we'd already read.

Tomorrow.

We're all going to sit and have a nice little chat about this fuckery tomorrow.

"I'm going to bed," she announced, grabbing a threadbare white t-shirt from the shelf of the closet outside the bathroom and tossing it on her bed before snatching up a throw blanket that was haphazardly draped over the top of her purple covers.

"Here," she said, pushing it into my hands.

"You going to make me sleep on the floor?"

"You can if you want to," she replied sweetly. "But I'm not going anywhere. Take the couch. You'll be more comfortable."

Her words didn't match the lack of sincerity in her tone. I saw this for what it really was. Her walls were finally starting to come down, and she didn't know how to handle it. So, like the Ava Jade we knew, she was going to fight it with everything she had.

It was a fight she'd lose.

"Did I do something?" I asked. "Because as far as I could tell, you thoroughly enjoyed yourself the other night."

"I don't sleep with other people."

"Good. Apparently, I don't, either."

Her nose wrinkled at that, confused at the dual meaning.

"No. I meant that I don't *sleep* with other people as in; I can't sleep when there's someone in bed next to me."

"You did just fine in my bed."

She opened her mouth to reply, shut it, and seethed. "That was different."

157

"Was it?" I challenged, brushing past as I left her bedroom. "Sleep well, Ghost. Maybe if you're lucky, I'll be the one haunting your dreams tonight."

A cute growl preceded the slam of her door behind me, and I laughed to myself, not bothering to try to hide the sound.

Becca stared at me from the kitchen, pausing after she finished filling herself a glass of water.

"What?" I asked.

"Nothing," she muttered, shaking her head as she walked to her own bedroom, but I caught her gaze fall to my cock beneath my jeans, and I knew why she was staring. Looking for the outline of my stainless-steel *accessories.*

Ava Jade told her. I wondered what she said. I glanced back at Ava Jade's door and smirked, mindlessly grabbing the pack of cigarettes from my back pocket.

"Could you, um, *not* smoke that in here?"

I blinked, coming back to myself before I could tug a smoke from the packet to find Becca hesitating in her doorway.

"I hate the smell."

"You smoke pot in here."

"That's different."

I raised my brows, and she dropped her gaze, clearing her throat as she closed herself into her bedroom. She wouldn't push the matter, but I would never hear the end of it from Ava Jade.

She said she wasn't going anywhere. Guess now was as good a time as any to test that. Corvus had left her to her own devices for hours yesterday, and she hadn't run, what was another hour? I could use the fresh air. It was late, but after hearing those messages, I wasn't fucking tired.

For once, I might get a taste of what it was like for Corvus. Exhausted but unable to shut my eyes.

I ditched the blanket on the couch and slipped a finger under the collar of my leather jacket hung on the back of a stool in the kitchen and shrugged it on. My teeth clenched as I wrapped my fist around the door handle, hesitating to leave.

Whoever was texting her had sent threats. Maybe Corvus was right and it was all talk, but what if it wasn't?

On a whim, I dipped my fingers into the pocket of Ava Jade's jacket on the hook by the door, digging for keys. I pushed past a thick piece of paper and heard them jingle. Drawing them out, I tossed them in the air and caught them, stepping out of the shared apartment and locking the door behind me.

I pocketed the keys and thumbed a quick message to Ava Jade.

Rook: Going outside for a smoke. If you hear the door, it's just me coming back in. I locked it behind me.

She didn't reply, but the message showed as *read* after a second and that was good enough for me.

I hustled down the stairs and out the back door, stalking towards the basketball court protruding from the back of the academy. Automatic lights flicked on and I grimaced at their ridiculous brightness, lighting my smoke for a long drag as I leaned against the rough brick beneath the basketball net.

The academy grounds were quiet at night and everywhere outside of the ring of white security lights appeared so dark I couldn't see more than a few feet into it. Frowning, I moved away from the lights and settled myself just out of range from where they would detect me.

The dark swallowed me up again, and I waited for my eyes to adjust, the orange glow of the cherry on my cigarette now the only light as far as I could see toward the north lawn and gardens.

I scanned the trees, my fingers twitching toward the knife in my right boot. Corvus wouldn't let me bring a gun, and maybe that was for the best. Especially if Diesel chose tonight for her next trial.

Normally they were more spaced out, just long enough between them to make you start to get comfortable. Start to get complacent. But he was known for running a few back to back, just to mix things up.

My Ghost would pass the surprise attack with flying colors. Fuck, she almost had *me* that night out behind the apartment buildings. If she hadn't panicked, I had no doubt she'd have gotten free of my hold, too.

I rubbed out my smoke on the brick and walked back to the door, satisfied to have seen no threats lingering in the trees outside.

The keys jingled in my pocket and I plucked them back out as I neared the back door to the academy, but my arm jerked when I tried to open it.

I tried again, but it wouldn't budge. Locked.

Someone locked it.

Rook: Did you fucking lock me out? Really?

No reply. No read receipt.

My stomach twisted.

Diesel.

It was fucking Diesel.

Or rather, whoever he sent after her. They knew I was a loose cannon at the best of times. They wouldn't want me interrupting her trial, and I gave them the perfect opportunity to lock my ass out.

I chuckled darkly to myself, heat making my leather jacket unbearable. I slung it off, discarding it onto the concrete as I rounded the building, picking up speed.

She can handle herself.

I believed it. Really, I did. But I didn't like being locked out. Chained up. Held back.

I wanted to see my Ghost go full poltergeist on their asses. I wanted to watch. I needed to be there *just in case*.

If she somehow failed the trial and was taken out, Corvus and Grey would blame me. Rightly fucking so.

It took me only a minute to find what I was looking for; the slim half-window at the base of the building on the west side, leading down into an old file storage room in the basement of the academy. A regular meeting place for Mrs. June and me before they cleared it out and added a space for the teachers' *quiet reflection*.

I bent and threw my elbow into the glass, sucking in a breath at the sting of air on a fresh cut. Licking my lips, I twisted, booting out the rest of the glass with the sole of my boot before pulling myself through.

I shouldered through the locked door to the filing room and stalked down the hall, taking the stairs up to the main floor three at a time.

"Hey!" Mick, the round-bellied security guard who was absolute shit at his job shouted as I rounded the corner into the main atrium, making for the stairs. I was surprised he'd even left his office, but by the disheveled look of him I'd woken his ass up from his one a.m. nap with the window breaking.

His flashlight beam caught on me, and I gave him a half a second of time. A single look that had him dropping the beam.

"Oh, fuck. Sorry, Mr. Clayton. I thought it was—"

I was gone before he could finish, up the curving staircase and down the hall, keys out, metal slipping into the lock, It was already open. *Fuck.*

I walked in and Becca appeared in her doorway, her

161

eyes wide and wild and face pale in the moonlight as she took me in, confused. Her nightgown all twisted.

A loud *bang* echoed through the apartment and Becca cried out, her attention jerking to Ava Jade's closed door. Not a gunshot. Something hard knocking into an even harder surface.

I gritted my teeth and clenched my fists, the desire to go straight for that door and mow down whoever was behind it stronger than any urge that'd possessed me in a long ass time.

"*AJ*," Becca breathed as the sounds of a struggle came louder through her friend's door. She made a break across the apartment and I headed her off, catching her around the waist. A bit surprised at her willingness to run into danger for her friend. I'd misjudged her.

"You can't help her," I muttered in Becca's ear, the smell of her essential oil perfume filling my nose.

She struggled to get free and shoved me, making me jerk a step back. "Don't you have a gun or something?" she blurted, and I sighed, my back muscles going taut as the sound of something else crashing in Ava Jade's room echoed all around us.

I snatched Becca's wrist and jerked her back when she made another go for Ava Jade's door.

"Go back to your room," I ordered her. "I'll handle it."

She frantically looked between me and Ava Jade's door, her eyes gleaming with frustrated, confused tears. It wasn't fair for Ghost not to tell her friend.

"She's taking the trials to become a Saint," I explained simply. "This is one of them. She's going to be fine."

Becca's brows drew together, but after a beat, her shoulders lowered slightly, and she closed her mouth on a heaving breath. "It doesn't sound like it."

162

Ava Jade cried out and a tremor of wrath flashed up my spine like lightning.

"Just go to your room," I growled at Becca before turning for Ghost's door, my vision darkening at the edges. Hot air pushed out from my lungs as I waited outside, listening carefully to the sounds within.

A male grunt.

A hard blow.

A cry of fury that could only be my Ghost's.

I was inside in an instant, dodging an elbow as Ava Jade tackled the tall masked man to her bed. They rolled off onto the floor, and she gasped for air as they struggled.

She has this.

He'll back off any second. Tell her she passed.

She managed to get on top of him, and I strode farther into the room, watching her as her fist connected with his jaw, knocking his head violently to the side.

Yes. Come on, Ghost.

I groaned at the violence of it. At the look on her face as she hit him again. A quiet determined fury edged in something sharper.

Wait…

She wasn't detached like she was that night with Bri at the Docks. She was on edge. Something about this attack spooked her.

I didn't like that.

Not one fucking bit.

Who was this guy? He was in a mask for the trial, but still, I should've recognized him. He was tall. Wide through the shoulders. Crowley? No, maybe Derrik?

My Ghost's eyes alighted on me for an instant and it was the opening the Saint needed to turn the tables. He flipped her onto her back, and I saw a flash of something silver in the moonlight.

Ava Jade shrieked, stopping whatever it was with a forearm, her teeth bared.

I couldn't help her.

It would render the trial void, or worse, result in an immediate fail.

She would either have to go through something like this again, or her trials would be at an end, and I shuddered to think what that could mean.

Shit.

"*No,*" she hissed, and then frantically, she shouted. "Rook!"

My beast responded. It didn't matter who he was anymore.

I didn't even register what I'd done until he was off her and I'd knocked whatever was in his hand onto the floor before throwing an elbow into his face. The window shattered and he sailed through it. Tossed out like trash to drop the two stories to the ground below Ava Jade's window.

The *thud* of his body against the earth was followed by silence only broken by the sound of Ava Jade's coughs and strained breathing.

I stomped to the wall and flicked on the light, finding her clutching her throat where a ring of quickly darkening bruises were rising to the surface of her skin. Heat seared along the back of my neck, and I bristled, nostrils flaring as I knelt and drew her against me. She fought my hold, her voice hoarse and cracking, making her cough as she tried to speak.

"*He…*" she managed hoarsely, getting her voice back. "*…in…*"

I rushed into her bathroom and filled a glass with water, hurrying back to kneel once more and put it to her lips.

164

She took it greedily, sitting up straighter and wincing as the cool water snaked down her throat. "He was trying to inject me," she said after another watery cough.

"What?"

Her mouth opened in surprise as she darted forward, almost knocking me over as she retrieved something from beneath her bed. She stared at it in her hand, barely breathing.

A slender plastic syringe with a short, needled tip was gripped there. A clear substance in the chamber.

I snatched it from her, turning it over in my fingers before looking her over for injection marks. "Did he get you?"

"No," she breathed. "No, I don't think so."

She coughed again, rubbing and massaging her windpipe.

"What the fuck was he going to inject me with? I didn't sign up to be fucking drugged."

I shook my head, my stomach turning. This wasn't right.

There was one trial that involved ingesting a substance, but not drugs. Never drugs. He wouldn't dare. Not after what I went through. What many Saints had gone through, the lives they'd come from and left before joining the gang.

I raced back to the window, leaning out, ready to climb down and demand answers from what was probably a corpse but...there was no one there. No body, living or dead. I jerked my head up, searching through the trees to the left and the edge of the parking lot and curving road leading to town to my right.

Nothing.

"Fuck," I hissed, pocketing the syringe in favor of my phone.

165

Corvus answered on the first ring.

"What is it?"

"We have a problem."

"Tell me."

"Get over here now. Bring Grey. Either Diesel's lost his damned mind or there's a bigger problem."

"Get out," I heard Corvus growl, and Tiny began to protest when I heard the Rover door shut and the engine rev.

"Be there in ten minutes," he snapped a second later, and the line went dead.

Ava Jade stood, her baggy white t-shirt torn to expose part of a breast. Stained red with blood dripping from a shallow cut in her forehead. "Do you want to tell me what the hell is going on?"

"Depends," I snapped, the fury still making my vision blur with patches of darkness not so easily released this time. "Do *you* have anything you want to tell me?"

A muscle in her jaw clenched.

I ran my hands through my hair and inhaled sharply, trying to get control. Bending forward, I planted my palms on my knees and leaned against the wall until my vision cleared.

"Rook?" Ava Jade hedged and I couldn't stand it anymore. I shoved the door to her room open, making it bounce loudly against the opposite wall as I stormed out.

What was Diesel thinking?

If this was Diesel…

And if it wasn't Diesel…

Someone was going to pay for this. We just needed to figure out who.

Corvus

FIFTEEN

The tires skidded as I drove us into the parking lot, not fast enough to cut the wheel before making us knock into a low cement piling. Grey and I both jumped out, slamming the doors behind us. I could inspect the damage to the Rover later. I had a gut wrenching feeling whatever I was about to walk into would put that damage to shame.

Rook rarely sounded like he had on the phone exactly nine minutes ago.

I braced myself for whatever was bad enough to get him that worked up, the muscles in my arms flexing and unflexing with the clenching of my fists as we found our way into Briar Hall through the front door. I'd already called ahead and told security to have the door open.

"She's okay, right?" Grey asked in a solemn tone as we shoved through the front doors unimpeded and marched up the stairs.

"I don't know."

"Was it a trial?"

"I don't know."

"Well, did Rook say anything about—"

"*I don't fucking know anything,*" I growled at him, slicking my hair back as we neared her door.

I hadn't seen my Sparrow or heard from her since this morning. I didn't know how I'd handle it if she asked me to leave.

Watching her break this morning opened some long-forgotten wounds deep inside. I *felt* for the first time in a long time. I felt her pain as acutely as I once felt my own before I learned to block it out.

I'd never wanted so badly to be someone who had the ability to comfort someone else. And that song. *My* song.

I couldn't get the sound of her voice singing my words out of my head all fucking day. I got why Rook had taken to calling her Ghost. She was haunting me, too.

The door was open when we got to it, and we pushed our way inside with ease, my hand unconsciously going to the butt of the gun tucked neatly into the back of my jeans.

Rook sat, elbow on knees on the couch, his fingers steepled against his lips. Ava Jade and Becca sat on the couch opposite him, and it seemed we'd interrupted some hushed conversation between them. Becca was deathly pale. Her bloodshot eyes strained with the knots in her forehead.

I shouldn't have been surprised to see her there, and yet I was. Did this have something to do with her?

That's when I noticed the bruises. In a ring of purpling flesh around Ava Jade's throat. The crusted blood in her hairline and the shallow cut it'd come from. How pale she was, too.

"AJ," Grey said on a breath and her eyes snapped to

168

mine for an instant before falling away as Grey approached her, going down on one knee before her on the couch to reach up and gently touch the bruising on her neck.

I wanted to break the hands of the person responsible. Saint or not.

"The attack trial?" Grey asked, and I cleared my throat, drawing his eye. I looked pointedly at Becca.

"She knows," Rook said, finally dropping his hands and sitting up straight. "We should have told her from the start."

My jaw ticked, but arguing wasn't going to help whatever the hell this situation was right now.

Rook pushed to his feet and gave Grey a nudge with his boot before shouldering past me towards Ava Jade's room. His face betrayed a storm cloud of dark emotion he was working hard to keep under control. "A word," he muttered as he passed, and I glanced between Ava Jade and him, jerking my head to tell Grey to follow.

Becca tucked herself into her friend's side, avoiding the blades strapped to Ava Jade's thigh and the one clutched in her hand. The one with the crow etched into the handle.

I made myself leave her there; it took everything I had not to demand answers right there and then. I wanted to shake Rook. To shake *her*. Make them tell me exactly what the fuck happened and why the fuck she thought it was okay to lie to us about her mystery texter for so damn long.

But that wouldn't win me any fucking points now, would it? And with the sound of her broken song still in my ears, I found I just couldn't do it.

Rook shut the door behind us and drew something out of his pocket. It took me a second to register what it was.

169

"What the fuck is that?" I asked, even though it was obvious. My skin prickled, burning up like my edges had been ignited and I was nothing but paper. "Is she on drugs?"

Rook's dark eyes met mine, and he shook his head once.

I noted the broken window behind him and frowned.

"She was attacked," he explained. "And whoever attacked her tried to inject her with it."

He was fucking playing with me. There was no way...

Grey snatched the syringe from Rook and pressed on the plunger enough to let a drop of the liquid slip out the top of the short needle head. He rubbed it between his fingers and sniffed.

A smell like limes tickled my nose. Familiarly mixed with the tarry scent of pine. I leaned in towards the substance coating Grey's fingertips, but it wasn't whatever the liquid in the syringe was. That was odorless, this was something else. So faint I could barely detect it, but it was there all the same. So familiar it grated on my nerves that I couldn't place where I'd smelled it before.

"Do you know what it is?" Rook asked.

Grey shook his head, but he already had his phone out. He dialed a number. Hung up and dialed again. On the third attempt, the line connected. "I need you to ID a substance for me."

A pause.

"Greyson Winters."

An exclamation on the other end.

"I need you to come and get it from Briar Hall. It'll be waiting for you with security. I need to know what it is within the hour."

Another pause.

"Tell no one of this. You are only to give the

170

information to myself or my brothers. *No one else*."

He ended the call and pocketed the phone.

I didn't know who it was, didn't care, my mind was still reeling. I stared openly at the syringe, my blood going cold. "Diesel wouldn't…"

"If not Diesel then I can think of only one other potential," Rook put in, his anger flaring across his cheekbones.

"Her stalker," Grey uttered, curling his fingers tight around the syringe.

"Tell us the rest," I demanded, and Rook explained the entire thing from front to back, humoring me each time I asked for clarity.

He'd left her alone, like a fucking idiot, but it was too late to fix that. And the lack of anything useful in his story drove me near to madness.

"You didn't know who he was?" I asked for the third time. "Are you sure?"

Rook pinched the bridge of his nose. "I told you, I couldn't tell. It was dark. He was masked. Could have been a Saint. Might not have been."

"It could've been a Saint and still you threw him through a window two stories above the ground?" Grey asked, raising a brow as though that was surprising.

"Could *you* have stood there and let someone strangle our girl?" he challenged Grey and that shut him up. He dropped his gaze, pensive as he considered the implications of his response.

I began to pace the narrow slice of carpet between her bedroom and the bathroom, thinking. Connecting. Formulating a way to move forward.

"Okay," I said after a minute. "Okay, so we can't ask Diesel if this was him because he'll know something is up, and I'm not sure we want him knowing if this is something *other* than a trial. At least for now. He doesn't need more reasons to want her gone."

"We can find out ourselves if a Saint has been injured," Rook suggested, and I'd been getting to that. "He'd been fucked up pretty good after that fall. Wouldn't be hard to pick him out."

I nodded.

"This couldn't have been Diesel," Grey said, repeating what we were all thinking, and I felt like an absolute piece of shit for even considering it.

But he'd made his obvious distaste for her clear. He didn't want her around us. He didn't trust her.

"How far would you go to protect your family if you thought there was a threat?" I asked, meeting each of their hard stares, nodding when neither replied.

"We can't rule him out, but I don't think this was him. If it were a trial, he'd be ringing your neck for interrupting it," I told Rook, and his upper lip curled.

"Not if he felt guilty for trying to alter the results with whatever's in that syringe."

"We need to explore the other option," Grey said, his eyes fixed on the door and the Sparrow beyond it.

He was right. This wasn't going to be pretty, but it needed to be handled. After tonight, there was no way she was being left alone again. Not even for a second. She needed to know why. She needed to know that we knew what she'd worked so hard to hide from us.

I followed Grey through the door and back out to the living room where Ava Jade was placing a warm mug of tea in her friend's hands. Leave it to her to comfort her friend after she was the one who was attacked.

"She doesn't need to be here for this," I said before I could soften my tone, indicating Becca. "Do you have somewhere you can go?"

Sparrow curled a hand around her friend's wrist to stop her from standing. "She stays. I don't want her going anywhere alone right now. Whoever that fucker was could still be outside somewhere."

Becca shuddered and remained sitting.

"Fine," I managed, resisting the urge to press my argument.

Grey walked into the living room, sitting on the edge of the coffee table facing Ava Jade so there was only an inch of space between their knees. He leaned over, and I could imagine the gentle expression he would wear as he told her.

"We know about your stalker," he said, his tone somehow managing to sound hard and gentle all at once. It brokered no room for argument. He was stating a fact, and giving her an opening to tell him the truth.

Her mouth pressed into a hard line. "I don't know what you're—"

"*You should have killed the dark one while you had the chance, but now I see I'll have to do it for you. Nobody touches what's mine,*" Grey said, repeating the text message from where it's seared into his memory.

Her brows drew together and a flash of hot fury danced in her eyes.

"*Don't worry, my love, I'll help you...but if you let them touch you again, I'll have no choice but to punish you.*"

"Stop," she growled in reply, and I saw how Becca was clutching her friend now, worry in the tight lines around her eyes.

"Aves?" Becca prodded. "Why didn't you tell me?"

"I was handling it," she all but hissed in reply, fixing her stare on Grey. "You went through my phone?"

He nodded slowly. "The, *uh*...the day at the diner. It was all planned. I had the laptop ready when you got out.

Took a while to decrypt the files, though."

Her face reddened and she opened her mouth to speak, but I beat her to it.

"You should have told us," I said as gently as I could, given the situation. "Especially after whoever this clown is threatened Rook. Definitely after he threatened you."

Some of her anger seemed to burn off at that, and I placated myself in the knowledge that she clearly knew what I was saying was true, even if she didn't want to admit it to us or to herself.

I knew how hard it was to ask for help. To admit you might not be able to handle something alone. I'd chosen the harder path, but if I could go back and change that choice, things might've been different for me.

I might've been different.

"Has he sent anything else since the messages about fight night?"

Her ice-cold stare burrowed into me. "I didn't read it," she admitted. "He sent something, but I only read the first line. *I warned you…* then I deleted the message."

"Can you recover it," I asked Grey.

He nodded. "Yeah."

"Give him your phone."

Ava Jade balked at the command, and I gritted my teeth. I wanted to punish her for this. I wanted to bend her over my knee and bring my hand down on her bare ass until it was cherry red. I wanted to make her admit her mistake and apologize for putting herself and my brothers in danger.

But what I wanted didn't matter right now. What mattered was keeping us all safe, and the only way to do that was not to scare her into running or make her pull away from me even more.

"Please," I barely got the word out, and I sensed Rook

174

stiffen beside me at the request, his eyes boring into the side of my face. "We need to know what it said."

"You think this was him, don't you?" she asked. "It couldn't possibly be your perfect gangster pops," she scoffed.

I shook my head. "We aren't ruling that out."

She was taken aback at that, and thought quietly to herself for a second before plucking her phone from her pocket and handing it to Grey.

"Do you have any idea who this person is?" Grey asked, catching her hand in his. He gave it a reassuring squeeze before she pulled away.

She shook her head.

"Someone from your past, maybe?" Grey asked. "A spurned lover?"

What?

I stared at the back of Grey's head, wondering what other messages he'd recovered along with the ones from the apparent stalker. Clearly more than we knew.

Ava Jade glared at him. "No. It's not Kit."

"Because you don't want it to be or—"

"It's just not him. Trust me."

He nodded. The conversation done for the moment and already I'd committed the name to memory, ready to scour every inch of Lennox for this guy.

"I'm going to take this downstairs," Grey said and held up the syringe as he stood, leaving the apartment to bring the syringe down to whoever was waiting on him.

Rook sauntered back into the living room and fell onto the sofa opposite the girls with a deep sigh. "Until we figure this out, you can't stay here," he told Ava Jade. "The window will take time to fix and the Nest is more secure."

"No. I already told you I'm not staying there. Besides, I won't leave Becca here alone. What if he comes back?"

175

Rook nodded. "Okay. Fine. She comes, too. You can both stay in the loft above the garage."

Surprise flashed in Sparrow's eyes, and I mirrored the sentiment. What the fuck was he thinking? But if it got Ava Jade to agree to stay with us, I'd deal with it.

"*Uh*, I'm good," Becca croaked, speaking up for the first time. "I really don't want—"

"At least until the window's fixed and you can have your dad install a security system," Ava Jade interrupted her, suddenly liking the idea if it meant she could ensure her friend's safety. Clearly that was more important to her than her pride. "Please? I can't leave you here."

Becca slumped. "Fine. Yeah, I guess that wouldn't be too bad."

Honestly, I expected her to put up more of a fight, or request to stay elsewhere. I was sure her millionaire daddy would happily put her up at The Vandermark just outside of town. I would have rather that, but if I wanted to stay on Ava Jade's good side, I could allow this. At least temporarily.

"Pack up," I said, planting my hands on the back of the couch either side of Rook's head. "This is your last night at Briar Hall for a while."

Grey

SIXTEEN

Diazepam.

Sally from the twenty-four-hour pharmacy in town took longer than I'd requested, but at least she managed to ID what was in the syringe. Enough Diazepam to sedate someone for hours. It would have taken effect within fifteen seconds.

Rook had been pummeling the heavy bag non-stop since I told him and Corvus on Monday night after moving the girls into the loft. Rook knew that drug better than most ever could. It was what they used on him at the psychiatric hospital in Stockton. The one Barrettes Home for Boys sent him to after they found one of the group leaders with a broomstick up his ass in the janitor's closet. The words *Rook was here* carved into the meaty flesh above his tailbone as he cried against a dirty rag in his mouth.

I never asked why he did it, and he never told me. It was just one of those things I knew was off limits for discussion, but my imagination came up with the worst things. Which was why after Diesel adopted us and made us what we were now, I paid a visit to that group leader. I didn't ask *him* what happened, either. I put two pieces of lead between his eyes and never said a word to a soul about it.

Helped me sleep better knowing that whatever he'd done to my brother, he would never be able to do again.

Rook was at the psych hospital for two months before they cleared him to return, and he was never quite the same after. The brooding, angry Rook I knew came back from that place aloof. Without a care in the world for anyone or anything except me. And that made him more dangerous than he'd ever been prior to that.

He only told me about his time there once, when he was blind drunk and all his words were slurring. For a month straight they injected him with Diazepam to put him down for not following orders like *take your pills,* or *paint a picture of a tree,* or *wait your turn.* They were happy to jab him with that needle at even the smallest infraction.

"Rook," I interrupted, stepping into the garage to a wave of warmth and the heady smell of sweat and aftershave. Heaving, he paused, blinking as his eyes focused on my face. He dropped his fists, shaking them out as he bounced from foot to foot.

He was getting super wound up. We were going to need to find the time to peel back his lid and let out some steam soon. Julia still had nothing for us, but I held onto the hope that she would soon.

We could always widen our net like Rook suggested several months back. Post the helpline fliers in the neighboring cities and towns, but then we might wind up with the opposite problem. Too much work to handle instead of not enough. If we left even one kid in a lethal

178

situation…

If even *one* died because we didn't get to them in time after they called the hotline…

It would be one too many.

"Yeah?" Rook asked, swiping the moisture from his upper lip.

"It's almost time to go. You coming?" I asked, but it wasn't really a question. Diesel had sent us all the group message on Monday night after the girls got settled in.

Diesel: Saturday night. Sanctum. Bring the girl.

Well, it was Saturday now and getting dark. Dies hadn't given a specific time, but nine was a safe bet and it was nearing eight thirty now.

Rook shucked off his gloves and methodically peeled some tape from his knuckles and fingers. "We still don't know what this is about?" he asked, his slitted gaze finding my face.

I shook my head. "No. We have to assume it's another trial."

"So soon?"

I shrugged. "It's not that soon if he had nothing to do with the attack last weekend."

Rook's lips pressed into a tight line.

We hadn't found a single thing to indicate the attack was at Diesel's request. None of the Saints were injured or unaccounted for. Diesel hadn't come to ring Rook's neck for interfering or given Ava Jade a fail.

There were no prints on the syringe.

None anywhere in Ava Jade's room.

Rook was still skeptical, but I believe this wasn't Diesel. This was her stalker. It had to be.

"Anything more on her phone, then?" Rook prodded, flexing his fingers before taking a long swallow from the glass of whiskey he had perched on top of a wooden stool by the wall.

"Nothing."

He slammed the glass back down and a muscle in my jaw ticked.

Ava Jade's stalker had been eerily silent since the attack last weekend. She hadn't received a single message. Either we scared him off or he was biding his time. Or, maybe he was just recovering from the two story fall out the window of her room.

There was no way he'd escaped unscathed from that drop. We'd checked the hospitals though. Every one within fifty miles. Of the few patients admitted with injuries that would've been consistent with the fall, none fit his description.

Tall. The same height as Rook—give or take an inch. Strong with a slender frame packed solid with wiry muscle. Neither Rook nor AJ thought he was very old. Maybe older than them, but not by much. Certainly less than thirty-five.

Only one man fit that description. And he'd met the cold barrel of Corvus' gun and wet himself two days ago when he was released from the hospital. It wasn't the guy. He was paid enough for a new pair of designer pants and sent on his way with a warning.

Rook licked his lips, and I could see the spark of madness in his eyes as they flashed in the overhead lights.

"We're going to find this fucker," I assured him. "We're going to find him and then you're going to take him apart piece by piece. I'll help you."

His gaze narrowed on me, a curious furrow in his brow. The unspoken question on his lips. *You will?*

I nodded.

Rook nodded back.

"I'm going up to get the girls. Corv is nearly ready."

As I said it, we both heard the front door close in the house beyond the door to the garage and the engine to the Rover start in the driveway. It was cold as fuck out there tonight, chances are he was just warming it up, but he wouldn't want to be kept waiting long.

Rook finished his drink and went in, headed for the shower.

I took the old entrance up to the loft. The one that required the use of the narrow staircase at the back corner of the garage.

Corvus had one of Diesel's contractors in on Monday while the rest of us were in classes. They finished the small renovation within six hours as requested and by the time we returned after last class, there was a new entrance to the loft, accessible through the other end of the upstairs bathroom.

Corv hadn't liked my loft idea, but instead of arguing about it, for once he just shut his mouth and found a quiet solution. One I was angry I hadn't thought of myself.

If he didn't have the new entrance made, they would've been sealed off from us. It would take too long for us to get to them in case of an emergency, and would leave them with only one route in and out—which was why Ava Jade was keen on the idea, too.

I rapped twice on the door and waited a beat before hearing Becca call for me to come in.

The loft opened up before me as I crested the last few steps past the threshold and into the little studio we never used.

Becca was perched on the edge of an oversized desk chair, pausing in painting her nails to inspect them for imperfections before sliding her hand beneath a UV light dome.

"What? Sometimes they need a fix between

appointments," she explained. "And I haven't been able to get to the salon all week."

I wasn't going to ask, and I wasn't wondering, but I nodded all the same. "Where's AJ?"

She jerked her head toward the other end of the loft. "Shower."

I started into the loft but Becca's next question stopped me. "Got an ETA on those door handles yet? As much as I love showering with an open door in a house full of dudes...oh no, wait...I *don't* actually love that."

Fair enough. "Corv says they'll be here Monday."

"Thank fuck for that."

"Anything new we should be aware of?" I asked Becca, lowering my voice. "Messages, or…"

She looked at me like I'd sprouted another head. "Ask AJ," she said with a heavy sigh. "You really think she's still going to lie to you about it after that shit last weekend?"

The truth? I wasn't sure.

I wandered to the bathroom door, tapping on the wood pane lightly so it wouldn't open under my touch. "AJ? We have to get moving."

"What?"

The shower was off inside, but the exhaust fan likely made it difficult to hear.

"Time to go," I called louder, and she growled inside. The only response I was likely to get.

I sat heavily on the small chest snugged up to the end of the bed Ava Jade and Becca shared. The loft wasn't anything special, but it was enough for the two of them temporarily.

The bed was a queen, the mattress and bedding brand new. It had a small kitchenette in the farthest corner from the door and a sectional facing the wall in the opposite corner with a modest thirty-inch TV mounted on the wall. And the desk, of course, where Becca watched me warily as we waited for AJ.

The space was meant as a gift for Corvus. One Rook and I thought would help him get the peace and sleep he so desperately needed, but he never moved out here. Now that there was easier access to the rest of the Nest, I wondered if he would when the girls were gone.

I felt a pang in my chest, and I cleared my throat as Ava Jade exited the bathroom in ripped jeans and a tight-fitting, cropped tank top with no bra beneath. Her nipples like little Hershey's kisses beneath the dark fabric.

Her makeup was done, but her hair was still damp from the shower, falling down her shoulders and back in soft, wet waves.

"You got a blow dryer?" she asked.

I shook my head. "No. No time, either. I think Corv is already waiting in the car."

Right on cue, a long, blaring horn sounded outside.

"You going to be okay here alone, Becca?" I asked, and she opened her mouth to reply, but it was Ava Jade who spoke instead.

"You said it was safe," she spat back accusingly.

"It is."

"It better be. It's definitely safer than getting her any more involved in my shit than she already is. The last thing I want to do is parade her in front of Diesel."

I tipped my head to one side, pursing my lips. She had a point there.

"Besides she won't be here all alone anyway. You have plans tonight, don't you, Becks?"

Becca smiled at AJ meekly before shaking her head. "No. No, I'm just going to stay here."

AJ crossed the floor to her friend, lowering her voice

as if I couldn't still hear her clear as day. "You haven't been out at all this week. Did something happen between you and your mystery guy?"

Becca shrugged, sighing again. "Fuck if I know. I think he's avoiding me. He does that sometimes," she shrugged. "Gives me time to catch up on some BioChem homework though, so whatever. I don't need him."

AJ squeezed her friend's shoulder. "You sure as shit don't, babe, but nobody ghosts my bestie and gets away with it. Want me to track him down? Drag him over here for a little chat?"

Becca barked a laugh that quickly died in her throat when she saw AJ's expression and realized her friend wasn't joking in the slightest.

"*Uh,*" she said, laughing for a different reason now. "I'll let you know, 'kay?"

AJ nodded. "Hopefully we won't be long," she turned to me. "We won't be long, right?"

"Sorry. We haven't been briefed. No idea what's going on. Could be twenty minutes. Could be all night."

I hated admitting it but there it was, we were carting Ava Jade to Sanctum with absofuckinglutely no idea what was going to be waiting for us when we got there. It wasn't for a lack of trying to find out. We'd been snooping around Sanctum and the warehouse, and I'd even made an excuse to go and *pick something up* from Diesel's house just to have a little snoop there, too. Straight up asking him had gotten us nowhere, either. So, here we were.

"Is it another trial?" Becca asked, and AJ visibly tensed.

She'd had no choice but to come clean to her friend after the shit that went down at Briar Hall. It was about time, really. And as much as we didn't like it, it wouldn't have been fair to leave her in the dark, especially not if she was going to continue to stay here with AJ, which seemed like it might be the case.

AJ lifted her hard gaze to me, and I sighed.

"We don't know," she admitted, echoing my thoughts.

"You'll take care of her, right?" Becca asked me, fixing me with a venom laced stare that made me pause. I understood that she was pissed about what happened at BH, and that AJ was being swept up in all this, being out in danger, but there was more than worry there. There was hate.

And then it was gone, erased with Ava Jade's short laugh at her friend's demand.

"*Them* take care of *me*?" she said, grinning at her friend. "Don't worry, Becks. I don't need anyone to take care of me. I'll be back before you know it."

Becca's expression darkened, but she nodded. She really was in a foul mood. I hoped her boyfriend called her back soon. Otherwise, I was afraid her claws would only get longer. Her bite, harder.

"All right, then," AJ said, snatching a faded jean jacket from the back of the chair Becca was sitting on, sensing the tension in the air and wanting to leave before it got any thicker. "Don't wait up. Keep everything locked. You remember how to use that blade I left you?"

"Stick 'em with the pointy end," Becca replied, miming a stab gesture that needed a *lot* of work. AJ laughed at that.

"And the other part?"

"Stab first, ask questions after."

"You're going to be a pro in no time."

Becca waved us off after Corvus honked for the second time. "Go already before he blows a fucking fuse."

Ava Jade checked the door twice before we left to

make sure it was locked and secure. She checked the garage door and the front door, too, wistfully tilting her head up to the small illuminated window set above the garage doors, worry creasing her forehead.

"She'll be okay. Corv installed all those new cameras. If you want, I'll put the app on your phone on the way there. That way you can check them whenever you want."

She smiled at me with her hand on the door handle to the back seat. The first smile I'd seen from her in a week. "Can you?"

"Yeah," I said and held the door as she slid into the seat next to Rook, who was staring out the window like the trees themselves might grow claws and fangs and come for his girl.

I cleared my throat, nudging the back of the passenger seat. "Corv, can you drive?"

"What the fuck for?" he growled.

"I'm going to put the app for the cameras on AJ's phone."

He grunted. "Give it here," he said, holding out his hand for AJ's phone without turning around. "I'll do it for her."

She hesitated, but reluctantly unlocked her phone and placed it into his hand, sitting up straighter in her seat to watch over his shoulder.

Either she had something to hide or she wanted to see if he would try snooping so that she could give him hell.

My skin bristled at the former option, wondering if there were any new messages between her and *Kit*.

I clenched my jaw as I circled the Rover and hopped into the driver's seat, pulling us out on the road.

"Nothing more from the stalker?" Corvus asked in a tone that I knew was trying hard to sound casual and not demanding but failed on all counts.

186

"Nope," AJ replied, popping the *p*.

Turned out the last message Ava Jade deleted before reading the whole thing was just that first line. Recovering it and decrypting it was a total waste of time.

But seeing the three words for myself was enough to make my blood boil anew.

I warned you…

He warned *her*? Ha! Motherfucker was a dead man walking.

We'd considered the option that he could have crawled off somewhere and died of his injuries, but somehow I doubted that. It would be a waste. There was a deep, dark part of me that wanted him to still be alive so I could have a hand in killing him myself.

"Grey," Corvus said, edging my name in a question, and I realized how tightly I was holding the steering wheel and forced my stiff fingers to relax. Made myself slow the speed of the Rover as we pulled into the back lot at Sanctum and Corvus handed AJ back her phone.

She was the first to hop out, appearing to not be at all worried about what might await her inside.

I sighed after her door closed and flinched when Corvus gripped my upper arm in an uncommonly gentle gesture. "You good, man?"

I swallowed and gave him a quick nod. "Yeah. I'm good, just…"

"I know," he replied before I could properly articulate what I wanted to say. "We got this. She's going to be fine."

The Rover rumbled to a standstill as I twisted back the key and stepped out into the crisp night air, inhaling deeply through my nostrils.

Food.

I needed something to eat. The banana I ate at breakfast and the pizza pocket I warmed up at lunch

187

weren't even a fraction of my normal intake. No wonder I was so fucking irritable. No wonder my hands felt like they were trembling.

AJ flipped through the newly installed camera feeds through the app on her phone as we made our way inside, seemingly satisfied to find nothing but the shuddering shadows of trees moving in the wind and the quiet house on the screens.

"All clear?" I asked her with my best encouraging smile.

"Yep. Looks fine. She knows to call if she hears or sees anything. She'll be fine."

I wasn't sure if she was telling me that or herself, but either way, I agreed as we entered the main floor of Sanctum and the music from inside washed over us along with the smell of beer and whiskey.

I gave Sasha a nod as we entered and upon seeing us, she drew out Rook's favorite bourbon and poured him a glass without asking.

"Hey, sweets," she called, drawing the attention of the others. Sasha set the bourbon down on the bar for Rook and grimaced before taking it with a grateful nod. "Anybody else want anything?"

"No," Corv growled, his gaze tracking across the pub in search of Diesel.

"I'll take a water," AJ asked, and I caught her gaze dipping to Sasha's chest. It was hard not to, the way she wore her tits almost hanging out of her shirts. They were some nice tits, too. Fake, but sometimes those were even nicer than the real kind.

"Sure thing, hon," Sasha replied and filled a glass with ice and water, plunking in a slim black straw before handing it to AJ.

"You, Grey?"

"Nah, I'm good," I replied as I began looking for Diesel, too.

It was busy enough for a Saturday night and Sasha was quickly called away to help the other bartender fix drinks at the other end of the bar. Mostly Saints and their girlfriends or fuckbuddies graced the bar and tables. Pool balls knocked noisily into one another from the area at the back. A few locals drowned their sorrows in cheap beer at the bar and a handful of girls in too-short dresses eyed the leather-clad Saints not already spoken for from a booth near the door. Giggling as they adjusted their cleavage and hair.

I couldn't see Diesel anywhere.

Which meant he either wasn't here yet, or he was in the private room around the other side of the bar out of sight.

"Diesel here yet?" I went to ask one of the servers, a girl called Cat.

She shook her head. "Haven't seen him, but the others got here about an hour ago. Who's your friend?"

I glanced back at AJ. "That's our girl," I said before I could change my mind. "You get her anything she wants and if anyone so much as looks at her funny, I want to know about it."

Her lips twitched into an awkward tight-lipped smile as she replied. "Sure thing. I'll make sure everybody knows."

Rook growled behind me, and I turned to see him staring after a stumbling drunk asshole, leaving me to wonder if the guy'd accidentally bumped into him. He downed his bourbon and took off after the guy.

"Rook!" I called, but he was already gone, lost to the crowd.

"He muttered something about going to the

189

bathroom," Corvus said, giving me a strange look. Obviously he hadn't seen the look on Rook's face. Or maybe I was just overthinking it.

I grunted, giving a nod.

"I'll do a lap," Corvus offered, he and Ava Jade stepping up behind me. "Grab a table and wait."

"No, I'll go," I said, stopping him. "I need to stop by the kitchen and grab something to eat."

He looked like he might argue, but upon studying my face, stepped back to allow me to go. I must've looked as shit as I felt.

They found their way to an empty booth near the pool tables, Corvus slipping into the booth seat opposite Ava Jade.

"Hey, man!" Axel shouted over the music, clapping me on the back as I made my way through the crowd. His blue eyes hooded and glazed with intoxication. "Where's your pops at? I wanted to—"

"Don't know, Ax. He should be here soon," I interrupted, leaving no room for more conversation, but that didn't stop him.

"Hey! Hey, Grey, man I just wanted to let you know it's all set up like he asked. I didn't start drinking until it was done, you know. They're ready for him in the back."

What is? I wanted to ask the question but didn't. Then he'd know I had no fucking idea what he was talking about.

"Where?" I asked instead. "I need to check on them."

His face screwed up in confusion, and I worried I said the wrong thing but I stood my ground, waiting. "Well?" I pushed. "Where are they?"

"Kitchen," he said as another Saint began tugging on his arm for a reply to a question. "Bottom shelf of the cooler. I did it exactly how he asked, man. Just like always."

Like always?

Fuck.

"I'm sure you did, man. Thanks."

I left Axel to his friends and hurried through the back end of the bar, pushing into the kitchen. At this hour, it was closed and every stainless-steel surface gleamed. Satisfied it was empty, I crossed to the walk-in cooler and yanked it open, a blast of chilled air wafting into my face as I stepped inside.

Down low on the shelf to my left were two chalices made of heavy silver, the Saint emblem of a fleur-de-lis with a dagger protruding from the bottom embossed into the sides of each cup. Inside of each, a golden liquid reflected the horror on my face.

I swiped a palm over my face and began to pace the narrow slice of concrete floor, going over the limited options to prevent what was about to happen.

Ava Jade

"I told you," I groaned as Corvus pushed the pool cue into my hand. "I don't know how to play."

"It's easy," he told me, snatching a cue from the rack for himself. "It's all angles and calculating force. Grey tells me you're ahead of him in your math class. You'll pick it up quickly."

I fumed quietly by the edge of the pool table Corvus just cleared of players with a single look. My teeth ground together as he gathered up all the colored balls on the table and put them into a triangular frame, plucking some out to move them around to the right spots.

I hated that I could still barely look at him after the other morning. There were only a handful of people who'd ever seen me like that, well, maybe *handful* wasn't the right word. My dad was the only other person who'd ever seen me cry. And now there was Corvus.

It'd done something between us, and I wasn't sure I

liked it. He was being *nice*. Cautious. Like he was afraid if he said the wrong thing, I'd shatter again. It was driving me fucking mental.

I cried. So fucking what. He needed to get over it. *I* needed to get over it.

If he kept treating me like I was made of porcelain, I would show him just how sharp my broken edges could be.

Grey appeared behind me at the pool table, lightly brushing my elbow with something cold and wet. I whirled on him with a snarl to find him holding out an iced drink with a slim black straw. It smelled like dark soda with a bite of...rum, maybe?

"Here," he said, pushing it toward me. "I got you a drink."

"No thanks, I'm good."

His face fell, lips parting as though I'd just refused a fucking proposal of marriage instead of a damned drink.

"Jesus," I said on a laugh. "It's not like I kicked your dog. I just want to keep a clear head."

He cleared his throat. "Right. No worries. I'll just, *uh,* hold onto it in case you change your mind."

I lifted my brows. *"Okay,* then. You do that, Superman."

Grey's face pinched, his lips quirking up into the tiniest smirk before he stepped past me to go and sit in the booth next to the pool tables. Rook slid in a second after him, appearing out of nowhere. He leaned back in the booth, plucking a napkin from the silver dispenser on the table to wipe something that looked suspiciously like blood from his fingers.

"What?" Corvus asked and followed my line of sight to where Rook was now discarding the napkin atop the table and flagging Sasha for another drink.

194

"For fuck's sake," he cursed, and I followed him back to the booth in time to hear Grey hissing over the table at Rook.

"What the hell did you do?"

Rook gave a one shoulder shrug, his eyes looking lighter than they had in days. "He called her a whore," Rook said offhandedly, his wicked gaze flitting to me and away again.

Was he talking about me?

Corvus leaned over the table, his fingers splaying over the worn wood. "Who?"

"Some idiot."

"Rook?" Grey pushed. "Where is he?"

Rook sighed, graciously accepting a fresh bourbon from Sasha with a wink. "He's alive."

He didn't seem particularly thrilled about that. "He just won't be talking shit about our girl anymore. Or...talking much at all I'd imagine."

Oh my god. "You cut out his tongue."

It wasn't a question. I knew it, and he loved that I knew it, grinning at me wildly.

"Bingo."

That...that was kind of sweet. In a super fucked up, totally psycho kind of way. I bit my lip, hoping the sting of it would quell the rise of heat in my bloodstream.

"Fucking hell, Rook. You know the rules. No bloodshed at Sanctum. Diesel's going to shit," Corvus said, his face reddening.

"Relax, brother." Rook rolled his eyes. "I took him out back. I know the rules."

Grey relaxed some, nodding absently. "Fucker kind of deserved it," he muttered, making something flutter in my belly. Corvus didn't disagree, but he groaned, standing upright as he pinched the bridge of his nose.

"At least he didn't kill him," Grey told Corvus. "Progress."

Corvus shook his head, fixing his stare back on Rook, who was sipping his bourbon like he didn't have a care in all the world. "All right. Just...just fucking clean yourself up. There's blood on your jacket."

Corvus grabbed my elbow and steered me back to the pool table, away from the *situation* that was his brother.

"You want to break?" Corvus asked, indicating the neat triangle of colored balls on the table.

I knew enough about pool to know what he meant, but that was about it. Besides I was still reeling from Rook's blood display of affection. "*Uh,* I don't even know how to shoot."

"Come here," he offered. "I'll show you."

I snorted, imagining it. Imagining Corvus adjusting my hands on the cue. Him telling me to bend over and get a good line of sight down the cue to the ball while he positioned himself behind me. His warm body wrapped around mine. His warm breath on the side of my neck as he guided my cue into position with his hands on top of mine.

It was probably the fantasy of any girl in this room, and I'd have been lying if I said it wasn't tempting. But I didn't want to reenact cliched scenes from romantic comedies. Besides, I could figure it out my damn self. Just as soon as I shook off this feeling still heating my cheeks and making my knees weak.

"Well now," a rough voice called over the raucous laughter and music in the pub. "You boys didn't tell me she could play pool."

"Diesel," Corvus said, his jaw flexing as he stared somewhere over my right shoulder.

I turned, keeping any trace of discomfort from my

expression. I'd show him no fear. Men like him could smell it in the air. They thrived on that smell. Bathed in it. I wouldn't give him the satisfaction.

"I can't," I said for myself. "Your son was just going to teach me."

I couldn't help rubbing it in just a little—that his sons chose *me*. Had chosen to let me live despite what Diesel might've preferred. That they liked me enough to teach me how to shoot pool. To cut out a man's tongue for calling me a whore.

It was stupid and maybe a little childish, but I didn't care. I didn't ask for any of this, and I wouldn't go down easy.

"Is that so?" Diesel's question was meant for Corvus, and I turned back to him expectantly.

"Yeah. Passing the time till you got here. Took you long enough."

"We got held up," Diesel replied, and I watched him shrug off a busted up old leather jacket and pass it to an enormous guy to his left. I recognized him as *Tiny*. The bouncer from the illegal boxing ring downstairs.

Tiny carefully draped his boss' leather jacket on the back of a tall chair, as though he were afraid too much force might tear it in two. He wasn't wrong. The thing looked to be holding on by threads and a prayer. Not the sort of thing I'd have expected the leader of one of the largest gangs in Cali to wear.

"If you don't mind, son. I'd love a go," Diesel said, crossing the floor to hold out a hand for Corvus' cue.

The level of sound in Sanctum had dropped exponentially since Diesel's arrival and as I spun in a slow circle, I noticed how many of the Saints who'd been drinking merrily five minutes ago were now watching. Rapt at the exchange between Diesel and his sons.

Between Diesel and their potential *female* new recruit. *Fuck.*

Corvus reluctantly handed over the cue and Diesel flipped it over, holding it up to his eye to stare down the length of it.

Should I have done that?

"What do you say, princess?" he asked, his voice carrying in the pub as he set the cue down and fixed me with a ready stare. "Humor me with a game?"

"I told you, I don't know how to play. And don't call me princess."

He inclined his head, studying me from head to toe.

I took the opportunity to do the same. This was only the second time I'd seen Diesel St. Crow in the flesh and the first time, I'd been more than a little preoccupied.

The man was taller than I remembered. Handsome, for an older guy, with a trim, but muscled figure and bright eyes that I knew saw more than he let on. I normally didn't like beards, but somehow his suited him, long and tapered, mostly straight and groomed. I couldn't picture him without it. He had a relaxed sort of power. Like a lion at rest. He could spring up and strike whenever he wanted, but why would he when he had a pride at his back ready to do the work for him?

"Very well. Corvus? We're overdue for a game, I think. Why don't you take Ava Jade's cue? Or shall we just get started with the real reason we're all here?"

"Want to tell me what that is?"

Diesel smirked. "Why the rush?"

Corvus hesitated before coming to me. "Unless you'd rather just get this over with?" he muttered, holding a hand out for the cue.

I opened my mouth to reply *yes,* because *fucking duh,* I just wanted to go back to the house, but Corvus grabbed

198

the cue before I could reply, taking my split second of silence as a non-answer. Or maybe he just wasn't ready for whatever *it* was to begin.

Grey beckoned me to the booth, and I went while Corvus bent over the raised edge of the pool table and broke the triangle of balls apart with a loud *clack*.

"How about that drink?" Grey asked, sliding the rum and Pepsi over to me.

Why was he so insistent on me having a drink? I wasn't a joy to be around sober, if I started drinking I was liable to knife someone.

"There's not much rum in it," he said. "It's just a single."

I met his gaze, finding a worried crease between his brows.

"I think you need it more than I do," I joked but took the proffered drink, swirling the straw before I removed it and downed the icy cold drink in two long swallows. The ice made my teeth sting.

Grey visibly relaxed, and I peered into the bottom of the glass. "If this was roofied or some shit, I'll kill you."

Rook smirked at that because *of course* Grey wouldn't roofie me, but with how bad he wanted me to drink the damn thing, it was a valid comment.

I noticed he hadn't bothered to clean the blood splatter from his jacket, wearing it as a badge of honor instead. The color suited him.

Corvus and Diesel's game was over in a matter of minutes, Diesel coming out the victor.

He went to his adopted son and gave his shoulder a squeeze. "You're distracted," I barely heard him tell Corvus. "Let's have another round later, yeah?"

"Yeah," Corvus muttered.

"Good." He clapped Corv on the back. "Let's get this

199

over and done with. Grab the girl and meet us in the back room. Her second trial is tonight."

Corvus stiffened.

Diesel's eyes cut into me like shards of ice before they flicked away and he turned his attention to Tiny and another man behind him. Together, they vanished into the crowd.

"Any idea what it is?" I asked Corvus when he got close enough that I wouldn't have to raise my voice.

He shook his head. "A couple of ideas, but no."

I looked at the others. Rook and Grey sat stone faced and silent in the booth.

Great.

"The trials are always different for each person. There are a few that get repeated, sort of like tradition, but they're almost never given in the exact same way," Corvus explained.

He held out his hand for me and I stood up without his help, the little bit of rum I'd just slammed going to my head. I ignored his hand and he dropped it, seemingly unbothered. "If you need a minute," he offered but I was already shaking my head.

"No. I want to get back. Come on, let's just go do this."

Rook and Grey slid from the booth and fell in behind Corvus and me as we wove through the pub, making for a set of double doors around the quieter side of the bar in the back of the building. We stepped through them into a dark antechamber. Ahead were swinging doors with windows in their tops that showed a gleaming kitchen. To the right was a sign for bathrooms and to the left a long hallway that led to a single black painted door with a polished silver handle.

That was where we headed.

I steeled myself, cooing to my darkness as it began to swell, coming to life in my gut.

Corvus held the door open and Grey stepped ahead of me to go in first. Rook followed right behind me. The lighting inside the large room was dim, casting an eerie glow over the space.

To my left, a bank of expensive looking sectional couches held a few Saints, lounging quietly, drinks perched between their fingers. To my right sat a large rectangular table made of what looked like polished black glass at first. But as we neared, I saw it wasn't glass at all, but some kind of dyed epoxy, a golden fleur-de-lis turned dagger embedded down the middle.

Diesel St. Crow sat at the opposite end closest to the wall, and only one other chair waited at the other end of the table. It wasn't rocket science to figure out who it was meant for.

Without being told, I stalked past Grey and folded myself into the chair, sitting up straight as I pushed myself into the table ledge. With my lower body concealed, it was easy to stealth a blade from my thigh through the wide tear in the denim. Style and accessibility. These were my favorite jeans.

I laid the blade on my thigh and lifted my hands to the top of the table, feeling more confident knowing it was only inches away if I needed it.

Diesel's biting gaze watched me carefully, his line of sight flitting low before rising back to my face. Either he knew what I'd just done or he guessed. I didn't give a fuck either way. He didn't really expect me to go anywhere unarmed, did he?

I knew he was packing a piece. I'd seen it in the pub. And I also knew all of his sons were packing heat, too.

What was a blade compared to guns? In the hands of someone less skilled, nothing. But in my hands…

Maybe one day Diesel would find out.

"Is this a staring contest?" I asked after another minute of terse silence. "Because if it is—"

Just then the door opened again and Tiny stepped through with two silver chalices on a serving tray. He went straight to Diesel and bent, whispering something in his ear before setting the tray down and leaving the room.

Corvus cursed and Rook let out a growl so low I wondered if I imagined it.

This wasn't good.

"May we have the room," Diesel said, his shining eyes flicking over the many faces eager to watch whatever the fuck was about to go down.

The Saints left one by one, and I turned my head to see Grey, Rook, and Corvus still standing just a few feet behind my chair.

"Do I need to repeat myself?"

Diesel's jaw flexed.

"You can wait outside," he offered them. "I'll let you know when you can come back in. I'd like a word with our new initiate in private."

"Is this really necessary?" Corvus asked, and Diesel narrowed his stare on him. "It's an antiquated tradition. We should—"

"This isn't up for discussion."

Slowly, I turned back to face Diesel, saying nothing.

A prickle of unease skated down my spine, making my stomach sour with dread, but I didn't show it. Not even as Diesel's sons dutifully left the room as they were asked.

Something I don't think they would have done if any

of them truly believed he was the one responsible for the man who tried to inject me with fucking Diazepam.

That was enough to quell the rising dark within at least a little bit. Though we all knew Diesel wasn't interested in making me a Saint. That he didn't trust me and would do anything in his power to see to it that I failed. So, maybe the darkness could hang around just a little longer, in case I should need it.

"Ava Jade Mason," Diesel intoned, leaning back in his leather high back chair like a king on his throne. "Eighteen years old. Deceased father. Addict mother. Lived in Lennox your entire life until recently coming into the care of your aunt and moving here to Thorn Valley. Right so far?"

I didn't answer, but my fingers itched to reach for the blade in my lap.

"It was difficult to find very much information aside from that, however, given your street smarts and skill with a blade, I'd wager you had a *difficult* childhood. Is that right?"

"What does this have to do with anything?"

He shrugged. "I like to know what sort of snakes I'm inviting into my house."

"And?"

He tapped his fingers absently on the table. "And I like to know who my sons have invited into theirs."

"Well, now you know."

He pursed his lips. "Not nearly enough."

"If there's something you want to ask, just ask."

He cocked his head to one side, considering me in a new light. "I don't trust you, Ava Jade. I think you're a viper. All shining scales and alluring eyes. Lulling my boys into a sense of false security while you await your perfect moment to strike."

203

Officer Vick crossed my thoughts, but I pushed him away, afraid Diesel would be able to see the truth hiding just below flesh and bone.

"Then why agree to let me take the trials at all?" I asked instead.

He didn't like that question. It was clear in the way his expression soured. "My son asked me for this favor," he told me, surprising me with the truth. "Greyson has never asked me for anything. Not since the day I took him in. *Not a single thing.*"

His eyes found mine, holding me there with a warm intensity. "He asked me for *you*."

"And you think he made a mistake?"

"I know he did. I just hope they all see that before it's too late. There are some lessons I can't teach them. Ones they'll have to learn themselves."

Something in my chest cracked at his admission and in the haunted look darkening his eyes.

He snapped out of it after a second, sitting up straighter in his chair to fold his hands atop the table.

"I want you to know, Ava Jade, if you betray my boys—if you harm them—I will hunt you to the ends of the earth. You may think you know the meaning of pain, but you're wrong. You will hurt and you will bleed. And when I'm finished with you...you will die."

I let that sink in, his promise etching into my bones.

It was violent and a clear threat and yet…

I respected him for it.

An ache formed behind my breastbone, and I swallowed back a burning in my throat. The memory of my own father dredged back up from the depths where I'd banished it. I had to admire Diesel for his willingness to do whatever it took to protect his sons.

I loved my Dad, but if I'd had a parent as viciously

protective as Diesel, I might not have turned out the way I did.

"I understand," I replied with a nod.

"Good."

He rose from the table and lifted the two chalices from the tray at his side, carrying them both over to me.

He set them down in front of me on the table, one next to the other.

"Both have two ounces of good whiskey," he paused. "In one of them is a fast-acting poison."

My pulse quickened.

"You decide which one you want to drink. I will drink the other."

"You would poison yourself?" I asked dubiously, my mind racing.

He regarded me with cat-like eyes. "Yes. If you choose correctly. The poison is strong. The side-effects...unpleasant. But the likelihood of it being lethal is low."

Low, but not zero. Fucking awesome.

"What the fuck is this supposed to prove?" I asked, unable to help myself. "Blind obedience?"

"Sometimes obedience is necessary, even if it poses great risk to yourself. *If* you pass these trials, I need to know you'll do what is asked of you no matter if you don't agree. Even knowing it could cause you bodily harm. For the good of the many."

"And how is *this* for the good of the many? It's *poison*. This is some idiotic Princess Bride shit."

He smirked at that, but I wasn't joking.

"It's tradition," he added before indicating the chalices again. "Choose."

I narrowed my gaze on the chalices, grinding my teeth.

205

This is fucking stupid.

But...I realized a little belatedly, he'd just told me what this trial was meant to prove. If I didn't drink, I failed the trial. My refusal would prove my inability to follow an order.

If I didn't drink, *Diesel would win.*

Couldn't fucking have that now, could we?

I settled myself knowing that if Diesel killed me his sons would never forgive him. At least, Grey wouldn't. I didn't think Rook would be too happy, either. Corvus would probably get over it.

I could handle a little stomach cramping, right?

"Can I check them?" I asked and Diesel nodded.

I lifted each to my nose, smelling the bite of strong whiskey in each, but nothing else. I swirled them, angling the chalices to the light to check for swirls of a liquid that might have a different viscosity, or powder residue on the bottom. Both seemed clean.

Maybe there was no poison at all.

Maybe it was just a test of obedience and all I needed to do was drink to pass.

Too many maybes. Too little time.

I sighed, deciding on the chalice to my left, the one furthest from Diesel. I held it up, the cold silver damp with condensation. "To your health," I said with a wry smile, and he smiled back, all teeth as he lifted the other chalice and knocked it against mine.

I swallowed down the drink in two burning gulps and swiped the back of my hand over my lips, knocking the heavy metal chalice back onto the table.

"Boys," Diesel called loudly, giving me a knowing grin as he made his way back down the length of the table to his seat at the opposite end. With him gone from my side, I tucked my blade back into its sheath.

The guys came back in a second later, their faces shadowed as they took in the empty chalices in front of me.

A sharp pain lanced through my stomach, and I fought the urge to double over, clutching the underside of the table. *Fuck.*

"Go on, boys. Get her out of here. I don't want her making a mess on my floor."

Rook

EIGHTEEN

Ava Jade didn't make a mess anywhere as Diesel suggested she might. We brought her straight home, all of us tense with nerves as we waited for the inevitable pain.

But it never came. Nothing more than the knot between her brows to prove she was in any discomfort at all. I didn't know what the fuck to make of it.

I remembered the night after my poison trial and I wouldn't have wished it on anyone. Except maybe the motherfucker stalking her. The cramping had been bad, but it was nothing compared to the pounding headache that lasted days, or my stomach expelling every ounce of its contents and then some. And don't get me started on how badly I destroyed the bathroom.

I shuddered, hefting the massive water bottle onto my shoulder to trudge it up the stairs to the loft to replace the one Ava Jade and Becca had emptied.

I rapped twice on the door and Becca answered,

stepping aside for me to enter. She'd hardly left the loft at all since they moved in, and I was curious if she was too afraid to. I wouldn't blame her. Fear was a powerful form of natural self-preservation, that's what Diesel was always trying to remind me, anyway.

"Ghost?" I asked as I placed the jug onto the cooler, popping the seal so the water could flow down into the chamber.

"Bathroom," she replied with a sigh, and my stomach tightened. Had it finally started? Ava Jade went straight up to the loft when we got back last night, and we hadn't heard from or seen her since. We all agreed to stay clear of the upstairs bathroom to give her some privacy while she was sick, but I never heard a peep.

Even with my bedroom the closest. There were no vomiting sounds. No pained cries. I would have brought her water. A cold towel.

"How long has she been in there?" I asked, staring at the closed door across the room.

Becca lifted one of her dark brows at my question, hesitating before her reply. "Um, why?" she asked, like it was the most ridiculous question and she couldn't for the life of her figure out why I'd want to know.

I considered that. "Is she not sick?"

"Sick?"

The door opened, and Ava Jade stepped back into the loft, fixing her hair with a pin. My cock jumped in my jeans at the sight of her, my mouth going dry.

She definitely wasn't sick.

Looking more like a wraith than a ghost in all black with a leather skirt and a tight black shirt with little cutouts running up both sides from her waist to her underarms, exposing more than a little side boob. Dark makeup on her eyelids with wicked slashes of black liner making them look winged.

"Rook?" she asked, and I realized I was still staring.

I gave her all black outfit one last go over before reining in my expression. "Whose funeral is it?" I asked, my lips pulling upward on one side.

"I haven't decided yet," she quipped, smiling back with a wink.

She really wasn't sick. Had Diesel not poisoned her? That didn't seem fucking likely. He always poisoned both chalices. He'd done that trial in some capacity or other on every member of the Saints. He was used to the poison, had built up a tolerance to it over the years that allowed him to get by without too much discomfort. Plus, there was the antidote always at the ready just in case he should need it.

The antidote...

My brain worked to solve the equation, trying to figure out how she got away unscathed.

Grey. That sneaky son of a bitch.

I should have seen it before. He went off to do a loop of the bar, said himself he was headed for the kitchens. The poison needed to be kept chilled. He'd have found it in the cooler. But how had he gotten his hands on the antidote so fast? It was a ballsy move, but I couldn't say I wouldn't have done it myself given the opportunity.

We'd have to tell Ava Jade eventually. Diesel would want to know she suffered. The only way that was going to work was if she were in on the lie. A problem for another time.

"Are you almost ready, Aves?" Becca asked, leaning over the desk to look into a small circular mirror as she applied dark cherry lipstick. "We should get going."

"Going?"

"We have a concert to go to tonight," she said

211

offhandedly. "Thought I already told you guys'"

"You didn't."

"Oh. Too bad. If you're all busy tonight then it's no problem, Becca and I will be just fine without you."

Devious little fucker.

Why did her defiance just make me even harder?

I licked my lips, sucking in a breath as I bit my lip ring. Until I realized what today was and my amusement waned.

"I think not, Ghost," I replied without room for argument, not bothering to explain. She knew why we couldn't let her go anywhere alone. It was more than Diesel's orders now. There was someone out there who'd tried to put her down with a sedative. I could vividly imagine a thousand reasons why and none of them would *ever* happen if I had any say in it.

"Always such a buzzkill," Ava Jade muttered and I lifted my brows.

"No. That's Corvus. Not me."

She tipped her head this way and that, pursing her lips to show she agreed.

"What show are you going to?" I asked in an uninterested tone, leaning against the support beam at the center of the floor. "Anyone I'd know?"

"Doubt it," she replied with a haughty sort of disdain.

"Humor me."

She looked me up and down as she sat on the edge of the bed to tug on a pair of calf height boots, zipping them up tight. "Primal Ethos," she said finally, watching me for any trace of recognition.

"He's good," I said, eager to drag more detail from her lips. "Not amazing, but good."

An inside joke she wouldn't get, but inside, I was laughing.

WICKED TRIALS   ELENA LAWSON

Of course she would be a fan of Primal Ethos. I should've guessed it, but this? Her actually *going* to one of his shows? A bolt of wild anticipation tore up my spine.

"Ha!" she barked. "He's a fucking god and nothing less."

"*Amen*," Becca added, making a wicked sign of the cross as she shimmied her shoulders.

I couldn't keep the amusement from creeping onto my face this time, and my Ghost looked at me like I might have lost my final screw.

"What's so funny?" she demanded, and I cleared my throat, swallowing back my smile.

"Nothing at all."

She rolled her eyes, snatching up some cash and what looked like a fake ID from her nightstand. "Ready, Becks?"

"Yeah, just let me use the ladies room, first."

The door shut behind Becca, and Ava Jade adjusted her tits as she strode toward me. I let out a growl, loud enough for her to hear. She grinned at my reaction, leaning in close to my side to whisper in my ear. "So, will you be joining us?"

Her scent filled my nose, and I twisted a fist into her hair, knotting it in my fingers at the back of her skull to hold her there, inches from me.

Truth be told, I wanted to be there to see her face...but I had plans tonight. A little recon of my own. Off the books. All of us were carving out time to try to find the bastard who attacked Ava Jade, but so far we'd turned up nothing. I couldn't accept that. I needed his blood coating my hands. Splattering my face. I needed to hear his screams and watch the light leave his eyes so that I could sleep at night.

Tonight, I had one job. Find him. Or at the very least, find a fucking lead.

213

"Can't, I'm afraid," I murmured a breath away from her lips. "But I'm sure Grey would be happy to accompany you."

"Too busy for me?" she asked, her steely grey-blue eyes flitting to my lips and back up again.

I tipped my chin down, desire aching through me like a searing blade as I replied. "Never."

Her breath tripped from her lips in a quiet gasp as I tightened my fist in her hair, making her eyes squint with the bite of pain. She closed her eyes and moaned, but as the bathroom door opened, I released her, stepping away as though the moment between us never happened. She tripped forward a step, flushed and breathless, blinking at me standing three feet away like she couldn't fathom how I'd moved so fast.

"Aves?" Becca asked, staring at her friend's back. "You okay?"

She shook her head at me, the threat of returning my teasing ten-fold clear in her eyes.

"Fucking fabulous," she replied. "Let's go find Grey."

She sauntered past me behind Becca on their way out, and I smiled in her wake. I snatched her hand before she could vanish down the stairs into the garage, pulling her up short.

She glared at my hand holding her tight and lifted her chin with a question in her hard stare. But I didn't mean to stop her from going. "You're armed?"

She visibly relaxed and lifted the hem of her leather skirt, flashing me the twin blades strapped to either side of her thighs and a damn good view of her black panties. I clenched my jaw, nodding.

"Good."

I released her.

"Be careful."

"Ghosts can't die, Rook," she told me in a light tone. "We're already dead."

Grey

NINETEEN

Grey: Pick up your fucking phone, asshole.

I fired the message off to Corvus. The seventh message I'd sent him in as many minutes.

"Could you move your seat up?" I snapped, shouting over Primal Ethos' Gravedigger and Becca singing along to it.

AJ whirled around in her seat, her eyes gleaming in the neon dashboard lights. "Nobody asked you to come," she reminded me. "And I'm not scrunching up my legs so you can stretch out back there. Turn sideways or something. And stop being so grouchy. You're killing my vibe."

"Awe come on, Grey," Becca added once Ava Jade was finished, turning down the music a few notches. "Are you worried we won't be able to scalp you a ticket? I'm sure we'll—"

"No," I interrupted her. "I'm not worried."

Becca recoiled as though slapped and turned the music back up, leaning over to whisper to AJ. "What crawled up his ass?"

"Not a clue."

"Oh, I love this one!" Becca shouted excitedly, turning the volume up to ear ringing levels now as we took the Lodi exit. "Come on, Aves. Sing with me!"

AJ smirked, dropping her head as Becca began to sing, but she didn't join in.

"Come on, babe," Becca continued to prod. "This is my favorite part!"

I went back to my phone, flicking through unsaved numbers until I found the one I hoped was Maxine's. Hers was a number I had yet to memorize.

Grey: Max. We have a problem. Have Corvus call me as soon as you get this.

Fuck. This was going to be nuclear if AJ recognized him. Or worse, if he saw AJ in the crowd and knew I'd done nothing to stop her from coming. If he thought rationally, which I doubted he would, he'd realize that nothing I could've said or done would've prevented her from going.

If I'd said no, she would have found another way. If I'd taken the fuse for the fuel pump out of the car, they'd have just hired a cab, or fucking fixed it for all I knew. If I tried to lock them in, AJ was liable to break down a wall to get free, and kill me on her way out.

Apparently, Becca and Ava Jade had been waiting and planning for this concert for weeks. Over a month. There was nothing that was going to stop them short of fatal injury, and I wasn't going to go that far. I *couldn't* go that far.

If we were lucky, the tactics we used to conceal his identity from the masses would also work on Ava Jade.

218

But when had we ever been lucky? And when had AJ ever been fooled by anything we'd done or said?

It wasn't lost on me that if I hadn't slipped her the antidote to the poison that she would have been too ill to have gone. I guess this was karma coming back to bite me in the fucking ass.

Fuck. Fuck. Fuck.

On a last-ditch effort, I tried texting Rook.

Grey: Any brilliant ideas? I could use a hand.

The bastard had just walked right past me grinning when AJ announced where they were headed and said I had five minutes to get in the car or they'd leave without me.

His reply came a second later.

Rook: Enjoy the show.

Fucker.

He was enjoying this.

Becca elbowed AJ in the front, and she began to sing the chorus of the next song with her friend, her voice rising in Becca's Audi like a rogue wave. It took me a minute to process it, how incredible she sounded. Her voice weaving almost expertly with his voice as it poured through the speakers. I wanted to tell Becca to stop singing, just so I could hear her better.

She must've sensed me watching her because after the chorus, she stopped singing abruptly and sank back into her seat while Becca squealed excitedly.

"Shit, girl!" Becca said, shoving AJ lightly. "You didn't tell me you could sing."

AJ shrugged it off, staring ahead into the dark, but the tiniest smile teased at the edge of her mouth. At odds with the sadness in her eyes that I could see through the side view mirror.

The concert venue came into view up ahead and

219

swarms of concert-goers crowded in on both sides of the street, making their way to the main entrance from the parking lot we were turning into.

Grey: AJ is here. I'm sorry man, I couldn't stop her.

Concert nights were the *one time* Corvus set his phone aside to get his head in the game for the show. The only time he would ever ignore a call or a text. Max, his manager, usually held onto it for him until afterward, but even that bitch wasn't answering my goddamned messages.

It was just as likely that she'd read them, saw that the content might throw him off his game and decided not to tell him. He'd have her head for it, but at least the show wouldn't be ruined. Maxine was all about the money and when Corvus agreed to do another show, it was a guaranteed packed house. I wouldn't doubt it if the merch we'd ordered last minute was all gone before he even went on stage.

The mysterious Primal Ethos. The bone man, as some had taken to calling him. Everybody liked a good mystery. Maxine had been right about that, at least. Corvus' need for anonymity was part of the reason he'd grown in popularity so quickly. The ominous skull face paint added an edge of horror to the whole charade that matched his branding perfectly.

For a dead woman walking, even I had to admit Maxine was fucking fantastic at her job. It would be a shame to lose her. I might even miss her bossy tone and filterless attitude.

My phone buzzed as we stepped out of the car and I almost dropped it in my haste to tear it from my pocket.

Unknown Number: I don't know what's going on, but save it for post-show, alright? He's already stressed enough about the new song, he doesn't need whatever

shit you're about to bring to the table, 'kay. Thx.

Max.

"Grey, come on! We have to find you a ticket before the show starts!" Becca beckoned, locking her Audi and waving a hand to me.

"Just one sec," I lobbied back, stepping further away from the car as I dialed Maxine.

Come on.

It rang, and rang, and *fucking rang.*

"Hey!"

"Maxine, oh thank fuc—"

"You've reached Max. I hate voicemails so this better be fucking important. If it is, make it quick, otherwise, email me at—"

I ended the call with a deep sigh and nearly cracked my phone from clenching through the frustration.

"Grey!" AJ shouted, and I spun to find them both waiting by the sidewalk expectantly.

You know what...*fuck it.*

I tried.

Corvus said himself that AJ was one of us. If he meant it, then there was no reason for him to want to rip my fucking head off. If he didn't...well, that would be his problem to deal with because I couldn't very well go and hunt him down backstage and leave Ava Jade's side. Not with the possibility of her stalker still being out there.

He could be here right now. From his text messages, it seemed like he was always lurking. *No*, I'd stay with her and deal with the consequences later.

"Coming," I hollered, jogging over to them as I pocketed my phone, reaching for the joint dangling from Becca's fingers at her side. I put it to my lips for a good long drag and exhaled deeply, coughing a bit as the smoke scraped up my lungs. It was good shit.

221

"*Greyson Winters*," Becca trilled, taking her joint back with a look of approval. "Welcome to the party, handsome. Let's go find you a ticket."

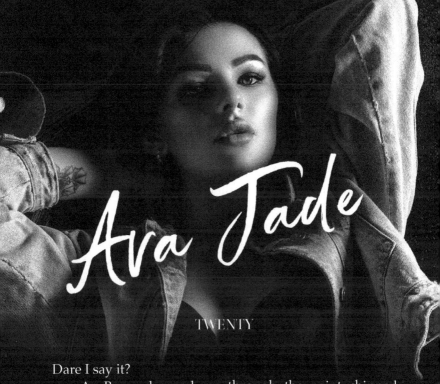

Ava Jade

TWENTY

Dare I say it?

As Becca dragged me through the paint chipped doors of the underground venue, jostled on both sides by other anxious fans, I had to admit it…I was having *fun*.

We weren't even in the main venue yet, and already I could feel it, a bubble of excitement in my chest ready to explode. As we were herded down the narrow corridor and out onto the floor, a smile pulled at my lips and lifted the edges of my eyes. Eyes that must've shone with the glow of the neon lights pulsing above in time to the music.

The band currently on stage was one I wasn't very familiar with but enjoyed listening to nonetheless. I let Becca pull me into the meat of it, brushing shoulders with her and Grey and about six other people as we danced.

Becca laughed as the song came to an end and those around us cheered, I tipped back my head to let loose a wolfish howl, raising my hands to clap with those around me.

I caught Grey staring and whatever bit of ice remained crusted around my heart began to thaw at the look on his face.

It was as though I could read his mind with that single glance. *I'm happy you're happy*, he seemed to say, but more than that. There was relief there, too. So deep that it hurt to look at. Had I been that withdrawn lately?

Thinking back to the night of the attack, I realized I had been. I'd hardly left the loft save for classes and the odd meal with the guys. And they'd left me to process everything on my own, only popping in every now and again to ask questions, showing that they were working to hunt down my stalker just as surely as I was.

They wouldn't like what I had planned to finally catch the motherfucker, but if everything worked out, whoever it was would be dead and then none of us would have to worry anymore.

If he wasn't dead already. My phone had been oddly devoid of threatening messages since last week, and I was starting to think the fall really had been too much for the bastard to recover from after all.

It would make things easier for me, that was for sure, but truth be told, I wanted to be the one to finish him off with my bare hands, and maybe a blade or two. It was a waste for a sadistic fuck like him to die without my being a part of it.

Too easy.

"Hey," Grey shouted as the band on stage announced that they would play one last song before welcoming Primal Ethos on stage. "Where did you go just now?"

"Hmm?"

"Come back," he urged me with an encouraging grin, slipping his hand into mine. But something pained flickered behind his amber eyes and I saw worry there that I hadn't noticed before. Something was going on, but whatever it was Grey seemed resolved not to let me carry any of the burden of it. Preferring to be a grouch the whole way here, at least until now.

"Stay in this moment, AJ. You deserve it."

Something fluttered in my chest, and I gave his hand a squeeze, nodding that I agreed even if a part of me thought I deserved all the misery the world could muster to give me. I'd ask him what was eating at him later. Help him if I could.

"Come on, Aves!" Becca screamed, twirling as the last song from the opening band started to play, holding her hands out to me as she came to a stop. "Dance with me, babe!"

How the hell could I say no to that face?

Grey stuck close by us as Becca and I danced and my eyes popped open when she stealthily drew a tiny bottle of Jack from between her breasts. I snatched it from her and looked around, making sure no one saw. "Are you trying to get us kicked out?"

She laughed. "Look around, babe! You see any security?"

I did as she asked and this deep into the heart of the floor, there was no security at all and in fact, I noticed several others drinking their contraband booze, and laughed.

"It's for you," she shouted, still swaying to the beat as the song began to slow to its end. "I have to drive."

I didn't comment on the fact that she seemed totally at peace with driving high, shaking my head at her instead as I held up the tiny bottle to Grey. "Want some?" I offered.

He gestured to me in reply. "All yours."

225

All righty then…why not?

I'd been handling my liquor pretty damn well these past few weeks and that was saying something since my life had been reduced to a pile of smoking ash.

"Bottoms up," Becca cheered as I downed the small bottle in one go and passed the empty to Grey when he reached for it. It seared a path all the way down to my belly, and a prickling warmth bloomed through the rest of my body, making me shiver.

But…

"Nasty," I said, shaking my head as my tongue recoiled from the flavor.

Becca laughed. "We'll try Crown next time. That's my favorite."

I had no idea what she was talking about, but I nodded, a heightened sense of ease taking root. "Whatever you say, boss."

The crowd broke into cheers, and we turned to give our attention back to the opening band, screaming and clapping with the others.

"That's it for us, Lodi!" the main singer called. "We had a blast tonight and we're fucking gutted to have to leave y'all, but it's time for the next act."

The decibel level as the crowd went wild reached an all-time high in anticipation of Primal Ethos.

I noticed how Grey had positioned himself behind Becca and me and was blocking several overly rowdy concert-goers from knocking into or jostling us. I smiled at him gratefully. Not that I couldn't have handled it, but it was nice to have him watching out for Becca, too.

"Let's welcome him back to the stage for the first time in over a year! Who are you here for, Lodi?"

"Primal Ethos!" the crowd responded, and slowly, a chant began to grow, echoing all over the tightly clustered space.

"Bone Man, Bone Man, Bone Man!"

Becca and I joined in while Grey remained silent at our backs, tense and so pensive I almost asked him what was wrong, but then the lights all went out, plunging the room into a darkness so deep that I couldn't even see Becca beside me more than her faint outline. I clutched her arm, reaching back to tangle my fingers with Grey's on instinct as the crowd hushed.

A black light flickered on the stage only a moment later, giving us a stilted, shuttering view of a bone-white skeleton face staring coolly out at nothing.

Becca squealed, her voice rising with the others as the black light flickered for the last time, now blooming to cast its eerie glow on the man standing center stage.

As the others around me screamed and shouted, welcoming Primal Ethos on stage, I could only stare, a deeply rooted emotion growing from deep within to claw up my throat, silencing me.

He truly was a real person. This man who sang of things few could ever really understand. Not in the way he did. Not in the way *I* did.

A beat started and the crowd began a new wave of cheers as the man with the skeleton face on stage lifted a microphone to his lips. He hummed the first notes with the beats, his smoke and honey voice reverberating in my chest just as surely as it was in his as he felt out the music, letting his body flow with it, too.

He looked like the devil incarnate. *The Bone Man,* they called him, and I could see how it fit. Dressed all in black with dark hair slicked back and white contacts covering his eyes, all that was clearly visible of him was his size, tall and muscled, but lithe. And his made-up face, done in a stark contrast of black and white that managed to look so

227

real you almost had to wonder if it was.

The Bone Man's voice rose with the first lyrics of Anthem of the Broken and my breath caught in my throat, stuck there, held back by a burning dam.

"We march up this mountainside alone.
Tired and broken, we push on.
One foot. Another. Do it all once more.
We crack and shatter while they rush past,
over jagged peaks with wings of steel…
…while ours are porcelain."

Becca's voice rose to meet The Bone Man's, lifting up and filling the space with hundreds of others all singing his anthem. But how many of them really understood his words? How many were crushed under the boots of the mighty? Forced into silence? How many could relate as he sang the verse about finding your hands red with blood and wondering what you'd done?

About not being sorry, but being afraid of finding yourself immobile, shut up behind bars, locked away with only the voice in your own head for company. About how insane that would make you. About how that purposeless life wouldn't just break your already crumbling wings, but shatter your soul, too.

As the song grew in strength building up to the chorus, I felt something in my soul lift.

"Find your broken crew,
'Cause they're the only ones who can save you."

My skin prickled as a new voice rose to join The Bone Man's on stage and the crowd absolutely rioted at the new addition. The female voice weaving with The Bone Man's on stage, mingling with his in a way that couldn't be described in mere words. I searched for the other singer, expecting a guest act to have joined him, but he sang alone, like he always did.

It shouldn't have taken me so long to realize why the voice woke something inside of me, but when I did, I almost hit the fucking floor.

How?

How had...

Tremors of fear and unease raced up and down my spine and a cold dread filled me all the way down to my toes.

"Oh my god, she's amazing!" Becca shouted, teary eyed and screaming as she swayed to the chorus. She hadn't noticed.

I turned to find Grey staring past me toward the stage, his lips parted and brows drawn.

Oh god.

I turned back and followed his gaze, pushing up on my toes to see.

Tall and lean, broad through the shoulders. You'd never know it if you hadn't spent weeks imagining what it might feel like to feel the crunch of his nasal bones under your fist.

No.

The chorus ended, segueing into the end of the song and the crowd roared. Not just for *him*, but for *her*.

For the new voice.

For *my fucking voice*.

My voice that Corvus not only heard in his little makeshift studio but *recorded*. That he'd edited and added to his song like it was his right to use whatever he fucking pleased. Because he *was* The Bone Man.

Primal Ethos.

That was Corvus *motherfucking* James on stage.

My stomach heaved, and I pushed free of the crowd, shouldering past Grey, tearing away from his reaching hands as I shoved through people all around me, itching

229

to use my blade when a few resisted.

Finally, I found cleaner air and fell forward, catching myself on my knees to try to breathe as my head spun.

"AJ!" Grey shouted, and a second later I felt his hands on me, curling around my shoulders, helping me up. "AJ, what's wrong?"

I tugged away and whirled on him, a little off balance, my stomach still in knots, the threat of vomiting a real and present danger.

"What's wrong?" I echoed, glaring at him.

His expression darkened, confirming my worst nightmare.

"Jesus fucking Christ," I spat, lifting myself back to my full height to push my hair away from my face and find somewhere to sit down, not bothering to check if Grey was following me.

Corvus...fucking *Corvus* began another song. Another one of my favorites and my skin bristled, every tiny hair standing on end.

I fell into a seat in a vacant row at the far right of the floor, up one level.

"AJ, listen—"

"Nope."

"Just hear me out—"

"If you say another fucking word, I will cut you."

Mercifully, Grey fell silent, and I leaned over my knees, head clutched between sweaty palms.

My mind raced in a million different directions, trying to come to terms with this new information. It was clear that no one else knew. I doubted even their dear ol' dad did. I doubted he'd approve of the spotlight, or of his precious second in command doing anything that might take away from gang business.

Those weren't the important questions, though. The

ones I really wondered about, I fought the hardest.

What did this mean?

I'd followed Primal Ethos for years. I'd loved his music for years.

Knowing that there was even a single other soul out there who understood me had gotten me through so much. His music had gotten me through so much.

Corvus' music.

Fuck.

I wanted to hate him, it was easier to hate him, but…

How could I when…

"I'm going to be sick."

Grey set a palm on my back, and I flinched, making him remove it immediately. "I'll go get you some water, okay, just…just don't move."

As if I even could right now.

"Becca, there you are. Can you sit with her for a sec," Grey said, and I wished I could disappear into myself as Becca rushed me, kneeling in front of me, right in the firing line if my stomach won the battle with my mind.

I swallowed my bile back as she set her hands on my knees. "Shit girl, you look like a ghost."

I almost laughed.

"Was it the Jack? We didn't really eat anything, maybe that was it. Do you feel sick?"

I shook my head and did my best to sit up, letting the chair back hold me up, but then he was in full view again. Up one level, I could see him clear across the concert venue, above the heads bobbing and swaying in an ocean of bodies on the floor.

I'd wondered before if The Bone Man had ever really experienced the things he sang about, but I didn't have to wonder anymore. Not while he sang about digging shallow graves. About the sound a bullet makes as it left the chamber of a gun. About how blood goes cold after a while, but still stains you forever, and no matter how many times you try to wash it off, it will linger, like an invisible tattoo only you can see.

Until you're just red. Nothing but red painted over shades of gray as you dig your graves.

"Incredible, right?" Becca shouted, and my heart squeezed painfully in my chest.

I couldn't reconcile them together. Corvus and The Bone Man.

I hated him for not telling me. For using my voice. For all the awful things he'd done and said. For every time he'd tried to control me.

But how could I hate him completely when now, through his music, I understood him?

His song, Protector, showed me why he had his need for control. How he couldn't survive without it.

And the others showed me...more than I wanted to know about him.

I sat there for so long, contemplative and numb that I didn't notice when Becca waded back into the crowd, leaving me alone, sitting there with Grey at his request so that at least she could enjoy the rest of the show.

I'd told her to go, or at least, I thought I did.

Somehow we'd been there for an hour or more because suddenly The Bone Man was announcing his final song of the night.

His voice, his non-singing voice, expanded into the cavernous underground space, and I'd have known it anywhere, even if he was adding an extra level of gruffness to it to try to mask it.

"I have one last song for you," he said and accepted a mic stand from a woman in black leather leggings when she walked it onto the stage and retreated with a quick red-lipped kiss blown into the crowd.

Corvus set his mic onto the stand and looked up into the black light. Something in his sharply defined skeleton face softening.

"You won't know it. It's something new I've been working on. It's…it's a little different from my usual, but I think you'll like it."

A few rogue shouts of *fuck yeah* and *whoop!* Went up.

He exhaled, the sound of it like a whispered prayer electrifying the air. He settled in as a beat a bit slower than his usual tempo began to filter through the speakers. All haunting piano keys stuck intermittently with the ominous sounds of breathing and an echoed beat. It made my skin bristle anew.

"This one's called *Sparrow*."

I snapped my attention to Grey, spine going rigid.

He offered me a small impish grin, nodding slightly. *Just listen,* he mouthed, as if I could do anything else.

"She makes me mad
She makes me mean
She haunts my dreams
I call her Sparrow."

Something cracked in my chest, and I got up abruptly, letting my feet drag me forward.

"AJ!" Grey called, but I was already gone, vaulting over the railing and into the crowd, dipping and weaving and pushing toward the front.

That motherfucker.

How dare he.

After everything…

The crowd pushed back, not allowing me past as I continued to find a way forward, realizing belatedly that I should have just gone around. There would have only been a couple of security guards to deal with if I had, it would've been easier than slogging through this.

"Wicked as they come,
I'm coming undone.
Hate, fear, pain, love
Don't you know what you've done?
Sparrow."

A guy attempted to grab me when I carved a space out for myself against the front rail in front of the stage, but a single look from me had him moving *far* away.

What now? An angry voice asked in my head, and the whisper of my darkness coming alive in the pit of my stomach warmed the chilled blood in my veins. I wanted to jump this fucking railing, climb up on stage and get my fist super acquainted with his jaw, but, I also didn't want him to stop singing.

Caught between warring desires, I stood there, smushed against the rail, sandwiched on both sides by screaming girls whose worst day probably looked something like a busted heel and a declined credit card, unable to do a damn thing as he sang of his Sparrow.

Me.

In that voice.

The one I should have recognized the very first moment he spoke. And maybe I had, but I'd denied just like I was trying to convince myself still that it wasn't true. Except, there was a part of me, however small, that wanted it to be true now, too.

However impossible it seemed.

It also felt right, in a way that was so so fucking wrong.

Confusing didn't even begin to cover this.

Maybe it was my lack of enthusiasm. Or my lack of movement that set me apart from the others, but something drew his eye to mine, and I saw the moment he

234

recognized me.

A muscle in my jaw ticked at the shock on his face, and my anger fizzled out when some emotion much stronger flashed in his white eyes.

He sang the last line, his eyes never leaving mine.

"She's the spark,

I'm drenched in gasoline

…I can't wait…

….I can't fucking wait to burn."

He stepped back from the mic, back from the black light to a raucous jeering of applause, until he vanished into the darkness backstage.

He wouldn't get away that easily.

Not a fucking chance.

I hopped the rail and kept low, racing across the base of the stage to the narrow corridor leading around to where I assumed the dressing rooms were.

"Hey!" A security guard bellowed somewhere behind me but I didn't stop, ducking below a velvet rope barrier.

Another guard ahead moved to mid-hallway, blocking my path.

"Now turn around, you don't want to get yourself arrest—"

I ran the last three steps, faking to the right so that I could clock him on his left temple, sending him down in a useless heap of overpaid muscle.

Nothing was going to stop me.

Corvus *motherfucking* James had some explaining to do.

Corvus

TWENTY-ONE

My phone screen blared with missed texts and calls, dropped off in the private dressing room by Maxine sometime during the show. She was fucking lucky she wasn't here or I might have had to murder someone tonight.

I slammed the phone down, wincing when I heard the distinct sound of the screen cracking.

Wasn't this what I wanted?

I knew writing that song with the help of the guys and deciding to perform it would mean having to tell her the truth eventually. *Eventually* being the key fucking word. Not yet. Not right now.

I thought I had at least until it was recorded and released to make sure this was the right call. I had to know I could trust her first. This wasn't gang secrets. This was *my* secret. One my brothers helped me keep.

Would she help me keep it, or would she use it

against me? I hated not knowing the answer.

A door down the hall outside opened, slamming into a wall.

"Corvus!" Ava Jade roared, her voice muffled through the heavy steel door of the room, almost drowned out by the still screaming fans out on the concert venue floor.

Another door opened. Another roar. *"Corvus!"*

Fuck.

I went to the door, with no other choice. If she kept calling my name, my very fucking *distinct* name, she was going to blow my damned cover. But when I got to my door, the handle was ripped from my fingers and the panel of steel flew open.

"You!" She seethed, breathing heavily. Her mascara smudged around her eyes. Her teeth bared.

So many roiling emotions in her eyes I couldn't peg down any particular one. It was like she was forcing herself to look at me against her own will. Making herself see me through the skeleton makeup still mostly intact on my face. Through the white contacts covering my ice blue eyes and the dark hair paint making my hair appear black.

My stomach clenched, fists balling as we stared at one another in a silent standoff for what could've only been a few seconds but felt like minutes. Or even hours.

I waited for the attack I knew was coming, resigning myself to stand there and take it, confident she wouldn't kill me. Maybe that confidence was misplaced, but the lyric rang true. If I would burn for anyone, it would be for her. I'd burn away just for her to be reborn from my ashes.

When she came for me, I stiffened, closing my eyes to accept my punishment for stealing her voice. For lying and hiding this part of myself from her. For everything.

But, when her claws dug into the skin at the nape of

my neck, yanking me down to her, there was no killing blow. She crushed her mouth to mine in a feral kiss, sharp nails biting down into soft flesh so deeply that I felt blood welling from the half moon cuts she was digging into me. But I wasn't focused on that. If anything, that pain only added to the perfection of it.

Of her lips on mine.

A growl rose in my throat and she moaned in response, making something tug loose in my chest. The growl louder now as I gripped her around her waist, lifting her to my height. Her legs went around my hips, and she fisted her free hand in my hair, pulling and twisting sharply against my scalp.

When her tongue pushed between my lips, I couldn't inhale her fast enough.

I hadn't kissed a girl, or been kissed by a girl, in years.

Fucked, sure.

Sucked off, often.

But this was a line I didn't cross.

Hadn't wanted to.

Until now.

My tongue warred with hers and her next moan almost sent me over the edge of control. Her shirt tore open at the back, ripped apart by my hands. She gasped, and I swallowed the sound, devouring her, body and soul.

"You're a fucking asshole," she whispered harshly between kisses, redoubling her efforts to cut me with her claws.

I grunted, twisting my neck to push into the bite of them.

"Never claimed to be anything else," I muttered, and she kissed me again before I could finish, tilting her hips forward so that my rock-hard cock pressed against her heat. Too many layers of fabric between us.

"I hate you."

"I hate you right back."

But that wasn't true anymore, was it. I hated that I wanted her. I hated that I recognized in her someone who could not just withstand me, but fit into the mold with me to be reformed as something new. Improved.

Twice as lethal and twice as strong.

It'd been there from the start, her spark. I thought it would be the end of us, but I was wrong. She was the ember that would ignite us, spurring us into a forest fire that would eat all our enemies away, render them to ashes. We would burn together.

She was the catalyst we'd been waiting for.

My Sparrow reached down between us, pulling and tearing at my dark denim jeans, trying to get my cock free and failing miserably. Even just the brush of her fingers there made me convulse with *need*.

I thrust her against the wall, no, the mirror, and it cracked. The narrow shelf beneath was covered in pots of dark and light makeup and I bent, clutching her to me to swipe everything onto the floor before dropping her on the ledge of the high shelf, pulling her shirt the rest of the way off to reveal a threadbare bra beneath.

We'd have to fix that.

I curled my index finger beneath the connective bit of cloth between her tits and ripped hard, the whole thing coming free with barely any force.

Her nipples were so hard for me. Breasts swollen and perky and begging to be worshipped.

"You're going to pay for that," she hissed, clutching the ledge of the shelf to keep from being pulled off. My dark makeup smudged all over her cheeks and down the slope of her nose.

"That's the plan."

240

A tentative smirk played at the edge of her mouth, and I kissed it, breathing in her scent. So sweet but with a smooth edge like fresh tobacco smoke or musk. I couldn't get enough of that smell. It was why I kept one of her shirts in the top drawer of my dresser, the urge to steal it having come over me in a way that I'd never experienced before. I just knew that I wanted something of *hers*. To touch when I wanted. To breathe in when I wanted. A part of her that I could control.

I sighed as the drug of her settled into my veins, getting me high.

Nothing beat the real thing.

Her fingers were surer now when they reached for the front of my jeans, jerking me closer. The top button popping easily now. The zipper racing down.

Fuck.

I gripped her hand, stopping her, and her lips froze on mine before pulling away.

"There won't be any going back after this," I warned her, unable to look her in the eyes. It was the truth, and she deserved to be able to make this call.

If we crossed this line, she would belong to me, and I would *never* let her go.

I could feel the beast in me swelling, taking over. Promising a possession so fierce there was no way I'd ever temper it. No point in even fighting it. She would be mine.

Ours.

She reached forward and clutched my chin, dragging my gaze up to hers. My nostrils flared as I let her see the agony there. The pain I kept pushed down so deep that sometimes I could forget it was even there.

It was, though. Always had been. I didn't think there could ever be anyone I could share that with. Nor anyone else I could want to be responsible for aside from my

241

chosen family.

But I would do it for her. If she would have me.

Please have me.

Her jaw clenched, and I braced for rejection, pulling my face from her hand, but she didn't let me go so easily.

"I don't make promises I can't keep," she said. "And a big part of me still wants to slit your throat…"

I snorted.

"But there's a bigger part that…" She trailed off, and the hope taking root in my chest hurt more than any pain ever could.

"I understand now," she said instead of finishing the thought, wading into safer territory. "I don't like it, and I haven't forgiven you."

Despite myself, I flinched, my teeth grinding.

"I want to, though."

"You do?"

"I think so."

I let out a shaky breath and put my forehead to hers, watching her eyelids flutter closed at the contact. "I can't promise to be better. I'm broken, Sparrow."

"So am I."

"No, you don't understand. I'll *always be broken*."

There was only silence in reply, and I watched everything I wanted vanish against the backs of my eyelids, but then she spoke.

"If this is *broken*, then I don't want to be fixed."

She finished freeing my cock with a flick of her fingers, and I groaned as she took it into her hands, stroking the silky length of it gently at first, then she gripped it tight, and I grunted again, eyes flying open.

"Now, fuck me, *Bone Man*, or I'll go find someone who will."

My beast growled with possessiveness at her threat,

242

but she didn't have to ask me twice. She'd made her decision. Now, she was mine.

I thrust into her palm, pushing my fingers into her hair to tug her head to the side, putting my teeth to her throat. I scraped them down the length of it to the nape of her neck and bit down, tasting her on my tongue, marking her for everyone to see. She shivered at the pain, and I pressed between her legs, knocking them aside to put my cock flush against her panties.

Her *wet* panties. She was drenched. Practically dripping for me, and I shuddered as her wetness soaked through, making the slip of my cock against them feel like a fucking dream.

"Panties," she panted, nails digging into my back, the word a plea.

I bit her again, resisting the urge to tie her up. Tie her down. Force her to her knees and tell her she was a good girl as I pushed my cock down her throat. Not yet. Not this time.

Not our first time.

"*Patience.*"

"Fuck that."

She reached between us and tore her own panties off, tightening her legs around my waist to impale herself on me. My glutes tightened, pushing me in deeper on instinct alone as Ava Jade held herself there, adjusting to me. And it *was* an adjustment. There was a reason the few girls I'd brought to bed in Thorn Valley liked to call me their Mount Everest. A summiting that could just as easily end in victory as it could in tears.

"*Jesus fuck,*" Sparrow said breathily against the skin below my ear, breathing heavily, and I smiled into her hair.

I started to move, aching to feel her clench around me

as I withdrew and thrust back in, but she whimpered, clawing up my back.

"I can stop."

"Don't you fucking dare."

My smile widened.

The kind of smile only she knew how to drag out of me.

"As you wish," I teased and flattened a palm against her chest, forcing her to retract her claws and return to clutching the ledge of the shelf. I wanted to watch her.

My Sparrow squirmed as I grabbed her thighs, spreading her wider for me as I withdrew and thrust back in with a stuttered groan.

She tipped her head back, letting herself be consumed by the sensations, moaning in a way that was driving me slowly to madness.

She was so fucking tight.

"Just like that," she said in a breath as I picked up the pace, pumping into her hard enough to rock the whole shelf she was seated on. To make the cracks in the mirror behind her head spider out, erasing the reflected image of me from view.

"Is this what you want?" I asked, my upper lip curling as I fucked her harder.

"*Yes.*"

She tipped her hips up for me, allowing me even deeper. So deep she could barely catch her breath.

"That's a good girl," I cooed, releasing one thigh to grip the side of her face, forcing her to look at me. I wanted to see her ecstasy. Needed her to know that this meant the end of everything. And the beginning.

"*Fuck*, Corvus," she whimpered, unclenching one hand from the shelf's ledge to rub her greedy little clit, eyes boring into mine. The sight of her touching herself while I slammed into her almost sent me over the edge, and I had to shut my eyes, slow my breathing.

What was she doing to me?

I truly was coming undone. All my carefully erected walls coming down. The cement blocks of my control crumbling to fucking dust.

Dangerous.

Incredible.

Terrifying.

"Fuck, I'm going to come," she announced, and I bit down, my own orgasm shuddering down the length of my cock.

I dropped my head and pulled a pebbled nipple into my mouth, making her back arch as I bit down on it, forcing her to that summit before I hit it first.

She cried out as her orgasm took her, her convulsions milking my cock of everything it had to give. The sound of my own release mixing with hers.

A loud *chink* was the only warning that the shelf was going down, and I was almost too slow to catch her before she fell, rolling myself to take the brunt of the fall with my jeans tangled around my ankles so that she could land on my chest, my cock popping free of her cunt.

A little squeal left her lips as she landed hard on my chest, knocking the air from my lungs. Makeup pots and brushes jammed into my back, and I groaned, coughing to get a full breath.

She rolled off and our gazes met.

Then, she laughed.

A laugh that started deep in her belly and reverberated up through her throat, filling the whole room with its musical sound.

I laughed too, the sound foreign as it found its way past my lips. Deep and rich.

245

She kicked my leg as though it were my fault we broke the fucking shelf, and I kicked her right back, laughing harder.

She swiped a tear from her eye and sat up, looking around at the state of the room. At the state of us.

"We're a fucking mess," she said.

"You are," Grey announced, and as one, our heads swiveled to the door, finding Grey standing there leaning against the doorframe with Becca next to him, covering her mouth with both hands, eyes wide as she took in her friend.

"Sorry!" Becca chirped and turned around, striding away from the door. I guessed she was one more person to add to the list of those that now knew my best kept secret. That was a problem. I glared at Grey, deciding to deal with him later.

"I was wondering when you were going to show up," Ava Jade said to Grey. "Ten minutes earlier and you could have joined us."

Ava Jade

"Uh, Aves..." Becca trailed off, and I groaned sleepily, refusing to open my eyes even though light was searing the back of my eyelids. "Wake up, girl. I think someone left you a present."

That had my attention piqued, but still my stiff joins protested movement as I rolled over in the bed to find Becca standing by the door leading down to the garage. She held up a smooth black box with a piece of paper taped to the top of it. Scrawled across it in black sharpie was a single word: Sparrow.

I pulled my pillow back over my head, the whole thing coming back to me now.

The concert. *Backstage* at the concert.

Me gathering my things and telling Corvus that I needed time to process everything. That I wanted space.

So much for that. He was already bringing gifts to my fucking door.

Prick.

My cunt throbbed at the memory of him inside me, and I clenched, feeling a pleasant ache still there from his size.

"You want me to open it?" Becca asked. "Or should we send it back?"

I moaned in response, disliking both options.

"I vote we open it, and since you're in no shape to be making any life decisions pre-caffeination, my vote counts for you too."

I pulled the pillow off. "No, wait—"

But she already had the top off the box and was staring excitedly down at whatever was inside. "Oh. My. God."

I sat up, the last remnants of sleep rolling off my shoulders like a bad vibe. "What is it?"

She tiptoed over to my bed like a crazy person and dropped the box in front of me. Black tissue paper spilled out, revealing something in a stunning magenta color. I used my pinkie to lift the dainty slip of lace fabric and my mouth fell open.

It was a thong. A lace thong.

"Look!" Becca trilled, clapping her hands before snatching something else from the box. "It's the matching set! Look at this thing!"

She held it up to her own boobs through her shirt as though checking to see if she might be able to borrow it.

I grabbed it from her and threw it and the thong panties back into the box, covering them back over with the tissue paper, my heart racing.

Becca calmed almost immediately, settling onto the bed with crossed legs. "I know we didn't talk about it last night, but I'm, like, hella curious what the fuck happened and—"

She caught my look and stopped babbling.

"Okay, so I *know* what happened. I just...I thought you didn't like him. I actually thought you hated him. Is it just because he turned out to be you know who? Because I *did not* fucking see that one coming. Corvus James: cold hearted prick, gang member, part-time psychopath, and *rock star?* You just can't make that shit up. Guess all the fan theories are wrong then."

She was wrong. So wrong, but I couldn't bring myself to correct her. I hadn't fucked Corvus because he was The Bone Man. I fucked Corvus because when I laid eyes on him in that dressing room...I saw him for who he really was. Not for the mask he wore.

I saw his soul. Bared. Naked.

And I wanted to claim it.

Becca laid her hand on mine, and I blinked back to myself, realizing I'd gone quiet. "Hey," she said. "You totally don't have to talk about it if you don't want to. I may kinda sorta be trying to live vicariously through you. I mean, since..."

She didn't finish the sentence, and again I was reminded that somewhere out there was an asshole who'd drawn her in and then ghosted her. If he didn't come back and apologize, I made no promises against finding his ass and forcing the apology out of him.

"It's fine," I told her with a forced smile. "I just don't really know how I feel about it yet. I do hate him. Or, I *did* hate him. I don't know. I'm just—"

"Confused?"

"Doesn't even begin to cover it."

She laughed. "Well, with a dick that big, I'd take my time considering my options."

I cocked my head at her, cheeks tinging red as something uncoiled in my belly.

249

He's not yours to get jealous over, Ava Jade. Cool it.

She held up her hands in a placating gesture. "No, I just mean it was a nice dick, that's all. I think I'm going plastic for a while. The real thing just isn't worth it sometimes."

"Ain't that the motherfucking truth."

My phone buzzed on the nightstand, and I grabbed it, catching Becca's barely concealed excitement at the sound.

"Is it him?" she asked, scorching closer.

I shook my head. "Just an email."

I almost set my phone back down before noticing who the email was from. *Vicky.* I didn't know a Vicky. I clicked on it.

To: Ava Jade Mason
From: Vicky Doyle
Subject: Swap Notes
Hey, Ava Jade, it's Vicky from English Lit. I was hoping we could swap notes for the upcoming project like we talked about. Can we meet? I was thinking maybe Sunday morning. I'm not going to be able to help you if you don't help me. Last chance. I'll send you the address later! Thanks.

My stomach dropped.

Vicky.

Officer Vick. He was trying to covertly set up a meeting without drawing suspicion.

Crafty fucker, and maybe a bit smarter than I gave him credit for. I had no idea how he got my email address. He was giving me exactly a week to make my decision.

An impossible decision, but one I think I'd already made.

"You good?" Becca asked. "Is it your hag of an Aunt

again?"

I clicked off my phone and shook my head. "Nope, just a stupid scam email."

"Ugh, I hate those."

Becca jumped up from the bed to check her face in the small mirror on the desk, rubbing a mascara smudge from beneath her eye.

Her phone went off, and she lifted it eagerly, only to frown at whatever was on the screen.

"All good?" I asked.

"Yeah. Just my dad. Asking if I'm coming home for Thanksgiving."

"Will your mom be there?" I asked, realizing she only ever talked about her dad, never her mom. I assumed they were separated, but I honestly had no idea.

Becca stiffened, swallowing as she turned back to me, a sadness in her brown eyes. "No."

"Oh, you don't get along, or?"

"We did," she said with a somber smile. "Before she died."

My heart twisted.

"Guess we have that in common," she pointed out, and it was easy to tell she was trying to play it off like it was no big deal when it was. She immediately began picking at her fingernails, an act I'd come to realize was one of her stress responses.

"You have a dead dad. I have a dead mom. And our other parents are mostly MIA, other than when they want something."

I hadn't told her much about my mom. Only that I hadn't seen her in years, and only heard from her exactly once. A phone call from a payphone asking me to bail her out of jail.

"What happened?" I asked, getting a sinking feeling

251

in my gut.

Becca clenched her hands together. "It was an accident. A bad one. The wrong place, wrong time kind."

Her lips pressed into a tight-lipped smile, and her gaze found mine before slipping away quickly. She sighed.

"I'm so sorry, babe. Do you want to talk about it?"

God, I was shit at this sort of thing. How were you supposed to comfort your friends if you couldn't slay their demons for them?

"It was a long time ago." She shrugged, and her eyes lit up, hands unclenching in her lap as she perked up.

"Hey! Do you know when Corvus' birthday is?" she asked after a second, turning a bit to lift a curious brow in my direction.

Um...talk about a one-eighty...

"Why?"

"I'm not sure if I pegged him right anymore, you know? I always thought he was a Scorpio, but now I'm thinking maybe Gemini?"

So, we were changing the subject then. Got it. I laughed for real this time. She really wouldn't give it up with this horoscope stuff.

"No, I don't know when it is. Rook's is next weekend though."

She gasped. "No way! I thought for sure he was Aries, but of course *he's* the Scorpio! Should've seen that one coming a mile away."

I hoped he liked his gift. It wasn't much, but I had a feeling it might mean something to him. Something more than chocolate cake or anything bought from Amazon. And I wouldn't make a big deal out of it since Corvus told me he didn't like to celebrate.

I shook my head at Becca.

"You figure me out yet?" I asked with a challenge in my tone, and she pursed her lips at me.

"You're a tough one. I think I've almost got you, though."

She wandered back to the bed. "You've got to help me figure out the other guys. They've legit never had a birthday party or anything in all the years I've been at Briar Hall with them. I'm starting to wonder if they were made instead of being born. Like crazy gangster robots."

We both burst out laughing, and it was hard not to picture it. Which only made it even more funny.

I sighed, swiping a tear from my eye as I calmed down. "Fuck, I think we need to get out more. We're laughing about fictional gangster robots."

Becca cut herself off mid-laugh and reached under our shared bed, drawing out two lumpy parcels with the Crow's Nest address on them. "Say no more," she announced and ripped into the first one then the second.

She waited for my reaction, but I just stared, wondering what in the actual fuck I was looking at here.

"For the full moon party!" she said when I didn't get it. "It's a few days before Halloween so everybody's dressing up. I got us costumes!"

Truly, I'd been planning to find a way out of going to that, but I couldn't do that now, not with Becca looking so excited. Though, if the rumors were true, Brianna, *the bitch*, was talking shit around Briar Hall about 'taking me down.' So, the night might not be a total bust. Maybe I'd borrow the trimmers from under the sink, give her a new hairdo. The idea made me smile.

I lifted silky black fabric from one package, noticing the Prada label on the sheath-like dress, and what looked like horned headbands from the other.

"Do you get it?" she pressed, and I winced, staring

253

between the two items with confusion.

"The Devil Wears Prada," she said, losing some of her steam. "You know, like the movie? Or the book, I mean, both were fucking phenomenal."

My lips pressed tight, and she gasped.

"You haven't seen it? Are you shitting me?"

"Sorry."

She shoved all the clothes and horns out of the way and took both my hands, hauling me up from the bed. "We're fixing that right now."

She pulled me through the bathroom, to the upstairs hallway of the main house. I pulled back, not wanting to face anyone just yet, but she only pulled harder. "It's just Grey, and he's working on something in his room, see?" She waved an arm to his open door. "No one else is here."

Grey lowered his headphones to his shoulders and spun in his office chair. "Hey, what's up? You need anything?"

"Just to borrow your TV," Becca said. "And to be left alone for a minimum of two hours."

Grey blinked, clearly as confused as I was but waved us on. "Our TV is your TV. Have at it."

"Come on, girl. Miranda Priestly is my fucking spirit animal, I can't wait for you to see this!"

"The guys are already out by the car," Becca said, peering out the small octagonal window at the front of the loft.

"They can wait another sec. My liner is almost out."

I shook the tube, forcing the last dregs of the black liquid eyeliner to saturate the brush tip. "Fucker," I cursed as a glob of black splattered on my black Prada dress that I was definitely going to pay Becca back for some day.

"Sorry," I muttered, trying to brush it off, but only managing to make a mess.

Becca laughed at my growly attitude, coming over to help. "You can't even see it. Here, give me that before you wind up looking like a raccoon."

I passed her the liner and reached for a makeup wipe, cleaning the black smudges from my fingers while she eyed up my eyes, getting a lay of the land. "Okay," she said, mostly to herself as she knelt and leaned in. "Close."

I closed my eyes, feeling the gentle press of her fingers at the edges of my eyes and then the cool swipe of liquid product over my lash line. She fixed the other side to match and then stepped back.

"Open."

She smiled. "There. Have a look. Maybe a bit bolder than your usual, but it's Halloween, so I think you can get away with it."

I checked my reflection, surprised at how the slight change in my liner could make my eyes look so much brighter than they usually did. And fuck if those wings weren't perfect. Combined with the dark lipstick, horns, and mega contouring, I really did look like a devil risen from the depths of hell. A sexy one.

"You're hired," I joked, trying to inject some real excitement into my tone.

She put her hands on my knees, and I found her staring curiously up at me. "You okay, babe?"

I nodded. "Yeah. Of course I am."

Becca's face fell a bit, but she recovered quickly, and I was reminded why I loved her too damn much. She didn't pry. Never pushed. But I knew she'd be there whenever I needed her to be. It made me feel guilty for never allowing Dom to get this close to me. Made me wonder if she and I could've had this. It didn't matter much now, though.

After a quick chat this week, it was clear Dom had moved on with her life in Lennox, and I couldn't blame her.

You could only hold out for your *non*-friends for so long.

Kit was still trying though. He'd even gone so far as offering to come all the way here to visit since I'd told him I couldn't—*more like wouldn't*—come to Lennox.

"Well, you know I'm here if you need me," Becca said, standing with a sigh as she adjusted her boobs, making them appear even fuller over the top of the black bustier.

I smiled at that, a real smile, and stood with her, double checking everything of mine was in place, too. Deciding to whip my mopey ass into a better gear.

Just because all three guys were being moody bastards who'd barely left their bedrooms this week, didn't mean my fun had to be ruined.

It was obvious, wasn't it? The fucker who'd been texting me crawled off into a hole somewhere and died like the rodent he was. It was sad—not getting the chance to maim him myself, but I was over it. Why couldn't they get the fuck over it, too?

I followed Becca down the stairs and out to the front, where the guys waited by the Rover under the moonlight. Corvus, with his arms crossed leaning against the hood. Rook smoking a cigarette like it was his fucking job, and Grey texting something furiously on his phone.

My stomach twinged with discomfort as Grey, seeing me approach, quickly stuffed his phone back into his pocket, the muscles in his jaw clenching.

I couldn't help wondering who he was texting. If it was Bri.

My fists clenched.

"Let me guess," Grey said, painting on a forced grin.

"The Devil Wears Prada."

Becca put a hand to her chest and smiled widely at him. "A man after my own heart." She tossed a wink my way. "He's a keeper, Aves."

"Good flick," Grey added, gesturing to the bag Becca was carrying. "What the hell are you bringing in that?"

I thought she just had her larger black purse with her, but I realized now that it was more like a mini duffel bag.

"I had a feeling you three would be lame asses and not bother dressing up for your own Halloween party, so I got you these."

She dropped the duffel down onto the hood of the Rover, earning herself a little glare from Corvus as she unzipped the bag.

"One for you," she said, handing one to Grey.

"And you, Rook."

"And you, too, *Bone Man*."

"Becca," Corvus warned.

"I know, I know. Only in private, oh powerful prince of darkness."

"What the hell are these?" Rook asked, seemingly annoyed as he stomped out the remnants of his cigarette beneath his boot.

But it was obvious, wasn't it? The shape gave them away, even in the minimal light pouring onto the front drive.

"Crow masks," I said, not even realizing I'd said the words aloud.

"Come on," Becca urged them, planting her hands on her hips. "At least try them on. I had them custom made."

Corvus' nostrils flared, and Rook lifted a brow at her.

"She said try them on," I repeated, adding an edge of violence to my tone that was just enough to spur them to listen.

257

"Aren't they great?" Becca squealed as the guys finished tying them on with the oiled black laces.

They covered half their faces from forehead to just below the nose and were both a shining and matte black with an iridescent blue in some parts. The beaks extended out, but not so far out that they appeared bulky or looked foolish. They looked badass. Like, straight out of a horror movie.

"What do you say, boys?" I pressed. "Becca went out of her way to have these made for you…"

Grey cleared his throat. "Thanks, Becca. These are great." He elbowed Rook.

"Yeah. Whatever. They're cool."

"And you're already used to wearing a mask, so I'm going to assume this suits you just fine, Corv." Becca patted him on the chest. "Though I like you better in skeleton makeup."

He growled slightly, and I steered Becca toward the back seat. "Okay. That's enough. Let's go."

We barely got outside of the town limits before Becca pulled a joint from the smaller purse she had hidden in the duffel and lit it up, blowing the smoke out the rear window while she hummed along to Boy Epic pouring out of the speakers.

"Here," she said, passing it. "You need this more than I do. Loosen up a bit. Tonight's going to be fun, and it's my last night at the loft."

I took the joint with a sigh. "I really wish you'd reconsider staying a bit longer."

"Why? The window's fixed back at Briar Hall, and besides, you barely sleep at all with me there."

I opened my mouth to argue, but she held up a hand, and I took another drag instead.

"I'm not taking any offense," she said. "So I hope you

258

won't either when I tell you that when you *are* actually sleeping, you're a terrible sleeping buddy."

"What?"

"Seriously, like, I'm pretty sure I have bruises from you kicking me."

I snorted. "Liar." I hardly moved in my sleep.

"Okay fine, I just miss my bed. Happy?"

I shook my head, and when I went to pass the joint back to Becca, Rook stole it from my fingers, lifting it to his lips instead.

"You mind?" he asked Becca, and her brows lifted.

"Not at all."

He smoked it down to the nub and tried passing it back, but Becca just gave him an unimpressed look. "You might as well finish it now."

I shivered as the cool night air pumped into the backseat from the open windows, and from the pot working its way into my muscles and making them tingle. It was stronger than her usual stuff, and I hummed contentedly to myself, leaning my head back against the seat as we veered off the main road and down towards the edge of Thorn Valley and the lake.

"Good shit," I muttered, letting the high sink deep into my bones.

"The best," she agreed. "I was saving it for—"

Her words cut off abruptly, and I was almost too slow to brace myself on the front seats as a black sedan peeled out in front of us, forcing Grey off the road.

Becca squealed while we swerved, the Rover's movements jerky and making my stomach fill with the bad kind of butterflies.

"*Fuck,*" I shouted as we skidded on the gravel at the road's edge, coming to a stop just a few feet from hitting the ditch.

I clutched my stomach, heart racing as car doors popped open all around and Becca screamed as black gloved hands dragged her from the Rover.

Her eyes went wide and wild as her body fell from the seat faster than I could snatch her back. My doped up fingers fumbled with my seatbelt as I shouted. "Becca! Someone get Becca!"

I got free and jumped from the car in time to hear a crude grunt. Headlights blinded me as I turned to find what made the sound, reaching for a blade.

"Aves!"

I spun, but it was too late. The blade was knocked from my hand and a black sack was pulled over my head, arms sharply hauled back and bound tight.

I kicked back, but my leg was only hooked by whoever had set upon us, sending me sprawling face first into the gravel. The earthy copper taste of my own blood filled my mouth, and I gagged as I swallowed it back, rolling to get back to my feet.

"Becca!"

Someone made a grab for my arm, and I bent my knees, throwing my whole body into the round house kick. I nailed whoever it was real fucking good, but without my arms for counter balance, I only ended up on the ground again, my shoulder aching from the fall.

"Sparrow, stop fighting," Corvus bellowed, and I hesitated as I rose back to my feet again, trying to see through the black hood over my head, but there was only light and shadows.

"What the fuck is going on?"

The hands came for me again, and I thrashed, but this time I didn't fight, choosing, maybe very stupidly, to trust Corvus.

"Awe, don't ruin the game, Son," Diesel's distinct

voice rose right after a car door opened somewhere far off to my right.

"Just let her go!" Becca cried, and I could hear the struggle in her voice. Someone was holding her back. Was someone holding my guys back, too? Or were they watching this happen and doing nothing?

My chest ached for an instant before I realized what this was.

Another fucking trial.

Of course.

I forced my breathing to even out and straightened my back.

"It's okay, Becks."

"What's going on? What is this?" she demanded, and I wanted nothing more than for her to be *far* away from this place. Far from Diesel St. Crow and his men.

"Take her away," I said, in no direction in particular, the order meant for the guys. "Get her out of here."

"You heard the girl," Diesel said. "Get her little friend out of here."

"What are you doing?" Grey demanded, and I could see his expression in my mind's eye from his tone alone. The tension that would be between his brows. The sour curl of his upper lip.

A pause before Diesel answered. "I didn't want to ruin the surprise, but anticipation sometimes makes it even sweeter. We're having a hunt."

"A hunt?" Rook asked, his voice a lethal rasp.

"Yes. Like we did for Foley a few years back."

"Foley died in the hunt," Corvus deadpanned, and my mouth went dry.

"What?" Becca all but screamed, and I could hear the scratch of heels against the pavement as she struggled some more, making my heart twist in my chest.

261

A shuffle of feet and I saw what I thought was the shadow of Diesel move closer to his boys. Their three shadows were surrounded by many others standing in front of the headlights.

"Yes, well, Foley had questionable intentions, and in the end, he just wasn't good enough. He would've been a liability. A risk."

The way Diesel said *risk* told me exactly how he felt about them. Like father, like son. Corvus was just the same.

"We're taking her with us," Rook said, and I heard him step forward, saw the shadows close it, and then nothing. No movement.

"If you interfere, she fails," Diesel told his son. "You know the rules. I've already made one exception. I will not make another."

"You boys have a party to get to," the man holding me added, tightening his grip on my arm. "You'd best get going. You know how shit is with the Aces right now. If you want to keep your *Docks*, you have to be ready to defend them."

"Diesel," Corvus said, his father's name on his lips like a plea.

There came no reply for his son, but an order hissed from his lips. "Take her."

I didn't struggle as they led me away, already trying to come up with a solution on my own, but my thoughts were slow. Addled by the third of a joint I'd smoked in the fucking Rover.

"Wait!" Becca shouted as we passed her, and her hands grasped my arm, trying to keep me there while the men holding us fought to keep us apart.

I slowed my pulse and swallowed. "I'm going to be fine," I said, in a voice that sounded so certain I almost believed it myself. "Don't worry about me, 'kay? I'll see you later."

"Promise?"

"Promise."

Her nails scratched my arm as she was pulled away, and I heard her gasp as she was passed off.

"I've got you," Grey said. "It's okay. She's going to be okay."

"Are you sure?" she asked, the watery sound of her voice making my eyes burn.

"Positive," Corvus replied instead of Grey, making me feel stronger.

"But what if she isn't?"

I was shuffled from warm hands to cold ones and a trunk opened. I ground my teeth as they shoved my head down, folding me into the dark, cool space and closing me in. My phone was taken from my back pocket just before the trunk slammed shut.

Rook's reply was the last thing I heard before the engine started and the menace in his voice woke the dark parts of me back to life. Stoked my fire back to life, burning me back to a sense of sobriety.

"She has to be."

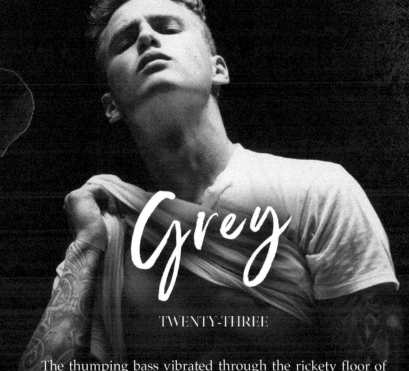

Grey

TWENTY-THREE

The thumping bass vibrated through the rickety floor of the Docks, reverberating up through my feet. Setting my fucking teeth on edge. Becca sat with us on our makeshift stage, picking her fingernails at the far end of the worn leather sofa, her stare distant, thoughtful.

I snapped my fingers, and a pledge rushed over. I gestured to Becca. "Get her a drink."

"What should I get for her?"

"I don't know," I snapped, heat rising in my core. "Why don't you fucking ask *her*."

He nodded before running away to do just that, and I pressed my palms into my eyes, trying to grind out the ache forming behind them.

Rook threw his flask at the pledge now begging Becca to pick something to drink so that he could go and get it.

"Refill," Rook snapped while the pledge bent to retrieve his flask from the floor. "Now."

The guy scurried off, and I turned to where Corvus sat next to me, hunched over his knees, fingers steepled near his lips in complete stillness. Utter silence.

"We need to cut that one loose. He's useless."

Corvus grunted in response, and I got the feeling he hadn't even heard me.

"Corv, are you listening?"

"Hmm?"

My head pounded, making it almost impossible not to throttle him. How could he be so fucking calm right now? How was he not freaking out?

The Hunt was the worst ever idea for a trial Diesel had ever concocted. And he'd only come up with it because he decided he didn't want Foley to make it through the trials. And Foley, the twenty-five-year-old college drop-out, already knew far too much to be cut loose.

Diesel was right, of course, like he almost always was. It turned out he was being worked on by a cop. And Foley, being the weak link Diesel was beginning to think he was, was close to folding. Close to becoming an informant. Close to being formally inducted into our ranks, where he would've had access to even more sensitive information.

The Hunt was designed for a single purpose, to *kill* the hunted.

My stomach soured, and I got up, needing to move. To *do* something. But black spots crowded my vision and a wave of vertigo sent me back to the couch with a groan. "Fucking shit."

"The fuck is wrong with you?" Rook asked, raising his voice to be heard over the music and the chatter of the crowd before us.

I shook off the fleeting feeling. "Nothing."

But when I lifted my head to the strobing dance floor,

the faces blurred in and out of focus, making my pounding headache that much worse.

Devil faces and witch faces and Barbie faces and every other Halloween costume that could be worn as a lingerie set with heels paraded past. They spun and jumped. Swayed and fell.

But none of them were AJ.

When the pledge came back, I snarled at him to get me some painkillers, hating my inability to control the rage I felt building inside.

Brianna's face filtered past with the others, trying desperately to catch my eye, her bunny ears bobbing as she sashayed past the raised stage, biting her lower lip.

I didn't know what part of *stop fucking texting me* she didn't understand, but obviously it wasn't sinking in.

She took a step toward the stage, and something in my face must've made her reconsider. Hurt gleamed in her eyes as she stepped backward instead, falling back into the crowd.

Good. I couldn't deal with her shit tonight. Not on top of everything else.

"The meet with the Aces coming up," Corvus said, his voice so low and deep it was almost impossible to distinguish it from the throaty bass. "I don't think it's a good idea. Something's up."

I couldn't keep the shock off my face. "How the actual fuck are you thinking about that right now?"

Rook stared off into the crowd, but by the tiny twist of his lips, I knew he was listening, too.

"Diesel wants us with him for the meet. I'm trying to come up with the best way to play it."

"Right now?"

I knew what he was doing, but I wasn't fucking having it. He was deflecting. Not thinking about the thing he couldn't control by thinking about something he could. A defense mechanism that wasn't going to save our girl.

He'd just fucked her, you'd think he could act like he cared whether she lived or died for five fucking seconds.

"I have an idea," Rook said, slipping from the arm of the couch to flop down onto the cushion next to Corvus. "Kill them all. Problem solved. Danger avoided. Risk factor? Reduced to a big fat fucking zero."

His dark eyes glimmered with drink and malice in the red-tinted lights. "We could start tonight."

Corvus finally broke his pose, fingers leaving his lips as he twisted to lay his eyes on Rook. "You can't just kill every person you have a problem with, Rook," he chastised our brother. "There are better ways of handling shit."

"*Smarter* ways," I added, not knowing why I was bothering to add anything to this pointless conversation right now.

Rook shrugged. "Not easier ones."

The pledge returned with some white pills and a bottle of water, and I swallowed them both down, guzzling the whole bottle before tossing it back at him. "Go."

Rook and Corvus regarded me with matching lifted brows, and I grimaced. "Fucking headache," I explained. "Lay off, okay."

I never took painkillers. *Never*. But if I didn't do something about the piercing, throbbing ache behind my eye sockets, I was going to snap.

A girl with light hair in an angel costume walked up onto the stage, swaying her hips as she approached Rook, bending to his eye level with her tits pushed out. I couldn't hear what she whispered to him, but I saw the way her gaze tracked to the Red Room door and back and how she bit her lower lip.

Rook gazed up at her with a haughty disdain, giving her a one-word reply.

When she redoubled her efforts, placing hands on his thighs, his entire body tensed, and he shoved her back, sending her sprawling to her ass with a yelp as his nostrils flared.

He snapped at her like a wild animal as she scrambled to her feet, sending her scampering off back into the crowd, red-faced and shaking.

His rejection only made *her* come rushing back to the forefront of my mind.

I pinched the bridge of my nose, pushing my thumb and index finger into the fleshy corners of my eyes. "She's going to be okay, right?" I asked, feeling something grow and clench behind my rib cage.

"I don't know," Corvus answered, and I let out a shuddering breath.

"Diesel wouldn't..." Rook trailed off, settling back onto the couch, but he couldn't finish the sentence and there was a reason why.

Diesel *would* if he knew something we didn't.

He *would* if he believed beyond a shadow of doubt that she would be our downfall.

"There's nothing we can do but wait," Corvus hissed.

"It's not good enough."

"You don't think I fucking know that?"

"Even if she lives, Diesel won't be finished with her," Rook mused, swirling his whiskey in the flask, staring down into the neck of it like the amber liquid inside might hold some secret to fixing this whole fucked up mess.

In a move so fast I hardly saw it coming, Corvus stood and flipped the low coffee table, throwing it into the unsuspecting crowd with a roar.

269

Becca squealed, and I heard the clack of her heels over the music as she backed away from the stage.

Corvus whirled on Rook. "What would you have me do?" he demanded of Rook, his eyes like burning embers. His teeth bared. "If we stop the trial, she fails, and she dies. If we save her, we've interfered, and she fails *and dies*."

"We could leave," I said, not even realizing I'd spoken out loud until Corvus' searing gaze found mine, his nostrils flaring. "We could save her and then leave."

He paled, and I felt the blood draining from my own face, too, giving the migraine wreaking havoc in my skull a pulse.

"No," Corvus said after a minute, saying aloud what I wished wasn't true. "We can't."

"You said she was going to be fine," Becca said, and the three of us turned at once to see her standing behind the sofa, her arms tense with balled fists and trembling at her sides. "You knew she was going to die, and you just *let her go*. You fucking liars! You fucking pieces of shit!"

I stood, hopping the back of the couch to grab her. She just needed to understand, we didn't have a choice. But Becca snatched her arm away before I could grab her and spat at my feet.

"If she dies, I'm coming for you. I'm coming for all your useless asses."

She shouldered past me, the blow shaking me all the way to my core. She didn't have to worry about retribution. If Ava Jade died tonight, I was coming for my fucking self.

Ava Jade

TWENTY-FOUR

The drive wasn't a long one. No more than five minutes and the car whose trunk I was currently folded into began to slow, and then stop.

Judging by the curvy path they took, and the steady inclination of the road, I guessed we were no more than a few miles from the Docks. Maybe three. Four at a maximum.

I didn't know if knowing where I was would help me, but I would take any information I could, tuck it away in the back of my mind in case I should need it.

Like the fact that there were at least five of them, but no more than seven. In two vehicles. One a sedan, whose trunk I was currently in, and the other, the dark SUV that drove us off the road.

I knew Diesel was here. And Tiny. The others I couldn't be sure of.

I also knew that I was fighting a high I wished to hell

I hadn't decided to ride, and that in about three more seconds, I'd have the ties binding my wrists together at my back completely sawed off.

One, the sedan's ignition shuttered to a complete standstill.

Two, the doors clicked open.

Three, a key slipped into the lock on the trunk, and the latch popped.

The ties snapped apart, but I kept my arms behind me as the trunk opened, the almost total darkness brightening some under the dappled light of the full moon through the black bag.

Roughly, someone gripped my arm, and I clutched my wrist to keep my arms from popping apart as he hauled me from the trunk and threw me against the rear fender. I grunted as the blow to the back of my knees almost sent me to the ground, giving me the perfect opportunity to play it up the injury, and bend, groaning so I could slip two fingers beneath the back of my dress and snatch a blade from the garter on my thigh.

I wondered if I could kill them.

I mean, would that be breaking the rules?

The guys said to try not to, but if push came to shove? If they actively tried to kill me? If killing them was the only way to 'pass' the trial?

The other vehicle pulled up nearby and the headlights flashed over me before going out as the ignition shut off.

I sensed more than knew it when Diesel St. Crow stepped out of the other car, like a shift in the air. Similar to how it felt when one of his sons entered a room. As though they disturbed the fabric of the universe, taking up far too much space for beings their size.

I lifted my chin, waiting.

A second later the black bag was pulled from my head, and I blinked, disoriented and a bit nauseous from the bumpy ride in the trunk.

My lips parted, and a tremor of dread ran down my spine like an icy fingertip. Before me were six men, but I didn't recognize any one of them. It was too hard to tell in the masks.

A wolf. A bear. A stag. A panther. A snake. And a crow.

Their faces were fully covered by their animalistic masks, dark hollows where their eyes should have been. And in each of their hands, a crossbow.

Motherfucking crossbows.

I assessed my surroundings, finding myself ensconced in dappled darkness, surrounded entirely by trees. The road we'd driven in on was a dirt one. The air smelled of cooling earth and still warm wood with an undercurrent of something unpleasant, like sour mulch…or decomposing corpses.

"Untie her," someone said, but when the bear, Tiny, stepped forward, I loosened my hands, showing him the empty one. No need to let them know I was armed yet.

"Hmm," someone grunted, a sound of surprised approval I thought might've come from Diesel.

"What is this?" I asked, folding the blade in my hand so it laid flat against my wrist, hidden from view, but easy to throw in a hurry if I needed to.

"Escape or stay alive until dawn and you will have passed the trial," the snake said in a voice I didn't recognize.

"That's it? There aren't any rules?"

The bear and the wolf shared a look, but no one replied, and I understood they didn't expect me to last very long.

273

"You have a one-minute head start," Diesel said, his voice ringing true even through the crow mask he wore. I hated that it looked similar to the ones Becca had custom made for the guys. "Don't waste it."

"Fifty-nine," the snake said excitedly, limbering up his legs for a chase. "Fifty-eight."

"Fifty-seven," the stag joined the countdown, adjusting his hold on his crossbow.

I sent one last look Diesel's way, letting him see that I would not go fucking quietly, before I bent, tearing the bottom of my dress away and kicking off my heels. And then I was running. Drawing on the part of myself that I would need to survive. My darkness bloomed to life, spurred to wake by the adrenaline pumping through my veins. Making my vision clearer. Senses sharper.

It was the darkness that whispered sweet nothings in my ear when a sharp rock cut deep into the fleshy underside of my left foot. And when a tree branch whipped across my face, leaving a potent sting in my right eye that forced it closed.

Speed was key here.

Escape was the goal. I had no doubt they would find me if I tried to hide.

But first I needed to outrun the distance their crossbow bolts could travel, and then I needed to find my way out of these woods, onto a road, to somewhere there were houses I could break into or cars I could hotwire.

If there were no rules that meant I could use any means to escape. I just needed to find those *means*, and right now it looked like all there was for miles as far as I could see were trees and darkness.

Twenty-two, twenty-one, twenty…

The countdown continued in my head, and I veered right on a whim. They would expect me to run straight forward, to put as much distance between me and them in sixty seconds as possible. They may not have expected a deviation.

Four, three, two...

The rest of the countdown finished out in my head, and a renewed burst of energy seared like white hot lightning down the length of my body, propelling me faster until I was sailing over the uneven earth, launching over fallen forest debris and dodging low hanging branches like it was my fucking job.

Just stay ahead of them. If they can't catch up to you, they can't shoot you.

It had to be a scare tactic. The guys had made it clear they cared what happened to me, which I was still processing, so the Saints wouldn't...they wouldn't actually shoot me, right? At least, not kill shots? Maybe that was why they were using crossbows. I liked my chances against a crossbow versus a gun a lot better.

An arrow *thunked* into the tree directly beside my head, and I hit the ground with a gasp, my eyes widening.

Wrong.

I was so wrong.

I was also up and running again, distantly hearing the brush of booted feet over the ground behind me. Someone shouting far off to my left. Someone else shouting back, also far in the distance.

Whoever was on my tail, though, they were closing in.

Was it wishful thinking to hope it was only one? That the others spread off into five other directions?

Gritting my teeth, I kept running, and the next low hanging branch I found, I grabbed hold of instead of sliding beneath, pulling myself up to the next branch and the next. Until I was at least fifteen feet from the ground and would be absolutely fucked if there were more than a few of them following me.

Or at a very good advantage if it were just one.

I held out my blade, peering down through the sparse leaves of the old oak tree, breathing quietly. I steadied myself with my free hand planted against the rough bark of the oak's trunk.

He came less than twenty seconds later, crossbow up and ready as he moved stealthily through the brush and bramble. The snake.

I leaned forward on my toes, trying to get a better angle as he approached and the branch I perched on creaked under my weight.

The snake jerked his head up, raised his crossbow, and fired. I dodged the bolt by a hair, falling, and threw, having to curve the blade to account for the lower branch.

I reached for a handhold, but my fingers clutched at nothing, just empty air as gravity worked against me, pulling me back down to earth. With a grunt, I hooked a leg out, catching myself on the branch below me to hang upside down. Brutally tearing something in my knee.

Dammit.

I drew the second blade as I flipped from the lower branch and prayed to land anywhere that wasn't on my face. It was a surprise to land on my feet, though the ache in my knee sent me bending to one side to account for it.

It surprised my attacker even more, though.

His eyes went saucer wide at the sight of me, more or less unharmed while he clasped his hands around the blade protruding from his gut. Hands slick with red.

His crossbow was discarded on the ground, two bolts scattered around it.

He went for the handle of the blade, but I lifted another and it flashed in the moonlight, drawing his attention. "As much as I'd love to have that back," I hissed, careful to keep my voice low. "If you take it out, you'll die, and I'm not entirely sure what that means for me."

I wasn't not sure what I expected, maybe for him to suck it up and take his defeat like a champ, bow out of this stupid *hunt* like the harmless reptile he was pretending to be, but that's not what he did. Not by a fucking long shot.

"She's over here!" he called, his voice carrying in the night, and my skin iced over with a new layer of cold sweat.

I reeled back and kicked him hard in the knee, satisfied to hear him cry out in pain as he slumped to the ground in my wake. I stomped on his crossbow too for good measure.

Run, bitch, I scolded myself. *You got this.*

But my knee was aching, and every step felt like another thread torn in whatever was holding the whole fucking hinge joint together. I pushed through the pain anyway, resolved to get the fuck out of here.

I stopped, only for an instant to hear sounds of pursuit, but I heard something else instead. Faint. Super distant, but it was there.

Music.

Dance music. A house party?

Or was it…

It could be…

I ran in that direction, trying to listen to the far-off sound of the bass to guide me.

It was almost impossible to hear it over the sound of my own breathing. And the thudding of my pulse pounding in my ears made it hard to distinguish one from the other.

Shit.

I rounded a boulder, crouched down behind it to

277

listen again, holding my breath even though it made my chest burn. *There.*

More to the east.

I jumped back to my feet and was thrown forward, a whistle the only sound before I hit the ground, the air leaving my lungs in a pained gasp. Dirt and blood filled my mouth and the pain came all at once. An increasing pressure in my shoulder that was reaching a volcanic eruption size breaking point.

Still gasping for air, I twisted my head and came face to face with the arrowhead protruding from the fleshy bit of skin connecting my right shoulder to my torso. Blood dripped from the black metal tip and on a stomach twisting glance back, I saw the rest of it, sticking out the other side. Wood fletching and speckled feathers.

Holy shit.

They shot me.

Good thing I was a lefty.

The shooter's footsteps approached and even though it went against every instinct screaming in my nerve endings, I rolled to defend myself, snapping the wooden back of the arrow on the ground as I threw my blade, brokering no fucking mercy.

The wound in my shoulder protested in blazing agony and white spots flashed over my eyes as I pushed myself to my feet.

The blade embedded in the stag's eye, and he fell, thrashing wildly on the ground. The mask saved him from the extra inch of the blade that would've been his death. Too bad I'd have to waste another because he was making way too much fucking noise.

I went to draw my last blade, but my hand came up empty, and I cursed, searching the ground for it, but I saw no glint of steel on the dark mulchy ground.

278

"*Would you shut up,*" I hissed, reaching for the last resort. The blade Corvus had given me. The one I still wasn't entirely comfortable with. I guess now was as good a time as any to consecrate it unless I wanted to tear the blade from his eye and risk him screaming bloody murder before I could slit his throat.

A loud *knock* made me jump, and I spun to find the stag fucker knocked out by the boulder, his body limp and blood running down his mask. He'd thrashed so hard he knocked himself out. I resisted the manic urge to laugh, snorting instead, wondering offhandedly if my own blood loss was getting to me because that had to be the funniest shit I'd seen in a while.

Did that make me crazy?

Guess it didn't matter.

"Okay, then," I said, and before I could think too much about it, grabbed the metal arrowhead and forced it out of my shoulder with a grunt. Nausea rolled in my stomach, and I swallowed back bile, kneeling on the less sore knee to tear another strip from the hem of my tattered Prada dress.

Becca was going to kill me for ruining it.

I used the swath of overpriced fabric to tie tightly around the wound, winding it under my armpit and pulling it tight with my teeth. Not my best patch job, but it would have to do.

I hesitated before leaving the half dead stag, fingers itching to retrieve the blade sticking out of his eye. Odd, how I felt absolutely no remorse for permanently blinding him, but all the guilt in the world for leaving that blade where it was to hopefully prevent him from dying out here in the dark.

He looked young. Strong. What if he was like my guys?

He could have his reasons.

Just as I had mine.

Try not to kill them, Grey told me.

I made no promises, but this was me *trying* like he asked. Fucker better appreciate it because my shoulder hurt like a bitch, and my left hand was happy to dole out revenge.

With one last groan, I took off again, slower this time. Methodical. Focusing more on keeping quiet and hidden than covering ground. Since the latter didn't seem to be working out for me.

One blade left. I'd have to use it wisely with four more goons stalking the woods looking for me.

I followed the sound of the music upward, which seemed odd since I thought the road was the opposite way. Unless my sense of direction was just completely screwed at this point.

The trees ahead thinned out and more moonlight pushed between the trunks, making their shadows slant down over the ground like black bars in a ghostly cage.

I shivered, my mouth falling open as the view ahead opened up.

I knew exactly where I was.

Gripped with a sense of foreboding, I pushed my aching legs to move me the rest of the way up the slope to its ledge and stared out over the lake.

Moonlight kissed the rippling black water seventy feet below me, and to my right, maybe a mile as the crow flies, the Docks perched on wooden stilts over the lake. Pulsing with music and light and *life*.

So close.

So fucking far.

The sound of an arrow being notched into a bow had me dropping to the ground, crouching to find my attacker, crow handled blade lifted, pinched between my thumb and forefinger.

He stepped out of the shadows of the trees to my right, unfurling to his full height like he'd been there this whole time. Waiting. Like Diesel St. Crow knew it would come to this. Here. Right now.

"You aren't throwing," he crooned, inclining his masked head to the blade in my fingers.

"You aren't shooting," I countered, swallowing hard. "Not yet."

Nothing in my periphery. No one else was here, but they would be soon. This cliff side ran the whole way around the lake, there was nowhere else for them to go.

Diesel, moving slowly, removed his mask from his face and discarded it on the ground, taking a deep breath as though it'd been suffocating him.

"Do you know how many bodies I've buried in these woods?" he asked, lifting the crossbow in a way that told me he knew very well how to use it. Maybe almost as well as I could use a blade.

I leveled out my breathing, deciding not to play his little game of intimidation. He was either going to shoot me or he wasn't, the rest didn't matter. I needed to keep my eye trained on his trigger finger. If it so much as flinched, I'd throw.

And wouldn't it be some kind of irony if Diesel St. Crow was killed by a blade his own son put in my hands?

"I've lost count," Diesel admitted after another moment, shifting to his left a bit, making me readjust my position to counter him.

He grinned at my movements, interest piqued.

"But there's one," he continued. "Buried right there."

His gaze indicated a spot only a few feet from where I stood. "His name was Foley, and he begged for a spot on my crew. I gave him a chance, and do you want to know how he repaid me?"

"Not really."

His lips twisted into a cruel smirk. "He was going to betray us. He was going to take down my son."

Something in my stomach fluttered, and I worked to clamp it down.

"Do you want to know how he died?"

"Let me guess. Crossbow?"

Diesel shook his head. "No. When I caught Foley in these woods, I fought him man to man. No weapons. Just fists. It was personal, you see. *No one* hurts my family."

A pang in my chest at his words made my brows draw together and my grip falter for a second before I was able to recover.

"I'm not what you think I am," I said in a low whisper, meeting his stony gaze, but the words sounded like a lie even to my own ears. And Officer Vick's face flashed in my mind's eye, making my throat tight.

When he didn't say anything, and I heard the muted sounds of movement approaching, I chanced looking away from Diesel and into the trees, trying to judge how much time I had left before I was fully surrounded.

I was fucked.

Was this his plan all along? Keep me pinned here until his minions could get to us? So that he could have one of *them* kill me. For him to be able to keep his hands clean of my death?

Idiot. I should have run.

I still could if…

"*Uh, uh, uh,*" Diesel chided, seeing what I had planned in the jerky movements of my gaze. "They'll be here any second. There's only one way off this rock that might end with your survival."

282

His cold stare tracked to the water below and back.

"Why not just shoot me?" I asked, my stomach already fluttering at the prospect of the long drop. There were rocks down there, too. Big ones. And smaller ones. It would be a small miracle not to hit any of them.

He hesitated, his hands tightening on the crossbow.

He couldn't, I realized. He wouldn't risk alienating his sons for good. He could let someone else do it, though. Or he could let me jump and hope the rocks below would do the job for him.

They might forgive him for that, in time.

"Make your choice, girl," Diesel snarled, his tension rising as the others closed in. "Do it now."

I inched closer to the ledge and a piece of stone chipped off under my foot, falling down to smash into another rock protruding from the waves below.

"And if I survive?" I asked, swallowing, my blood singing with what I was about to do.

Diesel tipped his head to one side, not understanding.

"If I survive, will you stop trying to kill me? Will you give me a real shot at passing these trials?"

He frowned, considering my requests, and maybe, my chances of survival.

"Perhaps."

Fuck.

It would have to be good enough. There was no time left.

"There!" someone shouted, and I sheathed the crow blade, backed up, took three running steps, and launched myself from the edge of the cliff.

The ground vanished and my body dropped like a stone, hurtling through chilled night air, my hair flung back from my face. I tried to right myself, knowing feet first was the only way that wouldn't result in injury, but

283

at the last second, the wind shifted and I turned, flipping until I was face down, staring at rock and water and my impending death.

Rook

TWENTY-FIVE

During the last hunt trial, Foley was dead within thirty-five minutes.

I jammed the side button on my phone, displaying the time and a text message from one of my contacts in Lennox. A drug dealer who'd sold to me when all the ones in Thorn Valley were threatened away by my brothers.

Dan the Man: Sorry man, no one with that description or injuries. I'll keep my ear to the ground though. Can I get you anything? I got some real good Columbian shit. Pure.

My mouth dried at the offer, and it took me a full minute before I forced myself to delete the message without replying. Keeping the knowledge in my back pocket for if Ava Jade…

No.

It was after midnight now. She'd been gone for over two hours.

It was either a very good sign, or a very bad one.

Happy fucking birthday to me. Putting her in the ground on the day I was born would just be the cherry on the bad memory pie. I already wanted to expunge this date from existence. Wipe it from the calendar completely and pretend it was never there. I didn't think it could get any worse.

As usual though, I was wrong.

Corvus had a drink in front of him, and though he hadn't touched it, it was the closest I'd seen him come to drinking in years.

Grey was a fucking wreck, getting up to pace every few minutes, only to sit back down. I knew the feeling. The sense of being absolutely useless dug deep into the marrow of my bones. Festered there.

Corvus had been right. There was nothing we could do but wait.

Ava Jade needed to prove herself, just like all the other Saints had to. Just like *we* had to. I could hardly blame Diesel for going harder on her given her history, but I would blame him if something happened to her. If she didn't come back…

I couldn't even imagine it.

Couldn't let myself go there, or else I'd lose control.

No one would be safe until I saw that she was with my own eyes.

Another drink. Another minute of blissful numbness.

Wait. And drink. And wait some more.

I hadn't worried about her at all in the previous trials, but this was something different. She was heavily outnumbered. Likely outgunned. I had every confidence in her, but with those odds?

I wasn't even sure any of us would come out the other side alive, and we had a fuck ton more experience than her, not to mention firepower where she only had blades.

The last of the whiskey in my flask flowed down my throat, and I lit up a cigarette, the last one in the pack, and sneered. "You going to drink that or just stare at it?"

Corvus' pale blue eyes slid to me with a murderous look before he lifted the short glass from the now-semi-busted coffee table and put it to his lips.

He paused, and I snorted, until I saw why he wasn't drinking it. Something drew his eye and I followed his line of sight, searching, the shriveled black thing in my chest squeezing ever tighter.

"Ghost?"

Ava Jade stood no more than fifteen feet away, and for a second, I thought I was hallucinating her. Thought she was a phantom come back from the dead to haunt me.

Pale. She was so pale. Her long dark hair dripping wet and hanging in her face. Mascara running to her chin. A bleeding wound in her shoulder. All her weight on her left leg. Her dress in sopping wet tatters.

It was the best costume here, but it wasn't a costume at all.

I saw it in her face just before it happened and rushed from my seat, off balance from too much drink, but not even that would stop me. I caught her as she collapsed, fingers curling over the back of her skull only a second before it would've connected with the wooden planks beneath our feet.

"Ghost!" I shouted, pushing wet strands of hair away from her face. "Hey. Hey, stay with me."

A hand came down on my shoulder, and I whirled, my upper lip curling at Corvus.

"It's me," he said, and Grey was there, too, looking white as a sheet.

Corvus tried to take her from me, but I held her

287

tighter, my mind in a fog filled with flashing lights and Ghost, Ghost, Ghost.

"Okay," Grey shouted, pulling Corvus back from me so that he could step closer.

Around us, a crowd of onlookers was gathering, and I glared at them, my vision wavering so their costumed faces looked as though I was seeing them through a fun house mirror.

"We need to get her out of here," Grey was saying and I focused, blinking to clear the haze from my eyes. "Take her to the back room."

Out of here. Yes.

I lifted her to my chest, almost losing my footing until Corvus righted me. "Hurry. She's lost a lot of blood, Rook."

No. She was fine.

She would be fine.

Her wetness seeped into my clothes, drenching me in a brutal cold, nearly as cold as where my hands held her bare arms. She was too cold. She needed to be warmer.

Grey ran ahead of me, opening the door to the back room. He flipped a breaker and the music and lights behind us went dead as the heavy door shut. The partiers screamed and shouted their protest, but already their footfalls seemed to be retreating, leaving the Docks. Good.

Corvus knocked bottles and glasses from the top of the short black bar where we kept our stock, sending them shattering to the floor. The intoxicating smell of good bourbon and very good whiskey filling my lungs.

"Lay her down," Corvus ordered, and I grudgingly set her down on the damp bar.

"She's cold," I managed, coming back to myself, the influence of the whiskey still churning in my stomach, waning in the face of an injured Ghost.

288

Warm. She needed to be warm.

I threw off my leather jacket and laid it over her chest while Grey worked to untie the strip of black cloth around her shoulder. The knot came loose, revealing a water-puckered wound. Too messy to have been a bullet.

"Diesel," I growled, picturing the crossbow bolt that would've gone straight through her. In one side and out the other. Invading her flesh, corrupting her perfection.

I'd kill him.

I'd kill whoever shot her.

It didn't matter who it was.

"Rook," someone said, but their voice was so distant I couldn't be sure it wasn't just in my head.

"Rook!"

I found Corvus' blue eyes and flinched as he clutched my arms, shaking me. "Hey. Stay with us here, okay. She's okay. She's alive. She escaped."

"She passed the trial," Grey added, using his teeth to rip open a packet of gauze and jam it into the wound.

Ava Jade coughed, squirming as Grey packed her injury with the gauze, her storm-cloud eyes going wide. "*Fuck*," she croaked, just barely holding onto consciousness.

Her fingers curled into my leather jacket over her stomach, pulling it tighter to her.

"Sparrow?" Corvus shouted, going around the other side of the bar to assess her. He lifted his phone flashlight high and pulled down her eyelids, checking dilation.

She weakly batted him away, her face screwing up in a sour frown. "S-stop," she stammered, her teeth beginning to chatter.

"What happened, AJ?" Grey asked, winding a clean bandage around her wound.

She blinked, her eyes coming more into focus, and

289

focusing on me.

I went to her, and when she reached for my hand, I let her take it, holding her clammy fingers tight until some color returned to her cheeks.

"I j-jumped," she said, and Corvus and I shared a look.

"Hold on," Grey muttered, running to the couch at the other end of our small private bar area and the arsenal of guns locked up against the wall. He tore down the woven Saints banner hanging from the wall there and brought it back over, draping it over my jacket and her whole body. She shivered, giving him a grateful look.

"You jumped from where?" Corvus asked, his gaze lethally steady as he waited for her to reply.

"The c-c-cliffs. A mile from here."

"You swam a mile injured?" Grey asked, incredulous.

"A mile…" Corvus trailed off, the realization I'd just come to dawning on his face. Diesel had taken her to the same place he'd taken Foley. The Deadwood. Where we'd been burying traitors and enemies for years. Which meant…

"That's a seventy-five-foot drop. At least."

"What the hell were you thinking, Sparrow? You could have died."

Her eyes flashed with malice. "I would have died if I *didn't* j-jump."

Heat rushed up my spine and warmed my face. This had gone too far.

The trials were meant to be a challenge and more than a few had died before they could earn a space on our crew, but the trials were always fair. A challenge, made to push the one taking them to the limits of what they could survive, but *fair*. There had been five Saints with Diesel. Six in total, against one.

Even with the head start I was certain he'd have given her, where was the fairness in that?

"Who shot you?" The question passed my lips without conscious thought. "I want a name."

"*Rook*," Grey warned, and I gave a look that dared him to challenge me again.

Ghost smirked, a tiny laugh stopped by her closed mouth that turned into a cough. "The stag," she said and my brows furrowed in confusion. "But don't worry, I took one of his eyes."

It was my turn to smile now, and I gave her hands a squeeze. "Of course you did."

"D-did you guys really think I wasn't going to make it?" She coughed again, her whole body racking. "Glad to know you have s-so much faith in me."

Her gaze slid from us to survey the dimly lit room, a knot forming between her brows. "Where's Becca?

Grey dropped the empty packets he was holding and scratched an imaginary itch on the back of his head. "She *uh*…she got kinda pissed at us and took off."

Ava Jade sat bolt upright, the color draining from her face again. Her eyes went unfocused as the sudden movement made her dizzy. "Well go and *find her*," she scolded, back to her fiery self already.

Corv gave Grey a nod, and he leaned in to kiss Ava Jade on her head before leaving. "I'll be right back."

"You should lie back down," Corvus said, but Ava Jade just looked at him like he'd grown a second head.

"I'm good." She winced as she tried to move her injured arm and peered up at me through her lashes. "I'll take a drink, though."

I rounded the bar and pulled a bottle of water from the small fridge beneath, handing it to her.

"*Not* what I meant," she said with an eye roll, but took

the bottle and drank half, shivering again. "I think I drank enough lake water to be hydrated for the next year."

Corvus' knuckles turned white where he gripped the counter, but he relaxed them when he caught me looking.

He was doing a shit job of pretending he didn't care.

Grey told me he and Ava Jade had finally fucked.

It wasn't exactly the kind of news I wanted after searching for endless hours and coming up empty handed in the search for Ava Jade's stalker, but that's life.

And Corvus deserved happiness just as much as any of us. More so than I did for sure.

Ava Jade passed me the other half of her water. "Drink," she demanded. "You look like shit and smell like a distillery."

"Shall I get you a mirror?" I joked, earning myself a glare, but I took the water, knowing a level head might prevent a few deaths tonight.

The door creaked open behind us, and Grey returned, a bit breathless. "The whole place is cleared out," he said. "I don't see Becca anywhere."

"What?" Ava Jade demanded, growling as she stepped down from the bar and almost fell flat on her face, grimacing as she gripped her right knee.

"You need to sit the fuck down," Corvus growled, hopping the bar to grab her from behind, picking her up off her feet despite her protests.

"Let go!"

"No. You calm the fuck down and *sit*, and then I'll let go."

Ava Jade, too tired to fight him, slumped, defeated in his arms as he carried her to the couch and tugged his phone from his back pocket. "Here," he said and handed it to Ava Jade. "Call her."

"Already tried that," Grey said, and Corvus sent him

a scathing look.

Ava Jade dialed her friend, tensing with each ring that went unanswered. She didn't leave a voicemail, instead hanging up to switch to messenger. She thumbed out a text to her friend and then waited.

Corvus crouched to her eye-level. "We can—"

"*Shh.*"

"She probably just—"

"*Shh.*"

The phone pinged in Ava Jade's hand a second later, and she sighed as they read the message on the screen.

"She's okay," she said, typing out a less hurried message. "She's with her boyfriend."

"She has a boyfriend?" I found myself asking, doubtful. A fuck buddy maybe. Rebecca Hart didn't seem the type to be pinned down.

"Something like that," Ghost replied, finishing off the message. "He's been ignoring her for a while. I guess he finally came to his senses and realized what he had. Good thing too because I was about twenty-four hours from tracking him down and forcing an apology out of his sorry ass."

She sighed, handing the phone back to Corvus. I read Becca's reply over his shoulder before the screen went dark.

Rebecca: I was so worried. Glad youre okay. Dont worry about me, Im just with you know who. Think Im going to stay here tonight so dont wait up, okay. Xx"

My jaw clenched, the lack of punctuation reminding me of the way someone else's messages often arrived on my phone.

Just a coincidence. It had to be.

I started for the door.

"Where are you going?" Ava Jade asked, stopping

me.

"To have a chat with Diesel."

To my surprise neither of my brother's protested, but my Ghost did.

"Can we stay together?" she asked, and when I saw the uncertainty in her eyes, I couldn't say no.

"If that's what you want."

She seemed to think about that for a moment, then lifted her head and got shakily to her feet. "Take me home?"

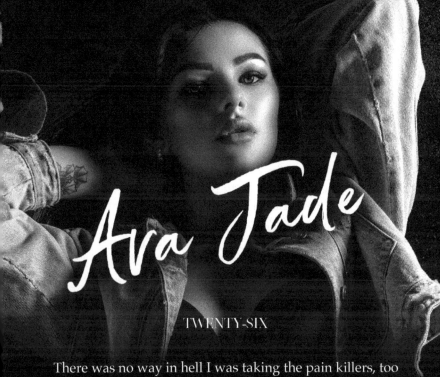

Ava Jade

TWENTY-SIX

There was no way in hell I was taking the pain killers, too afraid they'd knock me out to the point of full unconsciousness. So, sleep was just not a thing likely to happen.

Sighing, I hauled my achy ass out of bed, gingerly touching the bandage on my shoulder. The sharp edges of the stitches Rook sewed into my skin poked me through the gauze, and I winced but continued to prod the area, testing my motor ability with the new injury. My knee was feeling all right after some ice and a borrowed knee brace from Grey. But the shoulder was going to take some more time.

I could lift it until it was level with my face but no higher. At least the arrow hadn't pierced anything too important. Or at least I hoped it hadn't, only time would tell since going to the hospital was out of the question.

I flicked on the light switch and limped quietly to the

bathroom, trying not to make too much noise as I splashed cool water over my face and down my neck to staunch the feverish heat from getting any stronger. Honestly? I half expected to find Corvus in here.

Or Grey. Fuck, even Rook.

Each of them insisted I sleep with them or at least down on the couch where they could watch over me. I'd said fuck no on account of being absolutely exhausted and wanting to actually *sleep*, which I wouldn't be doing with an audience or a bed buddy. Turned out it didn't matter anyway. Sleep was a no go regardless of whether I was alone in my dark room or not.

I inched the door on the other end of the bathroom open and peered out into the dim hall, lit only by the pre-dawn filtering in through the window down at the other end.

Corvus' and Grey's doors were shut, but Rook's stood open, a draft whistling through to where I stood.

I bit my cheek, hurrying back into the loft to retrieve what I'd stolen from him a little while back. I wondered if he'd even noticed it was gone, but seeing as I found it tucked mostly behind an old photo on his dresser, I could see why he wouldn't.

Hell, it made me wonder if my brilliant idea for a gift was even a good one if he kept it hidden away. Maybe he didn't even like it.

Oh well. No going back now, and I had to return it to him eventually.

When I got back to his door, I pushed it open, poking my head inside. "Rook?" I whispered, squinting to see into the gloom as the smell that was uniquely *Rook* filled my lungs, making me smile.

"Out here," came his whispered reply, and I followed his voice to the open window next to his bed, the dark

296

curtain billowing inward in the breeze.

The dark shape of him sat outside on the roof, a blanket loosely pulled around his shoulders.

"Couldn't sleep?" he asked as I crawled through the window to join him, the chill of the early morning air brushing over the bare skin on my arms and legs.

"No. You?"

He shook his head and lifted one side of the blanket, holding it open for me.

A muscle in my jaw ticked, but the hesitation only lasted a second before I curled up beside him, letting him drape the large furry blanket over my shoulders. His body heat enveloped me as I tugged the blanket around myself, huddling in closer to his side.

His fingers wrapped around the dip above my hip bone, tugging me against him with a small grunt. "You're freezing."

"It's cold out here."

"Nice though, isn't it?"

I couldn't disagree. It was nice. The fog that'd been clinging to my brain while lying in the stuffy loft had been blown away, replaced by a clarity only gained by inhaling clean, crisp air.

It seemed to have affected Rook in the same way. Though he was still tense, this was the calmest I'd seen him in days. Maybe even a week.

I wondered if the clean air was the only culprit or if something else had contributed.

We didn't speak for a while, content to sit there, staring at the slowly brightening sky in each other's warmth and company, but I'd come out here for a reason.

"So, um…"

"Hmm?" Rook said, coming out of whatever thought had taken him. He turned to me, his dark eyes searching

297

my face.

"I'm not going to say it because Corvus sort of told me you don't like to celebrate."

His brows drew together.

Maybe this was a huge mistake.

"Everyone always forgot my birthday growing up. I mean, I didn't care that much because when they did remember all I got was a gas station muffin with a lit match as a candle but...I guess I just thought maybe—"

"What did you do, Ghost?"

I licked my suddenly very dry lips and reached into my Panama pants pocket, a slithering sensation of unease crawling through my gut.

"I found it in your room," I explained as I tugged his hand close to me beneath the blanket and peeled back his fingers. "It was broken, and I thought it might mean something to you so I...well I sort of gave it to this girl in my English Lit class whose dad owns a jewelry shop in town, and he fixed it."

I placed the necklace into his palm and felt him jerk at the feel of it, his expression darkening.

Shit.

He didn't speak for the longest moment, holding the necklace beneath the blanket while he stared off into the shadows of the trees across the drive.

"Fuck, I'm sorry," I spluttered, heat growing in my cheeks and the tops of my ears. "I don't even know what I was thinking. I should've just left it like Corvus said and—"

His wide hand closed over my mouth, muffling my next word. "Stop talking," he said, a strain in his voice as he slowly turned his attention back to me and dropped his side of the blanket to look down into his palm.

His warm hand came away from my face, and I stared

down at the necklace, too. It looked so small in his large hand. So delicate.

The black diamond caught the pink light of the rising sun, and the brand-new clasp that the jeweler had to have custom made glinted like it was made of pure starlight on the thin white gold chain.

That, too, had been broken. Bent and twisted as though it'd been snatched off the neck of whoever had been wearing it.

I was dying to ask, but it was clear I'd already overstepped my bounds so I just waited instead, hoping he wouldn't be too pissed that I'd touched it.

"It was my mother's," he said finally, just when the silence was starting to get too heavy to withstand.

"What happened to her?" I asked before I could stop myself, then added quickly. "You don't have to answer that if you don't want to."

His lips quirked up slightly, making the tension behind my breastbone ease enough to breathe.

"She died," he explained in a rough voice. "Childbirth."

My stomach twisted.

"She was going to be famous, you know? Julia Clayton. The rising star; that's what they called her."

"Is she the woman in the photograph?"

He nodded, and I remembered the black-haired beauty from the picture frame on his dresser. I'd honestly thought it was whatever had come stock with the frame. The woman in the photo too beautiful to not have been retouched and edited to within an inch of her life.

But it made sense, if Rook was her son. Beautiful, lethal, Rook.

"I'm sorry," I whispered. "Is that how you ended up at Barrettes Home for Boys?"

Something in his gaze shifted and his hand curled back around the necklace until his knuckles turned white.

"You've done some digging."

I shrugged. "And you haven't?"

"Me? No. But I can't say the same of my brothers."

I waited.

"Yes," he said on a breath. "But I didn't wind up there right away. I was put into the care of my aunt for years before that. She never missed an opportunity to remind me that I ruined her sister. That she died so a little shit like me could live. She didn't bat an eye when her boyfriend took out his very particular brand of violence on me. I think part of her wanted him to do it. To punish me for taking my mother from this world."

"He's the one who gave you these?" I gingerly brushed a finger over the scars on his arm, the ones hidden by all the ink covering his skin.

His upper lip curled and my inner fire burned hot, wanting retribution on his behalf. To scar the fucker in all the exact same places and in all the exact same ways as he'd scarred Rook before killing him slow.

"I thought I deserved it."

"It wasn't your fault she died."

"I know. I didn't back then, but I do now. I found this journal she wrote in just before my aunt finally had enough of my shit and sent me away to the group home. Everyone was telling her that having me would destroy her career. That she should abort me and never tell the father. She didn't ever tell him, because apparently he was a fucking monster, but wrote that she did want me. She wanted me more than she ever wanted anything else in her life."

"She sounds like an incredible woman."

He smiled a sad smile. "I like to imagine she was. I

300

don't know what would've happened if I hadn't found that journal, but soon after I went to Barrettes home for Boys, I met Grey. And not long after that, I went back to my aunt's house on Sycamore Street and burned it down. With my uncle inside."

"Good."

His eyes met mine and something unspoken passed between us before he shifted, turning slightly to face me. Rook lifted the necklace between us, his face growing hard. "Will you wear it?"

My stomach flipped and my lips popped open in surprise, but he said nothing else, only waited for my response as the first rays of morning sun broke over the horizon, painting him in brilliant gold.

Everyone thought he was the devil, but I could see it now. In just the right light, he wasn't a devil at all but an angel of justice. My dark prince.

Wordlessly, I turned, using my good arm to push all my hair out of the way, holding it up off my neck.

His hands brushed my collar, making me tremble as he draped the dainty chain around my throat, the black diamond weighing heavily in the dip of my clavicle.

Once he finished with the clasp, he brushed his thumb over the chain against the back of my neck, guiding me back to facing him.

His cheekbones flared as he took me in, in the dawn light, eyes passing between the necklace and my face. He smiled.

"It suits you."

I touched the stone with my fingertips, a sense of belonging taking me so strongly that it hurt. Mixing with a heavy guilt so crushing that it took all the breath from my body.

In less than twenty-four hours I was going to meet

with Officer Vick. And thanks to Diesel's admissions in the Deadwood, I actually had something I could give him. If Diesel killed Foley with his bare hands and buried him at the edge of that cliff, his DNA would be all over the body. I could take him down. I could take them all down.

But when I looked into Rook's eyes…

His trusting, bleeding heart eyes.

How in the world could I ever betray him?

How could I ever betray *them*?

Was it worth my freedom?

Did I even want to be free anymore?

Rook lifted a hand to trace the line of my cheekbone, pushing my hair back behind my ear in a move so gentle it sent shivers all the way to my toes.

"What is it?"

I schooled my face, blinking away what was definitely not fucking tears.

"I don't deserve this."

Amusement crossed his eyes, making them slant playfully as he leaned in to whisper against my lips. "You belong to us, Ghost. And we belong to you."

Corvus

TWENTY-SEVEN

The knock came at the door only a few hours after dawn. The distinct three rap cadence of it giving away who was on the other side, making my irritability skyrocket.

I set down the whisk and wiped flour coated fingers on my jeans. The sky might've been falling down around us, but I'd never skipped a birthday. Rook would have his cake, and he would fucking enjoy it. Ava Jade would enjoy it, too. She deserved it after that bullshit last night.

The door banged noisily into the wall when I ripped it open, finding Diesel standing a few feet away, peering up toward the octagonal window to the loft above the garage. Heat bloomed over the back of my neck, but I reined it in. I had no doubts that he knew she was staying here, but I didn't like the look on his face.

"What are you doing here?" I asked, unable to keep all the accusation out of my tone.

Diesel lowered his gaze to mine, hurt pinching at the

bridge of his nose.

"I came to return the girl's things to her," he replied, handing me two clean blades and her cell phone.

"Where's the other one?" I asked, knowing she was missing all three of her blades. She was going to be pissed if another one was gone for good.

Diesel shrugged, indicating the blade in my left hand. "I pulled that one out of Galen's eye."

So it was Galen who shot her.

"And that one out of Dimitri's stomach."

"She said you didn't give her any ground rules," I reminded him, my teeth on edge.

"A mistake I won't make a second time. I underestimated her."

A flutter of pride had me lifting my chin. I'd underestimated her once or twice, myself. I wouldn't make that mistake again, either.

Diesel's gaze tracked back to the window above the garage and my jaw tightened. "She's sleeping," I told him. "And I won't wake her."

He lifted a hand to wave me off. "I didn't come to speak to her. I came to speak to you."

"About?"

He jerked his head toward the drive behind him, where his car was parked up next to the Rover. I set Ava Jade's things down inside and followed Diesel out, words I wanted to sling at him battering at the closed barrier of my lips.

When we were clear of the Nest, he stopped, leaning against the back of the Rover, and before he could speak, some of what I wanted to say came rushing out.

"What was that bullshit last night?"

Surprise lit up his eyes, followed by the lowering of his brows.

"Six?" I pressed when he didn't answer. "*Six* men with crossbows against just her."

I jabbed two fingers into the air, pointing to where she lay now, safe in our Nest. A part of me wished I could keep her there, bar her in and guarantee her safety forever.

"She survived, didn't she?"

My fists clenched.

"The trials are meant to be fair," I ground out. "To test loyalty and strength and wits. That was a fucking massacre that Ava Jade somehow managed to escape and you damn well know it."

Some of the rage Diesel kept tampered down tight came surging to the surface, and my own fury fought to be set free at the sight of it. If he could lose control, then so could I.

"So she didn't tell you I had the jump on her, then?" he asked, his voice like a whip, cracking against my defenses. "I could've killed her. It would've been a fair death. Just her and me at the edge of that cliff."

I heard what he was saying without the need for him to speak, piecing it together in my mind.

…he let her jump instead, leaving her death up to fate.

It didn't absolve him from this, but it softened some of the blow.

He left out the part that if they faced off on the edge of that cliff, Ava Jade could just as easily have ended him with a toss of her blade. And she didn't.

There was restraint on both sides.

"I didn't come here to argue about a trial I had every right to put her through as the leader of our crew," he hissed, running his teeth over his lower lips. "I came to warn you."

I started, my beast roaring *what now* in a way that made my rib cage rattle.

305

"About?"

His gaze dropped to the ground, where he dug the toe of his boot into the gravel and worked his jaw. "It's going to get ugly," he said after a minute. "I know you don't agree with me, Son, but it's my job as your father to look out for you."

My stomach twisted.

"You don't want to hear this, but I'm going to say it anyway," he continued, this time looking me dead in the eye. "She isn't who you think she is." How the fuck would he know who she is? He hadn't even tried to get to know her, and he would only know the same things I did from looking into her past There wasn't much to find. Unless he found something I hadn't? Or knew something I didn't? But if that were the case, why wasn't he sharing with the motherfucking class?

"Don't say anything." Diesel cut me off before I could say a word. "Just listen. She's fooling you. She's a liar and a con artist and you, my son, all of my sons, are her long game."

"You don't know what you're saying," I argued, my nostrils flaring as the fury worked its way to a head, filling mine with steam.

Ava Jade wouldn't...

My Sparrow *wouldn't.*

He was wrong about her. He would see that eventually, but I couldn't let him kill her in the process.

"I'm going to show you who she really is," he promised.

"How many more trials do you have planned right now?"

He was caught off guard by the question but answered honestly. "One, though there are several others I'd been consider—"

"No," I cut him off. "*One.* You can have your one, but no more. If she passes it, that's it. It's over. You accept her as a Saint and make her one of us."

His upper lip twitched, but I could tell he was considering my not-so-subtle request. He knew that shit in the Deadwood last night was pushing it to the limits of what would be considered a fair test of skill. By the look on his face, he was willing to negotiate if it meant peace between us. As a way of admitting his mistake *without* actually admitting it.

"And *when* she fails?"

A chill wormed its way into my belly, reaching icy fingers up to squeeze my lungs and crust over the thing beating behind my rib cage. "*If* she fails...if she truly is what you say she is, then we'll deal with her ourselves."

Diesel's expression evened out, and he sighed, placated by my response. He closed the gap between us to place a hand on my shoulder, squeezing in a way that told me he was sorry without the need for words. "All right, Son. All right. One trial and no more."

"When?" I asked as his hand slid from my shoulder. "She's injured. She needs time to heal."

Diesel nodded solemnly. "I make no promises."

Ava Jade

TWENTY-EIGHT

I checked my phone for the fifth time since I texted Becca two hours ago, finding only another passive aggressive text from Aunt Humphrey.

Female Hitler: I finally got to speak to several of your instructors this past week. It seems all your grades are well above average, however that doesn't excuse your lack of attendance.

Her way of apologizing?

Another message came through before I sent it back down.

Female Hitler: Also, dinner will be at 7 o'clock sharp at the manor for Thanksgiving. If you're bringing anyone along, please let me know in advance so I can make the appropriate arrangements.

Um, yeah…hard fucking pass.

"Anything yet?" I jumped out of my seat at the desk and winced as the torn ligament in my knee stretched too far.

"*Fucking shit fuck,*" I cursed, bending to rub the ache out of it.

"Sorry," Grey said, raising his hands in apology. "Didn't mean to scare you."

I sighed heavily, falling back into the chair at the desk and shoving my history notes out of the way so I could rest my arm there instead. "No. I haven't. She hasn't texted me back at all, and she won't answer my calls."

Grey's frown deepened. "Are you worried?"

I shrugged. "A bit? I don't know. She's always slow to text me back when she's with him, but not like this."

"Yeah, she doesn't usually spend the night," Grey mused aloud, and he was right. Becca always wandered back into the apartment at Briar Hall sometime in the early hours of the morning. She was never gone this long.

I shifted my notes around on the desk, stacking them into a neat pile atop my textbook, officially done with studying for the test this week. I doubted anything was sticking in my head right now anyway.

I'd overheard Diesel outside with Corvus this morning. I didn't catch everything, but I did catch something about things getting ugly and one trial. Hopefully, that meant there was only one left. I couldn't decide if that was a good thing or a bad thing, since Diesel St. Crow seemed set on me not surviving to the end.

"Hey," Grey hedged, coming into the loft. "If she isn't back for class tomorrow morning, then we'll go and look for her, 'kay?"

I wasn't sure how we'd find her since I had absolutely no fucking clue where she went when she drove off to meet her—

That was it! However she'd gone to meet her guy friend last night at the docks, it wasn't with her car. That was still parked in the school lot. I'd walked there with Rook earlier to check, and to stretch out the shit that was all twisted up in my knee.

"Do you think the GPS in her car has passive tracking? Like, to see previous routes?"

The corner of Grey's mouth lifted. "Yeah. I think it probably would. Just have to hack in, and lucky for you…" He rubbed his knuckles over his chest, smug as fuck. "You happen to be sharing a house with someone who knows how."

I smiled back. "Thanks, Grey."

His gaze softened and some of that smugness faded, transitioning to something harder to name. He cleared his throat. "Can I, *uh,* get you anything? How's the shoulder? We should probably redress it."

I shook my head. "Already done. And it's good."

I rolled it to show him, unable to conceal all the discomfort from my face, but somehow, mercifully, the arrow hadn't hit anything important. So, while it hurt like the devil's asshole, it would be just fine.

"Right. Good. That's good."

He was stalling, and for half a minute I considered asking him to stay. I'd been isolating myself from them since the Primal Ethos show, and I knew they were all uncertain about what the shift meant. Hell, so was I, but it didn't change things. Even if Rook and I had a moment last night. Even if a part of me wanted to rip every bit of Grey's dark tracksuit to shreds and fuck him until I couldn't breathe. And even if I couldn't stop remembering the feeling of absolute freedom that'd come with letting myself *feel* something other than hate for Corvus.

A shred of doubt nagged at the back of my skull.

This wasn't what I came here for. I came here for a fresh start. A chance at a new life free of violence. Free of

311

gangs and guns and *hate*.

Each day that image of what I wanted when I set foot in Thorn Valley has shifted. Every day spent with the Crows has been another bar welded onto a cage that I might never escape from if I'm not careful.

And that cage would trap me in the life I swore I was leaving behind when I took my Aunt up on her offer.

I didn't know what the fuck I wanted anymore, and that was a terrifying thought. But one I needed to figure out before it was too late.

"Thanks," I muttered, but still he hesitated. Wanting to say something more? Wanting to feel useful? It was hard to tell, but I knew they all partially blamed themselves for the Hunt. For letting it happen even though they didn't have a choice. Or, at least, that's what I was trying to believe.

"Maybe, if you don't mind, I'll take another piece of Rook's cake?" I said with a shrug, and his eyes lit up.

"Yeah," he said in a relieved sigh. "I can do that. Be right back. I'll make you some tea. I have this Rooibos blend that'll be really good with the cake. Might help you sleep, too."

He was gone before I could say anything. Like, what the actual fuck is Rooibos? I didn't peg him as an herbal tea kind of guy, and the new information made a small laugh escape my lips as I shook my head. I could use the sleep aid, though. It was already half past ten and I wasn't even remotely tired yet. Probably something to do with my three-hour morning power nap in Rook's bed. With Rook.

I hadn't planned to fall asleep there. I'd just wanted to sit with him a little longer after the blinding sun got to be too bright for our overtired eyes. Next thing I knew, I was drooling on his pillow, not for the first time.

I slumped in my chair, but sat bolt upright again as my phone buzzed violently with a new message. Becca's name flashed over the screen.

About fucking time.

Lifting my cell, I saw that it wasn't a message at all, but a video. I unlocked it and hit play and felt my whole fucking world crumble around me.

Becca screamed through the silvery tape covering her mouth, her black eye makeup running four inches down her face. Cords of metal chains hung in heavy circles around her slender neck, the skin beneath red from her struggling.

The clip was only four seconds long, and played again when it ended, starting a loop of horror.

I jumped to my feet, rushing to the bathroom to scream for the guys when another message came in, this time, a text. Making my racing pulse stop dead in my chest.

Becca: She's at the warehouse in no man's land. Come alone. Your trial begins now. You have thirty minutes. D.

What?

I replayed the horrific video of Becca, my hands shaking, stomach in knots.

There was a red glow over her right shoulder. I paused the video. It was blurry, but clear what it was. A timer. The red numbers 29:32 telling me the countdown had already started.

The chains around her neck...

He wouldn't.

But the guys' words echoed clearly in my mind, and I had to clutch the edge of the desk to keep myself from passing out at the wave of adrenaline going straight to my head.

Anyone or anything is fair game.

313

Come alone.

I couldn't even remember getting my blades strapped on, or putting on my shoes, but suddenly the keys to the Rover were in my hand and I was sneaking out the garage door, rolling beneath the seven-inch gap to keep from making too much noise. At least until it was too late for them to stop me.

"AJ," I heard Grey call out from upstairs in the loft just as I got to my feet.

Fuck.

The Rover chirped when I unlocked the door and got inside, and I saw Grey's face in the octagonal window as I started the ignition. His mouth opened wide as he shouted something I couldn't hear. Something not meant for my ears.

But I was already gone, peeling out of the gravel drive and bumping down the road, the Nest flickering to nothingness in the red glow of my tail lights in the rearview mirror.

Becca.

Of course Diesel would use the one friend I had here against me.

She was never going to want to see me again after this. She'd run for the fucking hills without looking back. Would she blame me? Hate me?

My stomach soured, and I groaned as the choppy pavement switched to clean smooth blacktop with a hard bump in the road.

If Diesel hurt her…

All bets were off.

I'd promised to *try* to not kill any Saints during the trials, but I'd have his fucking head if she died. And the heads of any others involved.

The minutes slashed away as I drove, barreling down

314

side roads until I got to the edge of town, to the border of no man's land. They kept falling until ten were already gone. Then fifteen. Hedging on twenty even as I pushed the Rover to the breaking point of how fast she could go, nearly losing control more than once as the uneven pavement leading down to the old industrial area tried to slow me with potholes and scattered debris.

The tires screeched, and the throat clogging stench of burning rubber filled my nose as the Rover slid to a standstill, knocking against a cement barrier. The glass of the passenger window shattered, raining down over the seat and my lap as I shoved the door open and raced out into the night, making a beeline for the warehouse.

My peripheral sight expanded all around, tracking movement as I slipped a blade between my first two fingers, holding it loosely at my side.

I lowered myself to a crouch, skirting the edge of the warehouse, listening carefully as I neared the open bay doors at the front.

A soft whimper inside twisted my insides, and I grimaced, lifting the blade to throw as I stepped out of the shadows and into the gaping doorway of the abandoned warehouse, my mouth falling open.

Becca thrashed when she saw me, the tape covering her mouth muffling a fearful shout as her eyes widened.

A mechanical whir sounded from outside and a spotlight flared to life, blinding Becca, painting her in a halo of white.

She stood atop a rickety old pallet pack over twenty feet up at the other end of the warehouse. The metal chains around her neck were attached to a rusted metal pulley hanging from the rafters above. The other end of the chain reached down toward the ground where I assumed it was tied off, but I couldn't see where for all the walls and debris blocking my view across the space.

It didn't look the same as it had that night all those weeks ago.

There were stacks of tires and old pallets and crumbling partition walls like before, but they were moved. The low piles of dirt and loose stone on the cement floor in lines across the room gave it away.

It was a course, I realized.

Diesel had put together an obstacle course, and I needed to get through it to the other side in time to save Becca.

Shifting movement inside the maze gave away at least one Saint's position inside. Looking up, I saw Becca eagerly staring down into the maze and back at me, giving me his position somewhere close by on the left.

A chirp had me jerking my gaze upward, to the red numbers on the timer near Becca's head ticking down.

I had a little under ten minutes to get through it, but this time, I wasn't going to hold back.

A blinking red light drew my eye, and I found myself staring into the lens of a surveillance camera placed high in the far left corner of the warehouse.

Becca moaned and growled against the tape covering her mouth, and then sharply, she breathed in deep as the tape came loose, pried off with her tongue. One side fell from her lips, and she sobbed.

"It's okay, Becks," I told her. "I'm going to get you out of—"

"I'm sorry," she cried, the tears dropping from her cheeks catching the spotlight like falling stars. "I'm so, so sorry, Aves."

What?

What could she possibly have to be sorry for? This was my fault. If I hadn't made friends with her—if I hadn't

316

brought her into this—she wouldn't be here right now.

She was here because I cared about her and Diesel wanted to use that against me. To see how far I was willing to go for someone whose life mattered to me.

He was about to fucking find out.

"Just hold on, Becks!" I called, keeping low as I darted forward, ready with a blade to throw at the Saint waiting just inside the row of tires to my left. A sharp snare snapped around my ankle, slicing into skin as the crude trap dragged me upward. My head smashing against the concrete as I was hoisted high into the air upside down. My fucked-up knee protesting the pull of the thin rope.

Dark spots crowded my vision, and I worked furiously to blink them away, my head throbbing.

I groaned, seeing the attacker coming just a second before it would've been too late. He charged forward from his hiding place, upside down, a knife raised high in his black gloved hand.

Blades against blades this time. Diesel was trying to be fair.

I threw my blade and it sank into his heart, sending him staggering back with a grunt.

Except, it didn't strike his heart at all.

The Saint lifted his head with a grin spreading wide over his lips, gripping the handle of my blade to tear it out of the bullet proof vest.

Motherfucker.

I reached for another, the move also saving me from my own blade as it was hurled back at me to *thunk* into a pallet wall six feet to my rear, deeper into the maze.

This time, my aim was lower, and the blade found a home in the meaty flesh of his inner thigh. I heaved my body upward, climbing the length of my leg to reach the blade at my ankle. Unsheathing it and cutting the trip wire

317

holding me up in one fluid movement.

The air gushed from my lungs as I hit the cement floor, and I croaked even as I rolled, getting to my feet. I stormed forward, gasping as the Saint worked feverishly to staunch the flow of blood around the blade protruding from his thigh.

His eyes widened, flashing with terror in the ambient glow of the spotlight.

"Yield!" he hissed through clenched teeth, backing away from me. He released the pressure on the wound gushing his life's blood over the cement to tug another two knives from his belt and toss them to the floor. "*Yield*," he repeated as he knelt, lowering his head.

The muscles in my face twitched as I struggled to get air into my lungs, my left hand tightening around the handle of my blade as the darkness roared within, beckoning me.

Kill.

"Please," he muttered, and I growled as I rushed the last four steps to him, reeling back to kick him in the head, sending him off to dreamland. I grabbed his off-balance blades from the ground and threw them high, embedding them in some wood shelving twenty feet off the ground where no one would be able to use them. They would be no good to me. I wanted *my* blade back.

I tore it from the fucker's leg, unwilling to permanently part with another of my babies. He could bleed out for all I cared.

"*Yeah*," Becca said, but her voice boomed all around me, and I looked up to find her on her hanging block, head bowed as she sobbed. "*One of them is staying with her tonight at Briar Hall.*"

A recording. I searched and found the speakers placed high on other pallet racks around the warehouse.

318

"Which one?" A male voice asked, and a shiver rolled down my spine, making my toes curl.

"Grey."

"And the others?"

"I don't know."

"Think you could find out for me, baby?"

What…

What the fuck was this?

The tape skipped and a new recording played.

"They went out of town for something," Becca said in the recording, while my best friend sniffled across the warehouse, unable to look at me.

"For what?" the man asked.

"I don't know. She just said they would be back later."

"Do you know when?"

A pause.

"I could text her to find out."

My stomach soured, and I held back the violent urge to vomit, heat searing across my chest.

I remembered the timer, and I looked up to find I had less than six minutes now. I started forward again, pulling my other blade from the pallet board and tucking it away so I held just one in each hand.

Whatever Diesel thought she'd done, he was wrong.

He had to be wrong.

She was telling someone things about me and the guys, but so what? It probably wasn't what it sounded like. Or if it was, then she…she was being manipulated. Maybe even blackmailed. Maybe…

The recording started again, and I paused, my lungs wringing themselves of air in my chest.

"Listen, baby," the male voice said. *"You know they're monsters. Killers. They killed one of our men just last week. Diesel put a bullet between his eyes."*

My mouth fell open as it all began to fall into place in my mind, the jagged pieces fitting perfectly together where I wished they wouldn't.

Becca was dating an Ace. That was why she was so secretive about him. It wasn't because it was a teacher or an older guy or any of the taboo things I might've assumed. It was because he wasn't allowed in Thorn Valley. And if the guys had found out she was with someone from a rival gang, her life at Briar Hall would've been over.

The sound of something shifting on the recording alluded to movement I had to assume was Becca.

"If my crew takes Thorn Valley, it'll be safer, you'll see. And if the Saints were gone, your Dad could finally come back. If Diesel isn't here to keep buying up all the vacant properties, he'd have no reason to keep buying further south."

"I just..." Becca trailed off. *"I just don't see how feeding you information on my friend is going to help you do all that."*

A condescending laugh from the Ace. *"Don't you see? She's one of them now. The Crows are Diesel's best weapons. Take them out and he's just an old man with a gun."*

No. No, Becca, why?

"I don't—"

"Listen to me!" the Ace thundered and something banged loudly, crumbling as Becca gasped on the tape, making my skin crawl.

"You're scaring me!"

Heavy breathing. *"I'm sorry. I'm sorry, baby. I don't want to scare you. I just need you to listen to me."*

"But they aren't like you think. They're good guys. Ava Jade is my friend."

"You're so naive. You have no idea what the world is really like. You know the Saints are the reason your mother died. What more incentive do you need?"

320

Another pause. So long I thought the tape had ended, but then Becca spoke again, a resolve in her tone that hadn't been there before.

"If I help you," the recording said, making my blood chill in my veins. *"Will you promise to leave Ava Jade out of it?"*

Becca cried harder, her sobs echoing around the warehouse, but this time, I couldn't bring myself to feel empathy for her pain.

"All right. Fine. Now, tell me about the trials. And I want to know where they are at all times. Can you do that for me?"

"I…"

"This is for us. So we can be together. Isn't that what you want? Don't you trust me?"

Oh god. The betrayal stung more than I could've thought possible and my eyes burned with hot, angry tears.

"Yes."

"I didn't do it!" Becca said through her sobs, shouting from the top of the pallet rack. "I couldn't. I saw how you were with them. How they were with you and I…I couldn't. *I hate the Saints.* I hate that if it weren't for them my mom would still be alive, but I wouldn't do that to you! You have to believe me!"

But he *ghosted* you, I thought to myself.

This Ace, whoever he was, he'd cut Becca off. Stopped texting her. Stopped seeing her.

If he hadn't ghosted her, would she have told him the things he wanted to know? Would Becca have caused the deaths of my Crows?

"When he texted me from that unknown number," she said between sobs. "I mean, when *Diesel* texted me pretending to be him wanting to meet up, I was going to end it for good, Aves."

I forced myself to look at her, my chest a hollowed-out shell filled with dark, but she brought the light.

There was no lie on her face. She'd fucked up. She'd made a mistake. She fell in with the wrong guy. Becca was smart, but even the smartest women could be fooled by the vilest of men.

A miasmal sense of foreboding wrenched the air as I wondered what exactly Diesel and the Saints would do with this new information. An Ace was trying to infiltrate Thorn Valley, gather privileged information, and take them all out. Diesel had been right not to trust the Aces. They were working against him in secret all this time. This was how gang wars started.

Wars that almost always resulted in innocent casualties. Likely what happened to Becca's mom.

And I remembered.

I remembered why *I hated the Saints*. Why I hated all gangs.

They'd taken Becca's mother.

They'd also taken my father.

Would I not have done the same thing if I were in her shoes? Did I not promise myself that I would return to Lennox and collect on the blood debt owed for my father's life?

And then it clicked.

This trial was never *if* I could save Becca.

It was whether I *would* save her.

Which meant I'd already failed.

The timer began to beep as the countdown rolled to 59 seconds and Becca started crying anew, her whole body shaking.

"Oh god," she croaked through the tears.

"Call them out!" I shouted to her, racing around the pallets. "Becca!"

A gasp, and then she screamed, "On your right!" and I went skidding to my knees, throwing a blade for the Saint's neck. It sliced across the side of his neck as he dodged the throw, sending a spurt of blood cascading in an arc over the floor. He immediately went to his knees, choking as he tried to splutter a *yield* from his lips.

There was no time to disarm him or make sure he didn't get back up so I moved on, the crow handled blade and my blade at the ready in each hand.

I rounded a tower of tires and Becca screamed, "Watch out!"

I ducked just in time to miss an axe coming straight for my head, using the Saint's momentum against him to drive an elbow down into the back of his neck, hearing the satisfying *crack!* of bone as he went down. Went still.

"Hold on, Becks!" I called as she worked furiously to get her hands free from the binds keeping them tied behind her back.

The timer read twenty-seven seconds and my throat closed as I sprinted through the last of the maze, every muscle in my body burning. The wound in my shoulder and the tear in my knee begging me to stop, but I didn't dare.

I rounded the last wall of pallets and lifted my blade, not hesitating this time when Diesel came into my field of vision. He threw an ax, but I dodged it, rolling and up again before he could reach for an alternate weapon. I tossed a blade and it found a snug home in his Achilles, sending him to his knees with a look of utter shock on his face.

He reached behind himself for the gun my fingers were already on. I tugged it from the back of his jeans and aimed it at his head.

"She betrayed you!" he hissed just as the buzzer

sounded and two men, no more than shadows outside of the spotlight's reach, pushed against the base of the pallet rack, trying to knock it from beneath Becca's feet.

She screamed, and I fired two shots at the shadows. I didn't think either hit, I was a shit shot, but the deafening sounds were enough to stop them.

"Touch that fucking rack again and I'll kill him," I hissed, aiming the gun lower, level with Diesel's head.

"Boss?" one of them called.

"It's all right, lads," Diesel called in reply, his voice strained as his blood pooled around his ankle on the cement floor.

I found where the chain was connected to a metal beam against the wall and edged toward it, keeping one eye and the gun on Diesel while I freed the chain.

"Becca," I called. "Can you climb down?"

"My hands!" she cried, a hitch in her voice.

"It's just zip ties," I said, assuming they used the same thing they used to bind my hands for the hunt trial. "Pull your wrists apart to put tension on them and then reach your arms back as far as you can."

"Okay."

"Okay now as hard and fast as you can, pull in toward your body and apart. It'll hurt, but it should break them apart."

She grunted. "It didn't work!"

"It's okay, babe. Try again. You got this."

Two more grunts, and I heard the satisfying *snap* of the plastic.

"I did it!"

"I knew you could. Now just climb down."

"You're making a mistake," Diesel said, seemingly unfazed by this entire ordeal. He just kneeled there, grim, and angry on the cement floor, eyeing me.

I gritted my teeth, so angry I wanted to beat him to death with his own fucking gun. "No." I seethed. "*You* made a mistake. She's an innocent girl whose mother you stole. She was played. Manipulated. And tonight she almost died because of you."

"She was feeding an Ace intel on my *sons*."

"So, what? You thought, hey, two birds one stone? Your men could've swarmed me all at once but they didn't. You *wanted* me to save her, so that I would fail the trial. So that you could turn around and kill us both."

He didn't deny it and that only made me even angrier.

But even I wasn't stupid enough to think that I could kill Diesel St. Crow and get away with it. If I shot him, his men would shoot me. They'd kill Becca, too. I needed to get us out of here. *Now.*

The pallet rack squeaked and trembled as Becca made her way slowly down, holding onto the rusted metal for dear life until she was back on solid ground. She sighed when her feet connected with the concrete, but when she saw the Saints on the other side of the rack, she squealed and raced to my side, putting herself behind me.

"I really wasn't going to tell him anything," Becca said to Diesel. "I swear I wasn't. I was just—"

"You don't have to explain yourself to him," I snapped, cutting off whatever Becca had been about to say next. "You owe him nothing."

She fell quiet, and I saw her chin quiver in my periphery as she held back the urge to cry. "I'm sorry," she whispered. "This is all my fault. I should've told you about him from the very start."

As if she was blaming herself right now. She and I were going to have a good long chat, just as soon as I got her out of here. "Come on, Becca. We're leaving."

I glanced toward the two goons still waiting in the shadows. "And if *anyone* tries to follow us, I *will* kill them."

We backed out through the rear exit, and I kept Becca tight to my side as we made our way to the front. To the Rover I hoped would still fucking start after what I'd put it through.

"Stay close to me," I reminded Becca, and she rushed to keep up as we stepped onto the road. Headlights flared on the road and the roar of an engine had me picking up the pace, grabbing Becca around the wrist with my blade hand.

She winced when I accidentally nicked her but she didn't pull away, letting me guide her to the Rover. "Get in!"

"AJ!"

I whirled, stopping with my hand on the door handle as the car skidded to a halt and the three of them jumped out.

"Sparrow, are you hurt?" Corvus demanded, rushing to close the gap between us while Rook fed a magazine into his gun and cocked it back, eyeing the warehouse like he dared someone to come out of it.

"We saw what happened," Grey rushed to say, his gaze sliding to where Becca was hesitating to get into the back seat of the Rover. His jaw clenched.

The surveillance camera. Diesel had sent them the live feed. And by the way they were looking at Becca...

I aimed the gun at Corvus, making him slow his forward trajectory. His brows drew together as he finally stopped.

"AJ, what are you doing?" Grey asked, stopping too, while Rook continued to watch my six, his gaze jerking warily between my gun and the warehouse at our backs.

"Get back in the car and go," I hissed.

326

"Sparrow…"

"No." I shook my head. "Tonight I'm not your fucking Sparrow, Corvus James. I'm the girl who almost watched her best friend *die*. Because of you. Because of all of you. Saints. *Ha!* Fucking sadists."

"We can work this out," Grey said, inching closer.

"Don't."

I shot the ground barely a foot from Corvus' boot, but none of them even flinched. They all watched with unconcealed hurt and horror at what they were seeing, but I couldn't make myself stop.

They weren't saying Diesel was wrong. They weren't apologizing. They wanted to *work it out*. Work it out *how*?

I didn't want to find out.

"If you aren't going to leave, then get the fuck out of my way."

Corvus met my gaze and something inside me broke, twisting and shattering until drawing my next breath felt almost impossible.

"Ghost?" Rook asked, his gun lowering now, and I couldn't bear to look at him, because I'd already decided what I needed to do next. "This isn't right. Let me come with you."

The necklace still clasped around my throat weighed heavily against my breastbone, making it even harder to get air into my lungs. But as much as I knew I should, I couldn't bring myself to remove it. Not yet. "I can't do that, Rook."

"Just wait," Grey all but begged. "Let us talk to Diesel. Maybe…maybe this is all a misunderstanding. We can fix this."

My teeth ground together, bone creaking against bone. *"You can't."*

It wasn't something that could be fixed. Not by

anything they could say. Only by something I could *do*. Something that could ensure this never happened again. That no more mothers or fathers needed to die senseless deaths for the whims of a merciless kingpin. The Saints of Thorn Valley, The Iron Aces of Edgewood, or the Kings of Lennox...they were all the same.

I just needed reminding.

"Let her go," Corvus said, his tone the one I remembered from when we first met. Cold and detached. Emotionless.

"*Corv*," Grey tried to argue.

"Move," Corvus replied. "Let them go."

Becca hopped into the Rover, not needing any more incentive, and I got into the driver's seat, turning over the engine. It started on the second try, and the cement barrier scraped along its side as I put her in reverse and turned around just as Diesel exited the warehouse, the two goons helping him walk out. The other injured Saints limped and grimaced behind them. One fewer than there had been inside.

At least one dead, then.

I couldn't bring myself to care.

"Keep your head down," I growled to Becca and hit the gas, bearing us away from no man's land. Leaving the Crows and everything they were a part of behind before I could change my mind.

My throat burned as I drove, aching until I couldn't hold back the pain anymore and it overflowed, tracing warm paths down my cheeks. The gaping hollow spot in my chest where *they* used to be now scraped raw.

"Where are we going?" Becca asked quietly behind me, and I swallowed past the lump in my throat.

I pulled off to the side of the road, the Rover's tires bumping over uneven ground, and yanked my phone free of the side pocket of my pants. My hands shook as I found the email I was looking for.

To: Vicky Doyle
From: Ava Jade Mason
Subject: RE: Swap Notes
I have what you need. Give me a location. I'll be there.

"Aves?" Becca pressed, and I set down my phone, calculating the hours remaining until dawn.

"There's something I have to do."

Pre-order Twisted Games now!

Who wants a bonus scene from the POV of Mr.
'Unknown'? Get it free by joining my FB reader group or
my newsletter! Not into commitment? That's okay, I
won't hold it against you. This bonus scene will also be
added as a prologue to Twisted Games!

Loving this series? Leave me a review to let me know!

ACKNOWLEDGEMENTS

This series wouldn't have been possible without the unwavering support of my readers. You encouraged me to run with this crazy idea for a whole new series in a whole new genre and I am so effing glad I did. It's been a wild ride.

I would like to give a special thanks for my alpha crew. You know who you are. Thank you for the words of encouragement and for all the hours you carve out of your busy lives to read my words while they're still raw to help me shape them into something smooth and strong. I don't know what I'd do without you. Seriously, never leave me…

A big thank you to my fiancé, as always, for being endlessly supportive of my work, no matter how dark and depraved it gets. To my editor, for not batting an eye at my constantly fluctuating schedule and always finding the time to fit me in and buff my words to a polished shine. And to my interior formatter and the genius behind the gorgeous covers for this series, Dez. Thanks for being the amazing, chill human being you are, and for always going above and beyond to make my vision happen.

Lastly, a shout out to my readers and all the babes over in Elena's Lawless Lair. You are my people, and I love each and every one of you to pieces. Thank you for reading!

STALK THE AUTHOR

...she doesn't mind 😊

Facebook: https://www.facebook.com/ElenaLawsonRH

Instagram: https://www.instagram.com/elenalately/

Newsletter: https://subscribepage.com/ElenaLawson

TikTok: https://www.tiktok.com/@authorelenalawson

Milton Keynes UK
Ingram Content Group UK Ltd.
UKHW020653151024
2186UKWH00038B/463

9 781989 723319